ECHOES
FROM THE WHITE
BEAR INN

By

Gene McSweeney

ECHOES
FROM THE
WHITE BEAR INN

ABOUT THE AUTHOR

Gene McSweeney is a former professor and relationship counsellor. He now writes fulltime in a variety of genres on topics that peak his interest. He is married and lives with his wife, Nancy, in the foothills of the Blue Ridge Mountains in northern Georgia. Echoes from the White Bear Inn is Dr. McSweeney's third novel.

OTHER NOVELS
By
Gene McSweeney

The Truman Factor
Visible Horizons – A Love Story

PART ONE

ANGEL'S MANOR

CHAPTER ONE

FIDDLER'S POINT, OHIO—1828

A woman's agonizing screams echoed across a shimmering darkness between the two banks of the Ohio River. Finally, they disappeared downstream only to start anew moments later. There was less time between each scream now as the man paddling the canoe looked first to his left at the steep Kentucky hills and then to his right at the low bank along the Ohio shore. He was praying for any sign of a settlement. A nearly full moon followed behind him, casting its light off the swiftly moving water and the gathering clouds on the horizon. He could hear the low rumbling of thunder in the distance somewhere ahead of him—he couldn't tell how far.

Landon Walters' and his pregnant wife, Jane, set out on their 156-mile voyage from Gallipolis to Cincinnati four days earlier. He had calculated that with a good tailwind he could make his destination in about ten days if all went well—but everything wasn't going well. Jane had assured him that it would be a good month before their child was due, but he knew different now—she would not make it through the night.

Landon let the current pull him along for a minute or two as he rested his weary arms. The thunder was getting closer and the wind was picking up quickly.

It was mid-spring, and although Landon had never been this far west before, he had heard from other settlers about the violent storms that frequented the Ohio River Valley. He felt the canoe slow with the growing headwind and could see in the moonlight that the water was becoming choppy. He would have to get the canoe out of the river before the approaching storm arrived.

Walters, a tall, strong man in his early thirties had come to America from Scotland in search of a better way of life. An expert stonemason, blacksmith, and carpenter, he had heard that Cincinnati might provide the opportunities he was looking for.

Having heard that Kentucky was mainly used as hunting grounds for the Shawnee Indians and that most of the new white settlements were mainly in Ohio, Landon stuck his paddle into the water and maneuvered the canoe to his right. Lightning flashed and the exhausted man thought he saw dim lights along the bank in the distance. He paddled toward them. A second rumble of thunder was mostly drowned out by another piercing scream from his wife.

Fast moving clouds quickly blocked out the moonlight as Walters brought his canoe to a near stop fearing that a low-hanging limb might knock him from the canoe. Lightning lit up the sky again for just a split second, but just ahead, he saw the source of the lights better this time. It was a steamboat moored at a large dock. Walters' hopes soared as he pulled his canoe up onto sandy mud near the landing. He at first thought he might seek help from someone on the steamboat, but it looked deserted. Besides, he thought, if a tornado were moving up the river hidden in the darkness, a steamboat wouldn't be any safer than his canoe. With each lightning outburst, his eyes gathered in all that they could see, and this time they saw a wide and well-worn path leading up to higher ground through a stand of tall reeds.

He gently picked up his wife in his strong arms and began carrying her toward the higher ground. Once through the reeds, he could see a white two-story building a few hundred feet ahead. On closer inspection, he could see a green sign with a white bear painted on it. The hanging sign read WHITE BEAR INN in all large, capital letters. As he neared the front door, his wife screamed again. He turned and pushed the door open with his backside and carefully maneuvered himself and his sobbing wife into a room that appeared to be a makeshift hotel lobby.

"Help me!" he pleaded as he approached the lady behind a counter.

"Oh, my word, when it rains it pours," she replied, coming around the counter to direct Walters up the steps. "There's another woman up there getting ready to give birth—she's the wife of your steamboat captain."

"We're not from the steamboat. We came by canoe."

"Is she with a doctor?" Walters asked.

"No doctors in the area and no doctors on the steamboat. There's just a Shawnee midwife up there. She's good though."

Walters took his wife upstairs to the anteroom and placed her on a cot as directed by the midwife. She was wearing a loose-fitting poncho of sorts over a cloth skirt and short leggings secured at the knees.

"Your wife is Creek?"

Walters hesitated for a moment wondering how the midwife knew. His wife wasn't dressed in clothing that would hint of being Creek, but this wasn't important now.

"Yes...Creek...friends to the Shawnee," Walters' wife managed to say between moans.

The midwife pulled a split gourd full of water from a bucket and gave Mrs. Walters a small sip.

"You must...wait...down...the stairs," said the Indian woman in broken English.

"Yes ma'am."

"My name is Waapa...Waapa Jane," Mrs. Walters mumbled from a hastily made narrow cot placed against the back wall.

"White Jane?" the midwife said, putting the gourd back into the bucket.

"Yes ma'am...my mother was British and my father a Creek," Jane Walters replied as she cringed in pain but fought back another scream.

Landon Walters heard their conversation as he descended the stairs. He had never called his wife Waapa although he was aware of the name given to her by her father's tribe. It was probably given out of disrespect for her mother's color, but Jane never seemed to mind.

Walters stepped outside the hotel and felt a strong, muggy wind against his face. He glanced to his right toward the saloon that occupied the corner section of the large building and saw a man sitting on a bench.

"Looks like Mother Nature's gettin' ready to show off," Walters said.

"I guess you can call it that, but I've got a steamboat down at the landin' that I'm worried about and a wife upstairs 'bout ready to make me a father. Kinda wish Mother Nature would give us all a break and let this storm go around the village this time," the man said.

"Can't say I'd disagree with that. My wife's upstairs about ready to have a baby, too."

The man stood and walked toward Walters.

"I'm Captain Bonèt," he said, offering his hand to shake. "I'm the captain of the Lucky Lady moored down at the landing."

"Landon Walters...and that's an interesting name for a boat," he said.

"She's a lady and the first I've ever owned. My brother-in-law, Mr. Phyddle won it in a poker game down in New Orleans about a year ago. We decided to go in partners. I would captain the ship and he would manage the gambling tables. He's in the saloon playing poker with some of the locals right now."

"So you're all staying in the hotel to wait out the approaching storm, huh?"

"We dropped off our last passengers in Huntington. We didn't take on any new ones because Mr. Phyddle planned to stop here for several days to visit with his seriously ill father who built this hotel. We got here a few days late, though. They just buried him yesterday from what I'm told. With the storm raging toward us, and the baby comin' a little early, I decided to stay here 'til my wife and child are able to travel. Might as well come in and have a drink with me. It might be a long wait."

"I don't drink, but maybe I'll have some coffee."

The two men took seats across the room from the poker table. Waiting out the storm allowed Mr. Phyddle the time and opportunity to play poker with some new blood as he called them. Within a few hours, he had won a small stack of gold and silver coins.

A short time later, his good luck changed to bad and he lost nearly all of his ready cash. He excused himself from the game and approached Captain Bonèt with an offer. The captain slipped a small leather pouch from his inside coat pocket and tossed it slowly from hand to hand while the tall, well-dressed gambler wrote his name, Jesse Noah Phyddle, on the deed to the hotel he had just inherited.

"Would you care to witness his signature, Mr. Walters?"

"Sure. Just show me where to sign."

Once done, the gambler walked back to the poker table and rejoined the game.

"May I know what I was just witness to?"

"Mr. Phyddle certainly doesn't want to tie himself down to operating a hotel, so he just signed over the building and the land it sits on in return for a sizable poker stake."

"You've got a mind for business, Captain."

"What brings you and your family to these parts?" the Captain asked.

"Like most folks...I guess...I'm just looking for a better way of life in America than what I had in Scotland."

"Do you gamble?"

"Not really. I've played some for small stakes but mostly for fun. Never understood why a man would work hard to acquire something, and then risk losing it all in a game of chance. Not meanin' any disrespect for Mr. Phyddle, of course." Walters answered.

Captain Bonèt grinned.

"I understand, Mr. Walters. My wife loves her brother very much and wishes that he would quit gambling and settle down. Highly unlikely, though.

"Too bad...odds are he'll end up with nothing someday."

"There, you see, you speak of odds and that's what poker is all about. Why don't we sit in a few hands? I feel lucky."

Landon sighed. He had lied to Mr. Phyddle about his experience playing poker because he knew he was being suckered into a game. Truth was, he had spent many long, rainy days playing poker with his construction co-workers when it was just too wet to work.

"I don't have much money to lose...but I suppose I could play a few hands just to see how my luck is tonight."

The two men took seats around the poker table. In a short time, Landon had won several hands that produced a small pile of coins. It wasn't that he was lucky, or even a good poker player, but he was very observant, and watched for peculiar signals between players.

A local man known for his gambling skills entered the saloon. He was dressed well and flashed a sizable amount of cash when he ordered a drink at the bar. He picked up his drink, turned, leaned back against the bar, and watched every hand until another local got up with a huff and stormed out of the saloon a loser.

"Got room for another player?" the man at the bar asked.

"Sure, pull up a chair," the captain said, glancing at Mr. Phyddle.

As the stranger took a seat, Landon noticed the subtle glances between the captain and Mr. Phyddle. He could see that there was something unusual about this poker game.

The Lucky Lady was one of the many gambling boats that traveled the Ohio and Mississippi Rivers. It was also likely that Captain Bonèt and Mr. Phyddle were cardsharps and probably partners in the fleecing of the locals as well as passengers.

As the night wore on and the drinking continued, the game eventually centered on Landon and the captain since they were the only sober players left. With a few lucky hands, Landon not only had a sizable stack of gold, but the deed to the hotel.

***

Upstairs, Jane Walters' screams had turned to loud moans. It was well past midnight when the first large drops of rain splattered against the roof. Another flash of lightning revealed the midwife holding a newborn infant and placing it on Jane's bare breast. Moments later, she brought another infant and placed it on Jane's other breast.

Several candle lanterns produced little more than a flickering light in the room. As the lightning flashed, Jane, exhausted and only semi-conscious, thought she saw the midwife pull a blanket up over the other woman's face.

The wind howled outside and suddenly a tree limb blew through the nearby window. Moments later, wind and rain raged through the shattered window blowing out all the candles as Jane drifted into a hazy unconsciousness.

***

Hearing the crash of the tree limb, Landon and the captain raked their winnings off the table before the next deal began. Mr. Phyddle declared the poker game over and suggested they start again the next morning if anyone was interested.

The two remaining locals grumbled a bit because they were losing, but agreed without incident.

Mr. Phyddle followed the captain and Landon upstairs into the darkness, barking orders to several crewmembers to light candles. Landon moved directly to the cot where he had placed Jane. Captain Bonèt stopped short of his wife's cot and fell to his knees when he saw the blanket pulled over her face.

"Take your captain down to the saloon immediately and get him a drink of whiskey. Then, get some more men up here to clean this place up," Mr. Phyddle said to the three crewmen who had brought candles.

The men helped Captain Bonèt to his feet and escorted him down the stairs. Mr. Phyddle pulled the blanket down to Mrs. Bonèt's waist and stared down at his sister for a moment before glancing over at Landon.

"There's no baby here."

Landon could see that there were two infants with Jane. For a moment, he wondered if Jane had given birth to twins—the complications beginning to swirl around in his mind.

Landon looked back at the gambler as he pulled the blanket back over the body.

"The midwife is taking whatever she knows to her grave. I hope your wife can shed some light on this situation when she wakes up," Mr. Phyddle said, examining the midwife and the jagged limb that had knocked the life out of her.

While Jane and the babies slept, Mr. Phyddle returned to the saloon to help the captain if he could. There was nothing more he could do for his sister.

"Is there an undertaker in town?"

Nobody answered, so he sent a crewmember to find out. The crewmember returned shortly to report that a local preacher also prepared bodies for burial in the backroom of his general store. The bodies were taken up the road a short distance to the store and left for preparation.

Landon Walters sat on the floor beside his young wife's bed, falling into and out of a fitful sleep. His mind was full of questions that only Jane could answer.

CHAPTER TWO

When Jane awoke shortly after dawn, she still held two infants against her bare breasts. She had nursed them both throughout the night. According to her Indian tribe's traditions, her body was now part of both their bodies, and the babies would now not only be considered milk siblings—but blood siblings forever.

Landon Walters still sat at his wife's side.

"How are you feeling?" he asked, patting her hand.

"What day is this?" she asked, ignoring her husband's question.

"Uh...it's the twenty-fourth day of April."

"Oh...I feel okay, but I had terrible dreams of a storm being all around us," she said, still with a dazed look across her eyes.

"There was a bad storm, but it didn't last long. Caused a little damage and a lot of heartache," Walters said. "I saw something crash through the window. Is that woman okay?"

"No, honey, a tree limb went all the way through her body and pinned her to the wall. She never had a chance."

Jane's eyes filled with tears as images of the late-night events crawled back into her memory.

"The other woman?"

"No. She lost too much blood."

One of the babies began to whimper some while the other one nursed. Jane's eyes blinked rapidly as reality began to set in. One of the infants she was holding lost its mother last night and the woman who delivered both babies was also dead.

"May I see my child, now?" a man's voice whispered from across the room.

Landon glanced in the direction that the voice was coming from to see Captain Bonèt and Mr. Phyddle standing at the top of the stairs alongside another Shawnee Indian girl that didn't look older than sixteen or eighteen. Landon stood and walked over to the group.

"The man is here to see his child," Jane thought, "but which one is it?"

She tried to pull back even a faint memory of how the two babies were placed onto her breasts, but there was nothing. She had not really seen the faces of either child yet, but glancing down now, she could see only the tops of their heads. They both had dark hair, and both were wrapped in identical cloth. There was simply no way for

Jane to know which baby belonged to her and which was the dead woman's child. In her mother's heart, she already loved them both.

Landon and the Indian woman walked toward Jane's bed and she knew she must make the most unthinkable decision of her life.

"The father would like to hold his child now. Captain Bonèt has hired this nice lady as a wet nurse for the baby. They will all be going on to Cincinnati soon if the baby seems ready to travel," Landon said.

Jane's chin trembled. She took the woman's hand.

"What's your name?" Jane asked.

"Nikkipohok?" she replied.

The young woman smiled down at Jane.

"When did you lose your baby?" Jane asked.

The Indian woman searched for words. "Soon," the woman said, putting a hand under each of her breasts. "Full...hurt," she mumbled.

Jane figured the young girl had lost a child at birth a few days earlier and that her full breasts were becoming uncomfortable. Nikkipohok would make a perfect wet nurse for one of the babies, but which one? If the father were a good man, she thought, this arrangement would be beneficial for Nikkipohok and one of the babies. Without looking at the child on her left, Jane indicated to Nikkipohok that she should take that baby. The girl took the infant from Jane's arms and smiled.

Right or wrong, the decision was made...a heart-rending choice made by a new mother not much older than Nikkipohok...a decision that would likely remain Jane's secret forever.

"Ooooooh, baby wet. I clean up," the Indian woman said as she moved over to a table with a blue and white pitcher of water sitting on it.

Jane fought back tears as she watched Nikkipohok clean and dry the infant.

"Beautiful, clean little girl now," Nikkipohok said moments later, wrapping the child in a clean blanket before handing the newborn to the father.

"She's pretty as an angel," the captain said. "That would be a perfect name for her—I'll name her Angelina...after her mother," Captain Bonèt said, turning and walking downstairs with his daughter in his arms.

Jane slid her hand down under the blanket that covered the remaining baby who was now asleep in her arms. Her child was also wet and needed attention.

Moments later, Landon and Jane Walters were alone in the room with their baby. They didn't talk about the events of the night. They didn't talk about the female child that had just been taken from her breast. They talked about names for boys until they settled on Caleb for their fine new son.

***

Captain Bonèt decided to remain in Fiddler's Point for at least another day in order to make arrangements for the burial of his wife and the Indian midwife who delivered his daughter. Around noon, Landon Walters walked into the saloon to get some food for Jane. Captain Bonèt called him over to his table.

"Hello, Mr. Walters. How are your wife and child doing?"

"Jane's a bit hungry and it doesn't seem like my son ever stops eating. I...I'm very sorry about your wife."

"Thank you, Mr. Walters."

There was silence for a moment as Captain Bonèt just stared down at the full glass of whiskey in front of him before pushing it away to the side.

Landon went over to the bar and asked if there was food available. He learned that there was only a pot of brown beans sitting on a wood-burning stove near the corner of the room. He could also get some bread if he wished. He filled a bowl with the hot soup and got a loaf of bread. As he started toward the door, he nodded his respects to Captain Bonèt.

"What line of work did you say you were in?" Captain Bonèt asked, stopping Landon in his tracks.

"I didn't, but I'm an expert stonemason and carpenter. I've even done a little blacksmithin' several years ago."

"It must have taken a great deal of effort to learn those skills, and the nature of the skills means you're willing to work hard. Are you planning on staying around here or moving on down the river?"

"I had originally planned on looking for opportunities in Cincinnati but the baby came early...and now...and now...I own this hotel."

"Do you consider being a hotel owner an opportunity?"

Walters blinked his eyes several times, as the realization of what he had just said sunk in.

"Of course...it's a wonderful opportunity."

"Then, don't you think I had better sign the deed over to you?"

Landon slowly recalled witnessing Mr. Phyddle's signature a night earlier.

"With everything going on, I guess it slipped my mind," he said, tapping his shirt pocket to make sure the deed was still where he put it.

"Then let's do it now. The bartender can witness my signature if you'd like."

Landon agreed, and moments later, the White Bear Inn was officially his.

"I have something else to talk with you about, Mr. Walters. You are the only person I know in this town though I don't know you well. However, I trust you, and would like to ask a couple of favors of you."

"What might they be?"

"Two things...with your stonemason skills, could you prepare an appropriate headstone for my wife's grave and one for the midwife? I will pay you fairly for your work and materials."

"Doing that wouldn't be a problem if there's stone available," Walters replied. "I have the tools I'd need in my canoe. The problem is...it'll take every bit of two or three weeks to chisel a nice size headstone. I could make one from wood in a hurry and replace it with stone later."

"That'll be fine. I'd just like to see one on the grave by the next time I return. Mrs. Bonèt's first name is Angelique. She was born on the 6th day of November in 1803."

"What's the second promise?"

"I need someone to see that my wife's grave is tended to and not allowed to grow over with weeds."

"I can do all those things, sir."

"One last thing," the captain said. "The land included on that deed I signed extends all the way down to the river...including the dock. You might think about starting a fuel depot down there. It could make you a wealthy man."

In less than twenty-four hours after arriving in the small but growing town, Landon Walters had fallen into the opportunity of a lifetime. He was already planning it all out in his mind. Jane could run the hotel operations and care for their new son at the same time. He would hire a barkeep to help him with the saloon. There were plenty of local workers who would be happy to cut and stack wood for a small fee. The forested acreage around the hotel would provide enough wood to fuel the Lucky Lady and other riverboats for years to come.

***

After a single day in the April sun, Walters figured he needed to hurry to prepare the headstones for the two graves. He found some roughhewn lumber stacked inside a small lean-to behind the hotel. As he searched the lumber, he thought he heard a rustling noise coming from somewhere behind the stacks of wood. Motionless, he listened for a long moment but did not hear the sound again. He went on about his work.

By that evening, he had fashioned two whitewashed wooden crosses ready for the epitaph, but soon learned that he only needed one. Apparently, several members of the midwife's tribe had already collected her body and carried it into the forest to take care of their own according to tribal customs.

A short time later, Walters went to the saloon and informed Captain Bonèt that the marker was ready.

"Thank you, Mr. Walters. Would you consider walking up to the graveyard with me to help me select a proper plot?"

"I'd be honored, sir."

The two walked a short distance west to the town's only graveyard where they found a bewildering example of what Captain Bonèt did not want for his wife's final resting place. Only a few graves had markers and most of them were in poor shape. Some could hardly be seen due to the weeds. Makeshift fences marked off several different areas in efforts to identify members of the same family.

"Now, do you understand why I want someone I trust to tend Mrs. Bonèt's grave?"

"I promise she'll rest in a place you'll be proud of, sir."

Captain Bonèt selected an available spot near a large oak tree a short distance from the senior Mr. Phyddle's grave.

"If you want, I will pay you double to chisel a stone with Mr. Phyddle's name on it. You can get more information from Antoine if you need it."

Darkness came before any more could be done. The two men returned to the White Bear.

"I think I'll go upstairs and clean up some before I go to bed. It's been a long day," Landon said.

"I'm going to walk up to the general store and talk with the preacher about having a quiet graveside service sometime early tomorrow morning. Afterwards, I think I'll do the same as you and get ready for bed. Now that the storms have passed, my crew and I will be sleeping on the Lucky Lady tonight."

***

The following morning after the burial, the Lucky Lady slowly pulled away from the Fiddler's Point dock with Captain Bonèt at the helm and a young Shawnee Indian woman named Nikkipohok standing beside him holding his infant daughter.

With tears flowing freely down her cheeks, Waapa Jane stood at an upstairs window of her hotel and watched until the smoking giant gradually disappeared around a bend in the river far downstream.

Later in the day, Jane had Landon go to the general store and get her some writing paper, a pen, ink, and a small box suitable for holding the paper. That night, she began writing what she could remember about the canoe trip down the Ohio River. She wrote about the storm and the hazy, shadowy events of the night her child was born. She wrote about the heartache she was feeling.

April 24, 1828
Late last night, I gave birth to a
healthy baby...and I should be
the happiest woman on earth.
Yet, my heart aches with the truth.

***

In the weeks that followed, Landon spent several hours a day chiseling a short epitaph into a large piece of stone and placing it on Angelique Bonèt's grave. He did the same for Mr. Phyddle. He had no way of knowing that Mrs. Bonèt and Mr. Phyddle would be the last two people ever buried in the boot-hill style graveyard.

To separate the two graves from the poorly kept graves in the area, he built a tall picket fence around the oak tree and a small section of land large enough for maybe a dozen graves. Above the entrance, he placed a chiseled wooden sign with the last names of the only two people who were now buried in the fenced-off section. The chiseled sign read in all capital letters: BONÈT-PHYDDLE.

***

With the coming of the spring freshets, the lowlands west of Fiddler's Point filled with floodwaters that took on the appearance of a large lake as the water spread in all directions across the Soda Creek Valley.

Concerned that the small town's only cemetery might be inundated by floodwaters, Landon walked to the point every day to see how close the water was coming to graves. This spring, the water stopped short of the cemetery but it had not always been this way according to some of the townsfolk whom Landon had gotten to know over the winter.

There were rumors that some of the town officials were getting necessary permissions to establish a new cemetery far out on the north side of town. The proposed land was on high ground and safe from floods.

Others suggested that the old graveyard flooded nearly every year and that some coffins and bodies had been disinterred and washed down the raging Ohio River by the floodwaters.

By fall, the refueling site was filled to capacity with wood, and the White Bear was looking good from a woman's touch. The new owners looked forward to a visit from Captain Bonèt before cold weather set in, but, again, that visit never came.

Before the end of the year, Park Lawn Cemetery was established in north Fiddler's Point. In the spring of 1830, a town ordinance required that all of the bodies and coffins that could be found in the old graveyard be moved to the new cemetery. Landon made sure Mr. Phyddle's father and Mrs. Bonèt's remains and headstones were properly relocated.

With all the graves gone, Landon began a cleanup project by raking down the area near the old oak tree. He had no way of knowing how Captain Bonèt would feel about his wife's grave being moved, so he left the picket fence up and planted flowers along the front. If Captain Bonèt ever did return, he could see that his wife's grave was well kept as promised.

Landon also decided to provide one last thing that would mark the former location of Mrs. Bonèt's grave. He chiseled a small, flat stone with the words, IN LOVING MEMORY OF ANGELIQUE BONÈT born-1803—died-1828. On the southwest side of the large oak tree, he carefully carved out a precise space in which to set the stone. He filled the edges with resin to hold it in place. The plaque faced the congruence of the Ohio River and Soda Creek where the setting sun would shine upon it every day.

***

Major changes began to take place at the White Bear Inn. Because of frequent fistfights, and after a near-fatal shooting over a poker game, Jane became quite concerned for Landon's safety and the safety of their son.

After careful consideration, Landon posted a notice on the front door stating that alcoholic beverages would no longer be sold, and that the gambling tables were now only to be used for dining. Overnight, the saloon and gambling hall changed into a peaceful, family oriented café. Unlike the gambling hall and saloon that previously stayed open late into the night, the café closed just before dark.

***

In the days that followed, Landon began working on building some shelves for the renovation of the kitchen. While moving some lumber around in the rear shed, he discovered a small door on the exposed wall. He easily pushed the door open to discover it was an entrance to the basement that he never knew existed. He got several candles and began to explore the darkness inside.

The first thing he noticed was the variation in headroom. In some places, he had to move along on his knees, while in other areas he was able to stand. He soon realized that floodwaters had left sediment on the dirt floor, gradually reducing the headroom.

As he moved closer to the front of the building, he could hear footsteps of people walking in the above café. He moved to his left a short distance and spotted what appeared to be a trapdoor large enough for a person to enter.

Landon secured his candle in the soft, dirt floor so that it would cast light onto the trapdoor. Glancing from wall to wall, he estimated that he was somewhere beneath their living quarters beside the café. He pushed on the door and found that it was hinged with strong rope that made absolutely no noise as it opened. As he stood, he stuck his candle into the darkness above to find that it was the space beneath the stairs that led to the anteroom on the second floor. To his knowledge, there were no other openings into or out of the space beneath the stairs.

Suddenly, the candlelight reflected off a shiny object near the lowest step on the staircase. Landon crawled into the darkness and was shocked at what he found. There was an empty water bucket with a metal cup hanging on a nail above it. There were several bowls and spoons stacked in one corner. One bowl still had a spoon in it. Landon held the candle close and could see the crusty remnants of some kind of food.

His mind drifted back to the day he was looking for lumber to make the grave markers. He had heard a rustling sound behind the lumber. Now it dawned on him that someone may have been hiding in the basement. It could only mean one thing. The White Bear Inn was probably part of the Underground Railroad.

Landon made his way out of the little room and out of the basement. He returned to the café and waited patiently until Jane was free to talk.

"You're not going to believe what I just found," he said in a whisper as he looked over one shoulder and then the other.

"My goodness, what's gotten you so excited?" Jane said, pouring him a cup of tea.

Landon glanced over his shoulders again to see the last lunch customer walking out the door.

"Jane! I think this hotel has been used as a station for the Underground Railroad!"

"What makes you think that?"

"I found a trapdoor to the space beneath the stairs. The little room had a bucket for water and bowls for food. What else would those items be used for?"

"I don't know, but maybe you should check out the whole building to see what you might discover."

Landon agreed. He got some paper and a rule and began measuring walls and checking them for unusual construction. As a carpenter, he would recognize other hidden areas if there were any...and there were.

The back wall of the living quarters was a false wall providing a four-foot-wide hiding place. A hidden door opened from this space onto the landing at the foot of the stairs. This simple arrangement allowed runaways a place to hide with several escape passages from the basement to the attic above the anteroom. Landon made a detailed drawing of the floor plan so that he could become familiar with every wall in the building and every secret passage.

An empty oil lamp hung outside near the café's front door. Over time, Landon and Jane learned that the lamp was to be lit at dusk if it was safe for runaways to come to the station. Other than that signal, they knew very little about how a station was to be operated.

Landon was not an active abolitionist, but both he and Jane were sympathizers, as were the members of the Shawnee and Creek communities still living in the forest. Jane knew that she could get information from them, and soon learned the process used to help runaways make their way to Canada.

Even with all the secrecy that surrounded the Underground Railroad, word somehow got out to the runaways that the White Bear station was still active.

Those who made it to the hotel's basement found food, water, basic medicine if available, and a safe place to rest. When the runaways were ready to continue their northern trek, Shawnee women provided them with native clothing and weapons for hunting. They would sometimes pretend to be wives to the runaways if questioned by slave chasers. Most of the time, they pretended to be a hunting party and traveled by canoe at night. On average, they made it to a station north of Columbus in seven to ten days. From there it was only about a hundred miles to Canada and freedom.

CHAPTER THREE

The stormy night Caleb and Angelina were born still came to Jane often in her dreams. She grudgingly accepted the fact that she had very little control over ever seeing Angelina again. However, on the twenty-fourth day of April, 1840 things changed.

As he often did, Caleb Walters was up and dressed just before the sun began to spread its light on the river. He carried his fishing pole and bucket of worms along the dock to the western edge where he took his favorite seat on a large piece of driftwood beneath a willow tree. He wedged the thick end of his cane pole under the log and rested it on a forked stick to hold the pole at an angle over the water. He sat there for nearly an hour, but the fish just weren't biting. Probably because of recent storms, he thought.

He was barefooted with his pant legs rolled up near his knees. He often dressed that way hoping to catch an occasional soft breeze from the river. Caleb was enjoying himself because he knew that when he returned to the hotel, things would change. His mother would begin her instructions to take a bath and put on the clean clothes she had laid out for him. After all, she wanted him to look nice on his birthday.

A blast from a riverboat whistle caused him to glance up the bank at the dock. The riverboat had been heading upstream but apparently decided to dock to take on a load of fuel. He watched as the boat made a wide turn and glided slowly and perfectly along the dock as crewmembers moored it to the bollards.

Caleb watched the activities intently because he often wondered what it might be like to work on a riverboat. Finally, he pulled in his line and wrapped it around the pole so the hook fit securely into the soft pulp at the fat end of the pole. He knew there would be no more fishing in the wake of the riverboat.

When several passengers began to depart, Caleb decided to wait in the shadows of the willow tree. Even from a considerable distance, his attention was drawn to the fancy dress and matching parasol that one of the passengers was wearing. She walked beside another woman who was also carrying a parasol. Walking closely behind them was a man in a uniform. It was the first time Caleb had ever seen Captain Lucien Bonèt.

Caleb walked up the path to the inner edge of the reeds and stood there in the shadows as the three people made their way toward the White Bear. As the three neared the front door, Caleb watched as his father stepped outside and shook hands with the captain before nodding politely at the two ladies. Caleb thought he saw his mother watching from a window inside the café.

Moments later, Landon, the captain, and the young lady with the parasol began walking toward the old cemetery. The second lady walked into the café.

"Hello, Waapa Jane," the woman said.

"Hello, Nikkipohok. It's so good to see you again," Jane said, stepping forward and hugging the woman who now had a big smile on her face.

"Nikkipohok! I've forgotten how that name sounds. No one has called me by my whole name since I left this town twelve years ago. The captain insisted that I be addressed with "Miss" in front of my name. Miss Nikkipohok was just too much for everyone to handle, I think. Anyway, after Angelina began to talk, she called me Miss Nikki and that's how it's been ever since."

Jane's eyes brightened at the mention of Angelina's name. "No one calls me Waapa...not that I would care, but I wasn't fond of explaining what the name meant to my tribe. It wasn't very flattering."

"You have done well, White Jane, in becoming part of the melting pot as they call it in Washington."

"I don't think many of the politicians ever considered Indians or slaves as part of their melting pot plan. It was more for the white European immigrants in my opinion. You seem to have adapted well," Jane said with a feeling of satisfaction because she felt as informed as Miss Nikki did.

"It's much about education, I think. Captain Bonèt hired the absolute best tutors for Angelina. As her escort, I was always around. I made it a point to learn everything that Angelina learned. I'm still learning."

"You are very pretty and still young enough to have a family of your own. Have you ever thought of marrying again?" Jane asked, hoping to learn more personal information about the lady who was taking care of Angelina.

"You remember how things were when we were young and Washington's army gathered up members of so many tribes and marched them out west. My husband died along the way. I changed the kind of clothes I wore, spoke English, and passed for white in order to protect my unborn child that died anyway at birth. When the captain gave me a chance to raise Angelina, I promised myself I would not marry again...at least until she was grown."

"How about Mr. Phyddle?" Jane asked with a shy grin.

"Mr. Phyddle is a gentleman...and a very handsome one at that, but he has his life and I have mine," Miss Nikki said, a flush crossing her face.

"And how about Angelina...does she have all the boys chasing after her?"

Nikki raised one eyebrow. "Not yet...I don't think, but even if they were, I would run them off with a broom."

"Nikki...may I ask you a question about something that is very important to me?"

"Of course."

"What has Angelina been told about the events that occurred on the night she was born?"

Miss Nikki's eyes blinked rapidly as she inhaled deeply.

"All she knows is that her mother died giving birth, and that it all took place during a violent storm."

"Does she know that Caleb was born on the same night?"

"Yes! Does Caleb know?"

"No, I was going to tell him as soon as he was old enough to understand, but when Captain Bonèt never returned, I didn't see the need."

"Do you see a need now?"

"I think so...I mean...I think it would be nice that they know they have that in common. Anyway...I'd like to give Angelina something for her birthday."

"That would be nice," Miss Nikki said.

**

The reeds were thick this time of year but Caleb managed to move through them quietly until he was close enough to the abandoned graveyard to see everyone standing inside the rose-covered picket fence surrounding the large oak tree. The sign reading BONÈT-PHYDDLE still hung above the arbor entrance.

There were no headstones, but Landon led his two visitors to the backside of the old oak and pointed to the stone embedded in the tree.

Captain Bonèt removed his hat and stood with his head bowed staring at the plaque. Finally, Captain Bonèt patted Landon on the shoulder and shook his hand again.

Caleb could see now that the female was just a young girl about his age. She knelt down in front of the plaque as Captain Bonèt spoke to her for a moment before walking away in the direction of the White Bear. The girl remained kneeling, but seemed to be writing something on a piece of paper.

Landon and the captain walked back to the café.

"Hello, Jane. It's been a long time." The captain said.

Without speaking, a quick glance from Captain Bonèt told Miss Nikki that Angelina was alone at the old gravesite.

"It was nice talking with you...Jane. I must go now."

***

Angelina stood and exited the arbor. Caleb froze in his tracks as she looked towards the reeds and straight into his eyes. Neither of them spoke, but their gaze remained locked for a long moment.

Suddenly, the young lady's face grew taut as she glanced away from Caleb toward her traveling companion standing a short distance away.

"We must go now, dear," Nikki said.

Without another word, but with a quick glance back into Caleb's eyes, the girl stepped to the older woman's side and they walked away into the distance toward the hotel.

Caleb sat down under the oak tree and watched as everyone but his father disappeared into the café. Moments later, Landon pulled up with a buggy and he and the captain assisted the ladies into their seats. The captain sat beside Landon while Angelina and Nikki sat in the back. With a loud cluck from Landon's mouth, the horse turned around in the street and headed east toward Park Lawn Cemetery. Jane stood near the street and watched until Angelina was out of sight.

Caleb immediately returned to the café. As expected, his mother began insisting that he get cleaned up. Now, he was more than happy to follow her instructions.

He poured water into a tub in the back room of the living quarters and scrubbed himself harder than he ever had before. His body was slim, his skin quite tanned, and his shaggy brown hair bleached light from spending so much time fishing on the riverbank.

He thought about how he looked earlier as he scrubbed the mud from his feet and legs. She was so beautiful and so perfectly dressed...and those eyes...he couldn't stop thinking about the nerves that exploded in his body for that short, wonderful moment that they gazed at one another.

I must have looked like some kind of ragamuffin, he thought. Why didn't she come later today when I would have at least been in my church clothes?

When he finished dressing, he walked into the small front lobby where he found his mother standing in front of the window staring toward the river. He could tell that she had been crying.

"Is something wrong," he asked.

"No, son, I must be coming down with the vapors or something," she said, moving from the window to behind the counter.

"Do you know all those people who are here from the riverboat?"

Jane took a deep breath before answering.

"Some of them, but not well," she replied, swallowing hard.

"Which ones?"

"Well...I know the captain of the Lucky Lady and the young girl's nurse...I mean escort."

"And the young girl...do you know her?" Caleb asked.

"Do I know her? No...not really," Jane said, the words sending chills up her spine. "I met her father many years ago. That was way back when your father and I first got to this town."

Caleb never said another word, but felt something...some kind of twinge or uneasiness inside as his mother lowered her eyes and walked back toward the café window.

"Caleb, watch the café for me for just a few minutes. I need to hurry up to the general store for a minute. I'll be right back."

When she returned, she was carrying a small sack.

"That didn't take long," Caleb said.

"I'm going to the kitchen. Keep an eye open for your father to return in the buggy. Call me when he returns."

Jane went into the kitchen and removed the items from the sack. She quickly wrapped the two identical packages with paper and ribbon. Then, she moved a large frosted cake to a counter near the kitchen door. She had baked the cake for Caleb early that morning before the visitors arrived.

Moments later, Caleb returned to the kitchen.

"The buggy's back!"

Jane left the packages on the counter with the cake and walked into the café dining room.

Angelina, Miss Nikki, and Captain Bonèt walked back into the café while Landon took the horse and buggy to the back.

"Mrs. Walters, we've come to say goodbye. We need to get back aboard soon...it's a long trip to Pittsburgh."

"Please stay just a little longer, Captain Bonèt. I have a couple of things I would like to share with everyone before you leave."

Jane quickly disappeared into the kitchen and returned moments later with Caleb at her side.

Captain Bonèt, I'd like you to meet my son, Caleb. Angelina's mouth dropped open slightly for just a moment but she quickly replaced her surprised look with a growing smile. Captain Bonèt bowed slightly and Caleb returned the gesture. The captain then introduced Angelina and Miss Nikki. Caleb's bowing of his head to Miss Nikki was followed by a much slower bow to Angelina without taking his eyes off hers.

"Please take a seat around the center table while I get something from the kitchen."

Landon arrived during Jane's instructions and joined the group. Moments later, Jane returned with a large cake decorated with fluffy meringue icing.

"Since Angelina and Caleb were both born on this day twelve years ago, I want to wish them both a happy birthday."

Everyone clapped except Caleb as the surprise information about being born on the same day as Angelina left him slightly stunned. However, when he glanced at Angelina and saw that she was smiling back with approval, he returned her smile. Everyone had a piece of cake and seemed to enjoy the party.

"I'm glad you liked the cake. I have one other thing I would like to do before everyone leaves," Jane said, as she stood and walked back into the kitchen.

When she returned, she was carrying the two small packages she had previously wrapped.

"Angelina...Caleb...I want to give you both identical gifts for your birthdays. In return, I want you both to promise me that you will use the gifts to record the special moments of your life as they occur. As our paths cross over time, I would be honored to read about both of your lives as you grow up."

Jane could not hold back a tear as Angela and Caleb opened their packages at the same time. Inside each was a box of writing paper, quill, and ink. Angelina and Caleb stood at the same time and gave Jane a big hug. Angelina also had a tear in her eye as she whispered into Jane's ear, "I promise."

As the visitors made their way down the path to the landing, Jane walked on one side of Angelina and Nikki walked on the other. Landon, Caleb, and Captain Bonèt followed behind.

After the three boarded the vessel, Angelina and Miss Nikki leaned against the rail near the stern of the Lucky Lady as they waved goodbye. In those last moments, Caleb's eyes met Angelina's and the gaze held until the riverboat steamed out of sight.

***

During the next decade, more changes took place at the White Bear. Landon began building a brick addition to the rear of the White Bear. His plan was to build twelve new rooms and several secret doors from the basement to the top floor. In 1847, shortly after Caleb went away to study law and journalism in Cincinnati, Landon finished the exterior walls, roof, and subflooring of the new addition before injuring his back. He was never able to complete the project, but the subflooring was over a basement and did not obstruct the rear entrance for the runaway slaves. Under roof and dry, the new addition could only sit empty and gather dust.

The Underground Railroad station at the White Bear operated flawlessly for nearly three more years, but the arrival of slave chaser, Silas

DePriest, signaled danger. The former part-time preacher moved into a cabin on the hillside directly across the river from the White Bear. Frightening rumors immediately began to circulate about the cruel treatment of runaways captured by DePriest. It wouldn't be long until these rumors were confirmed as Jane and Caleb witnessed the cruelty in the street outside the café.

□

CHAPTER FOUR

The cracking of a bullwhip got the attention of several white people milling around outside the White Bear Inn on this hot, June afternoon in 1850. They watched but did not attempt to come to the aid of the three runaway slaves being treated like cattle.

Caleb, now twenty-two years old, was in the café talking with his mother when he heard the commotion outside. The bullwhip cracked again, this time ripping off the back of a female's dirty dress. She screamed and fell onto the dusty street in a heap.

Caleb started to walk out the front door to rescue the young girl, but his mother stopped him.

"You can't mess with those chasers, son. The law is on their side. You'll just get yourself hurt or killed. Please stay inside," Jane begged, taking Caleb's hand.

The large, no-neck brute of a man kicked the female in the stomach and demanded that she get up. Two other male runaways, tied hand and foot with course ropes, cowered down as if their posturing might keep the whip from finding either of them again.

"Who is that animal?" Caleb asked.

"His name is Silas DePriest. I understand he's a former hell-and-brimstone preacher and a full-time slave chaser. He's supposed to live in that abandoned log church across the river."

"Kentucky's still a slave state, but they talk of staying neutral should a war come along. It's all about politics and keeping a balance of power in the capital. The whole idea of someone owning another human being is disgusting!" Caleb said, shaking his head in a gesture of hopelessness.

"It's rumored that DePriest keeps crates of rattlesnakes in the church's basement to prevent captured slaves from escaping."

Caleb knew all about the various Fugitive Slave Acts passed over the years. The way the legal documents were written made it possible for slave chasers to come into a free state and forcefully remove escaped slaves. In fact, the act made it a requirement that certain law enforcement officers and even regular citizens assist slave chasers if necessary. However, the new law didn't mean the people from the state of Ohio had to like what the law demanded—Caleb was one of them.

There were a few folks along the northern banks of the river who helped runaway slaves whenever possible. This assistance was most often limited to providing food and shelter to escaped slaves once they got across the river. If caught aiding runaways, white people or free slaves could receive severe floggings, fines, and sometimes several years in prison. Caleb was determined to help in every way he could as soon as possible.

However, at this very moment, he could only watch as DePriest and his captured slaves disappeared among tall reeds on the dirt path leading down to the dock where DePriest had moored his canoe under the willow trees.

DePriest took his three captured slaves across the Ohio River to his log-cabin church near the mouth of Tygart Creek. He promptly chained the two males in the basement where he kept his snakes. There was a stout door at the top and bottom of the stairs. Ropes were rigged to open the crates if anyone tried to escape.

"If in ya happen ta get loose from your chains and try ta escape up these stairs...jist openin' either door from your side will open all my snake crates. Ya won't make it up two steps afore ya been bit a dozen times. Ain't no since in tryin'."

He shook several crates sitting on each side of the stairs just to get the rattlesnakes upset.

"Hear them rattles...no use tryin' ta escape."

The female runaway was not so lucky. She was taken to DePriest's living quarters at the rear of the church. He sat on a chair and had her stand in front of him.

"Whatcha name, darky?"

The young woman's lips tried to speak but could not.

"I said, "Whatcha name?"

This time, he eyed his bullwhip.

She followed his eyes to the door and somehow found the strength to answer.

"Dottie, suh...my name's Dottie!"

"Ya got some blood runnin' down ya back, Dottie, and looks like some on ya legs. Take ya clothes off and I'll tend them wounds 'fore they get infected."

The young woman just trembled. DePriest stood and walked to the door separating his living quarters from the larger room once used as a church. He locked the door and removed his bullwhip that was hanging on a nearby nail. He carried the whip back and laid it over the arm of his chair. The woman's eyes locked on the whip for only a moment before she began taking off what was left of her ripped dress.

"Ya married, Dottie?" DePriest asked the woman.

"No, suh."

"Ya got any little bastards, maybe?"

"No, suh. Ain't old 'nough ta be wid no husband."

DePriest looked closely at her face for the first time. She was so dirty and unkept that he hadn't even considered her age. She was with the two men whom he had identified as runaways and figured she had escaped with them.

"How long ya been hidin' with those men in the basement? Don't cha lie to me or I'll take the whip to ya again."

"From Memphis, suh, where we be all muh life. We be runnin' 'n hidin' uh long time tryin' ta git ta Candah.

"Did either one of them there darkies in the basement try ta lay with ya in all that time?"

"No, suh. One dem darkies my daddy and one my brotha."

"How 'bout your masta...ya ever been laying with him?"

"No, suh. He tell me dat he think I purty enuf dough."

DePriest walked over to a small table and poured water into a bowl.

"Ya got all your clothes off, even your shoes?" he asked with his back still to her. He watched in a dirty mirror as she removed a tattered pair of sandals. That was all she was wearing—a gray dress made of coarse cotton and a worn out pair of sandals. Now she was totally naked. He could tell that she was quite young. Her breasts were small and showed no signs of ever being nursed. She was probably thinner now than when she was on the plantation because food was hard to come by for runaway slaves. Her skin was not as dark as her father or brother.

Probably a mulatto, DePriest thought.

DePriest carried the bowl of water to the chair and set it on the floor beside her.

"Turn 'round now so I can tend them there welts on ya back."

He soaked a piece of cloth in the cold water and squeezed it until water ran down her shoulders and back. He wiped the dried blood away and continued down her back and across her buttocks—lingering there longer than necessary. He rinsed the cloth often and washed each of her legs. There was only one welt across both calves where he had used his whip to trip her when she tried to run from him.

"Ya stink!" he said, touching her elbow to indicate he wanted her to turn around.

"Weren't no way ta take no bath runnin' 'cept in cricks. Then mud 'n dirt git back over ya quick."

"The Bible says, 'Cleanliness is next ta Godliness.' Ya ever hear that?"

"My mistress read duh Bible to me 'n muh mammy eva day when we wuz cardin' and spinnin'. My mistress say dose words ain't nowhere in da Bible, but dat it still be good fa ya to keep clean."

"She musta lied 'bout that 'cause she couldn't find it in da Bible, but it's there...swear to God," the burly preacher said.

DePriest continued to squeeze water out of the cloth and onto the girl's shoulders at her neck. He followed the beads of water down to her breasts and lingered to wash each breast until the girl's nipples hardened.

"Looks to me like ya have secret desires to lay with a man. Can't hide secrets from a man when ya naked."

The girl did not respond, but tears began to run down her cheeks.

The preacher stood and returned to the table and poured more water into the bowl.

"Ya still stink. Didn't your mammy tell ya 'bout the places you need to keep clean or they stink?"

The girl shook her head nervously but didn't speak.

"If ya gonna be travelin' with me, you gotta be clean. Nothin' worse smellin' than a woman who don't wash her private places. Stand still now, ya hear. I'm gonna wash ya all over 'til ya don't stink no more."

She closed her eyes and stood still as he ordered. When the cold water touched her private parts, she gritted her teeth but did not move. When the cold cloth was dropped and only his fingers remained exploring her insides, she did not move for fear of the bullwhip hanging on his chair.

After he was finished with her, he told her to wash herself again from head to foot, which she did as instructed. DePriest fixed her and himself a bowl of soup and some bread. They ate in silence. When they were finished, he tied her hands to the bedposts. He stretched out on a wooden bench near the bed and began snoring long before Dottie cried herself to sleep.

Sometime before dawn, the no-neck brute visited her again and she let her mind drift away from what her body was doing. She wondered about her mamma and wished she were back with her on the plantation. She wondered about her daddy and brother in the basement with the snakes. She wondered about God and the Holy Bible. She wondered about cleanliness being next to Godliness, and why a man of God, like the preacher, would stink so badly. She wondered about how good a fresh peach might taste.

More than a week went by and the two male captives remained in DePriest's basement while the female remained in his bed. Within a few more days, a steamboat would stop at the dock across the river. Aboard would be a slave broker or the riverboat's captain who would pay DePriest for his runaways and take them off his hands.

Slave brokers might return runaways to their masters if the rewards were large enough. Otherwise, the broker might sell the runaways at any auction along the river for a good profit. Either way, DePriest would be rid of them and free to get back to earning his living capturing other runaways.

He fed the two male slaves in his basement little more than bread and water once a day, but gave the female whatever he was eating. In less than two weeks of this repeated treatment and dependency, she lost her spark of hope for freedom, and became more of a slave to DePriest than she had ever been to her owners on the Memphis plantation.

***

The Lucky Lady was headed downstream when it docked on a humid, late July morning. DePriest was there waiting for the captain. Caleb Walters was also there standing in the shadows behind a willow tree a short distance away. He could see the cruel slave chaser, DePriest, and the two male slaves. He wondered where the young female was.

"How many ya got this time?" the captain asked.

Caleb's chin dropped in disbelief. It was Captain Bonèt! Memories came flooding back into his mind...it was Angelina's father!

"Got two uv'em from Memphis. They 'mitted bein' runna's, but wouldn't tell me da masta's name. Don't make me no nevamind...you'll sell'um in Lou'ville more 'n not."

DePriest unlocked the chains around the ankles of the two runaways and then stuck out his hand for payment. The captain motioned to a very large, clean, well-dressed mulatto to do his job, and the mulatto re-chained the runaways. The oldest slave whispered something to the mulatto and the mulatto relayed the message in a whisper of his own to the captain.

"That older runner says you also captured his fourteen-year-old daughter. Any truth to that?"

"Yeah, I had'er for a time, but she throwed herself overboard whilst I wuz loadin' 'em up. Head never bopped up. 'spect she's floatin' down 'round Vanceburg 'bout now."

"That's your loss, not mine," the captain said, a look of disgust crossing his face.

The Captain handed DePriest ten dollars for both runaways—the average reward being five dollars each at the time for unadvertised runaways.

"Be back this way in mid-to-late August. Maybe you'll have some more for me," the captain said, stepping back toward the boat. "Keep in mind not to be starvin' 'em, or whipping 'em and leaving scars on 'em. They bring more money if they're strong and healthy.

Depriest grunted, stuck his money in his back pocket, hopped back in his canoe, and paddled toward Kentucky.

***

That evening, Caleb sat in the café with Jane while she closed up.

"Mother, do you remember the day I turned twelve years old and we had visitors from a steamboat called the Lucky Lady?"

"Yes, I certainly do."

"I know you and dad shared some events in the past, but how well did you know those people?"

"Not well. We all happened to be here at the White Bear at the same time the night you were born. Captain Bonèt and his partner got to know your father during a terrible storm. The captain was a wealthy businessman and his partner was a gambler."

"Do you trust them?"

"It was your father who dealt with them. Mr. Phyddle inherited this hotel from his father who built it. Being riverboat people, they didn't really want to stick around to manage a hotel. They didn't seem upset at all when Landon won the White Bear in a poker game. That's about it."

"Where does the girl...Angelina come in?"

"Angelina is...Captain Bonèt's daughter. She was born the night that you were born, but her mother died that night. That's why they stopped here ten years ago...to visit Mrs. Bonèt's grave."

"Is she buried under the big oak tree?"

Jane sighed heavily. "She was for a while. Then, the town passed a law and all the remains from that little cemetery had to be moved up to Park Lawn."

"So...that's where Father took them in the buggy?"

"Yes. They were kind of in a hurry. Captain Bonèt was taking Angelina to Pittsburg and then over to New York to send her and her chaperone to Paris to complete her education."

"I wonder if she ever came back."

Jane just shrugged her shoulders because she wondered the same thing. Landon walked in a moment later and the conversation ended without another word about Angelina and her family. However, since both of his parents were present, Caleb decided to discuss another matter that was on his mind.

"I think I'm going to take a trip to New Orleans."

"Why do you want to go way down there," Jane asked.

"I figure it's the best way for me to learn the truth about the slavery issues going on in our country. My problem is I'm stuck between wanting to practice law and being a journalist. I want to help in any way I can, but I only have textbook knowledge from college. I think I need real world experience."

"I think that's a great idea," Landon said.

"But, I don't want to go as a lawyer. People don't seem to open up to lawyers. Maybe I'll go as a businessman wanting to learn about the building of hotels."

"You're going to lie about your intentions?" Jane asked.

"No, Mother, I'm just going to stretch the truth a bit."

"You don't even have to do that. There seems to be a great deal of interest about building a large, fancy hotel in town. I might want to get into part of that as an investment. They have some of the nicest hotels in the country in New Orleans. Wouldn't hurt none to go down and take a look at some of them," Landon said.

"Great! I can go down and visit for a few weeks and get information on hotel design for you and the slave industry for me."

Caleb excused himself because he didn't want to get too deeply into his real reasons for wanting to go to New Orleans. A week later, Caleb was able to flag the Sister Sue riverboat as it approached the Fiddler's Point dock. Several weeks later, he was in New Orleans.

CHAPTER FIVE

It was on a Sunday morning in August 1850, when Sister Sue docked in New Orleans near Toulouse Street. Several men carried Caleb's footlocker and bags from the ship and loaded them on a buggy ready to take departing passengers to the hotel of their choice. Caleb watched as the exchange took place. Two of the workers returned to the riverboat while three others continued walking up the hill and into town.

If these men are slaves, why do they seem to move around so freely? Caleb wondered. Just a few weeks earlier, he had watched two male runaway slaves and a young female slave being abused by a slave chaser. Caleb speculated if the three runaways back in Ohio had started their ill-fated escape from one of the area cotton plantations around New Orleans. Probably not.

How would they manage such a long trek on foot? The three were probably from one of the big plantations in Kentucky or maybe Tennessee, he thought. Kentucky was a slave state. Ohio was the nearest Free State, but getting across the river was just the first step. It was difficult for fugitive slaves to avoid slave hunters, the law, and citizens who felt threatened by escaped slaves. Navigating the two hundred miles from Fiddler's Point to Lake Erie took courage, cunning, and help.

Assistance in the form of food, money, shelter, and directions was available from members of the Underground Railroad, but the arduous trek between friendly stations was fraught with danger and the fear of capture.

Caleb's mind was filled with questions about the future of his country, about the future of the runaway slaves who made it to Canada, and about the future of those who didn't.

He was halfway down the gangplank when he saw a lady in the distance near the end of the dock. She had her back to him as she gazed at the river and the landscape beyond.

Caleb felt his pulse racing as his heart began to pound in his chest. He had not felt such an unusual stirring in his chest since he turned twelve. Absolutely preposterous, he thought.

He could see that she had soft, wavy brown hair that cascaded down her back past her waistline. She was wearing what Caleb at first thought was a flowered dress. As he got closer, he could tell that she was actually wearing a plain white cotton smock over her dress and popular hoop and crinoline slips. What he thought from a distance were flowers—were in reality multiple smudges of paint.

Caleb handed the dark complexioned buggy driver some coins and instructed him to move his buggy further down the dock and wait on him while he looked at some artwork. The driver followed instructions and pulled his buggy alongside another carriage parked near the end of the dock.

Now oblivious to the other passengers and dockworkers, Caleb strolled down the pier in the direction of the young lady. When he got close, he slowly cut behind her at an angle from her left to her right hoping to get a better look at the lady, but could only see her profile. He was close enough to see the curve of her long, dark eyelashes, her small slender nose, and her open mouth that now held a short, stubby paintbrush between white teeth. He wanted to see more, but as her slender arm carried a brush to her work, Caleb's eyes were drawn to the canvas.

She was painting the landscape of the flat marshes across a narrow part of the Mississippi River where a loon bobbed up and down on the surface water, a blue heron soared across the horizon, and swamp grass pointed in the direction of what Caleb believed was the bluest morning sky he had ever seen.

He passed the sitting young lady for a short distance before stopping and turning back toward her. When he was close enough to see her face clearly, a single question in his mind held sway over all others. Could this stunningly beautiful young lady sitting on a New Orleans wharf in front of an easel really be her? Impossible, he thought. Absolutely impossible!

"Is your painting for sale?" Caleb asked, not knowing any better way of striking up a conversation with a stranger.

She glanced up for just a moment before her eyes returned to the canvas. She removed the stubby brush from her teeth.

"Do you like what you see?" she asked as her brown eyes met his blue eyes.

"Yes, I think it's...well...it's beautiful.

The slightest of smiles spread across her lips but an even greater smile was evident in her eyes.

"Are you a dealer?" she asked.

"A what?" he replied.

"Do you plan on buying my work to resell?"

"No, ah...of course not," he stammered from being caught off guard.

"Then you don't think my work is good enough to sell?"

Before he could answer, she smiled broadly.

"You're teasing me?" He said.

"I apologize. A dealer would have known that my work is not even half done. What do you like about it?"

"Really, I was attracted more to the floral design you have painted on your dress. Is it finished?"

"Now you're teasing me."

They both smiled.

"Angelina!"

Caleb's body stiffened at the sound of the name. The voice came from behind them.

Angelina rolled her eyes to indicate she was familiar with the voice. Caleb turned to see a woman departing the carriage next to his. She was maybe in her late thirties or early forties, fashionably dressed, and carrying a fancy parasol. It was the parasol that changed Caleb's hazy memories to a clear picture. She was the same woman who escorted Angelina during their visit to Fiddler's Point ten years earlier.

"It's best you be getting out of the sun now," she said, directing her carriage driver to load up the easel, paints, and stool.

"Oh, Miss Nikki, the gentleman only wants to buy my painting. I'm as safe as a baby in her mother's arms," Angelina said, as Miss Nikki looked Caleb over.

Caleb wanted to shout, "I know this woman," but he simply wasn't sure what to do at this moment. He had seen Angelina's father paying for escaped slaves. He hated slavery and detested all who promoted the inhuman activities. Finally, he decided to deal with that matter as it progressed, but it was time to make his identity clear. He hoped Angelina remembered him.

Caleb seemed to grasp the immediate situation of being a stranger. He walked directly to the older woman, bowed, and presented himself.

"I apologize that I'm traveling alone and have no one with me that can make formal introductions if they are, indeed, needed again. My name is Caleb Walters from Fiddler's Point, Ohio. We met ten years ago."

The woman glanced at Angelina and sent unspoken instructions.

"It is nice meeting you again, sir. My name is Miss Nikki," she said, glancing at Angelina again. "I would like to present Miss Angelina Bonèt...should you not recall her name."

"Now that Mr. Walters and I have formally met again, Miss Nikki, would you wait in the carriage while I finish talking business with the gentleman," Angelina said.

Miss Nikki and the driver returned to the carriage, but Caleb noticed her glancing over her shoulder several times as if to make sure Angelina was safe.

"Well, I hope I haven't offended anyone's Southern expectations," Caleb said, making full eye contact with the lovely lady.

"I believe everything will be okay, but you will have to purchase my painting when it's finished or Miss Nikki will consider it an insult."

"I will buy it right now if you wish."

"Oh, no, I'll have to come back early tomorrow morning to finish up."

"Then...I'll see you here tomorrow."

Caleb escorted Angelina to her carriage and watched until the carriage disappeared beyond the levee. His mind was reeling. He had only been in New Orleans a few minutes and had already become reacquainted with the beautiful young lady who once again captured his heart.

"Take me to the St. Charles," Caleb said to his carriage driver.

***

Even though the pitcher of water in his hotel room had an unpleasant odor, Caleb poured about half of it into a bowl and used it to wash his face, neck, ears, and hair. With his face still wet, he honed his razor on a whetstone before shaving. While most men of society were sporting moustaches, muttonchops, or goatees, Caleb was clean-shaven with sideburns stopping at the earlobes. His face was smooth but his square chin gave him a masculine—if not a rugged look. His nose had a slight ridge in the middle because of having it broken and reset on several occasions while boxing in college. With his hand speed and foot speed; however, he managed to escape many blows that left some of his teammates with flat noses and cauliflower ears. Just over six feet tall, he was of medium build and carried himself smoothly and confidently.

The large pitcher of water was empty by the time Caleb finished his sponge bath. The odor of the drinking water was not much better than the bathing water. His thoughts drifted back to Ohio where natural, fresh-water springs and wells provided excellent drinking water. It's no wonder so many people in New Orleans drink wine, he thought, as he toweled dry before dabbing on some toilet water.

***

By early afternoon, Caleb had visited each floor of the St. Charles, and even though it had been seven years since the hotel was renovated following a fire that destroyed the veranda and great, white dome for which it was famous, the smell of smoke seemed to linger within the marble. At street level, he found the wine room, the ballroom, several smaller meeting rooms, and a dining area. The lobby was full of people and what conversations that Caleb could overhear most often concerned the potential for a war between the South and the North.

Suddenly, many of the people near the dining room moved as a group away from the entrance. They murmured something about a champion of some sort. Caleb stepped into the crowd as a small entourage of men escorted a puffy-faced, bearded man into the room. Women stepped back, and most covered their mouths with gloved hands or rapidly moving silk fans even as they stretched their necks in curiosity.

"Morrissey! It's John Morrissey," the crowd whispered almost in unison.

"I'll be damned! It is Old Smoke, the champ himself," mumbled a man near Caleb.

Caleb's coach at college had used Morrissey as a prime example for the boxing team of how not to box; Morrissey was a brawler, not a boxer. Yet, the coach told stories of Morrissey's great courage and stamina.

"Do you know how he got his nickname, Old Smoke?" Caleb asked the man standing near him.

"No, as a matter of fact, I often wondered about that. Do you know?"

"Yes. During a barroom brawl in New York City a few years back, young Morrissey and his opponent knocked over a wood-burning stove, scattering hot, smoldering embers across the floor. Morrissey's clothes caught on fire, but he still managed to fight through the pain and defeat his opponent."

"You don't say?" the man replied, his chin dropping down. "What do you suppose he's doin' here in New Orleans?"

"Barnstorming around the country, I suppose, building up interest in a possible fight with John Heenan sometime in the future."

Once Morrissey disappeared inside the dining room, the crowd dispersed. Caleb moved on through the lobby taking mental notes of the ballroom, the wine room, and the ornate staircase that once led to the popular dome before the fire destroyed it. Stepping out the front door, Caleb delighted in the beauty of the marble steps set between porticos of six Corinthian columns.

"A little more than what Fiddler's Point is ready for," Caleb thought with a smile, as he began a stroll around the town. He found a small restaurant where he sampled the local seafood. He was back at the St. Charles just before dark and went straight to bed hoping to get a good night's sleep filled with sweet dreams of the angel he had seen on the dock earlier in the day.

***

The next morning, Caleb was up, bathed, dressed, and sitting in the shadows on the dock when a warm, hazy dawn spread across the marshlands. Not long afterwards, a carriage pulled up. The driver got out and unloaded an easel and other paint supplies. He set them up according to Angelina's instructions on the exact spot that they occupied the day before.

Caleb remained in the shadows out of sight as he watched Angelina prepare to work. She selected a small brush, dabbed it in several colors on her pallet and then painted the letters "AB" on the lower right-hand corner of the painting.

"Are you still interested in buying my painting?" she said without taking her eyes off the easel.

Caleb stepped out of the shadows, "How did you know I was there? I thought I was well hidden."

"Artists are trained to see minute details in whatever they are looking at—especially shadows. Why were you hiding?"

"I...uh...I mean...I just enjoyed watching you work. Even though we were properly introduced yesterday, I wasn't sure if I...I mean...we needed to be in the company of your chaperone for us to be permitted to talk. Doesn't southern custom require that?"

Angelina turned slightly on her stool to face Caleb as he approached.

"Perhaps...if I were a Southern lady...that would be necessary, but I am not."

Caleb stopped dead in his tracks. "You don't live in New Orleans?"

"Gracious no! You would never catch one of those...well...one of those 'ladies' here on the dock at dawn without half of her family being with her."

"Then where..."

Angelina smiled. "I'm not from anywhere. I'm from everywhere."

Caleb was speechless. He certainly didn't know what she meant by being from everywhere.

"But, you have to live somewhere...don't you?"

"I live on my father's riverboat. I visit New Orleans from time to time just as I visit Pittsburgh, Cincinnati, St. Louis, and everyplace in between."

Caleb was fascinated with this intelligent, beautiful young woman. He finally began to walk again and when he reached her, he stuck out his hand in a gesture of politeness.

She responded not with her hand ready to shake like men, but with her hand out...limp wristed...palm down. He was not sure what to do except react to her response by taking her hand. The moment he touched her, electricity shot through his entire body, his heart pounded in his chest, and he felt as if his knees were trembling. The moment seemed suspended in time—moving in slow motion. He leaned forward and kissed her hand softly...lingering for only a moment. When he straightened up, her eyes locked with his and she did not take her hand away.

After a long moment, she removed her hand, but not until that ancient message, delivered and received between men and women, was locked within their hearts and souls forever.

"Well, my painting is finished now. Are you still interested?" Angelina finally said, breaking the silent moment that they had shared.

"I thought you said yesterday it might take you until noon today to finish it."

"Oh, that was for Miss Nikki's benefit. I only needed to sign it for you. If you were truly interested...in my painting...I hoped you might be here this morning...and here you are."

"Yes...here we are...and where shall we go from here?" Caleb said, thinking of the long term.

"To breakfast!" she said without hesitation, speaking of the short term without revealing any hints concerning the long term.

They were playing a game that all lovers must play when getting to know one another better.

Caleb Walters, a young lawyer and humanist, was deeply committed to a social position of helping the victims of bondage, a cruel and selfish social and economic system. He was a man with opinions that he felt he must conceal while getting a first-hand look at slavery in all of its complexity. He wondered if he had already allowed his intimate thoughts and hopes to grow in the face of the great abyss between his social position and hers...or at least her father's.

But what about her? A young, beautiful, free spirited artist without permanent roots, a visitor wherever she may be, a woman that did not allow social etiquette to control her life, and a woman that seemed to have deep secrets masked by mesmerizing eyes and an innocent smile.

Angelina was wondering about some of the same things. She was only twelve years old when she met Caleb for only a few minutes on one day.

Did he remember those moments as fondly as she did?

"Breakfast sounds great, but this is my first time in New Orleans and I don't know the best place to go."

"The St. Charles has a great breakfast," she replied, waving for her carriage to move closer.

"The St. Charles? That's where I'm staying!"

Angelina smiled with a look of satisfaction before saying, "Me, too."

When the carriage grew near, the driver got out and loaded Angelina's equipment onto the buggy. Caleb bowed his head slightly, smiled, and greeted Miss Nikki.

"Good morning, ma'am."

"Good morning, Mr. Walters."

"Mr. Walters will be riding back to the St. Charles with us, Miss Nikki. He's staying there."

Her chaperone's eyebrows rose and remained there while she inhaled deeply, held her breath for a long moment, and then finally exhaled with a rather loud puff of air.

Caleb offered his hand to Angelina to assist her into the carriage before stepping up and sitting beside her. Again, Miss Nikki exhaled loudly.

CHAPTER SIX

At the St. Charles, Caleb, Angelina, and Miss Nikki sat at a table as a dark complexioned waiter prepared to take their order. Suddenly, a wry smile formed on Miss Nikki's face.

"Angelina!"

The voice came from behind Caleb and Angelina, but Angelina rolled her eyes at the sound of the male voice without looking around.

"Hello, Father."

With the second word registering in Caleb's mind, he immediately stood.

"Father, I think you'll remember Mr. Caleb Walters from Fiddler's Point, Ohio. Mr. Walters is interested in purchasing one of my paintings and we're about to discuss the price over breakfast. Would you like to join us?"

"The name, Caleb Walters, nearly took Captain Bonèt's breath away, but he recovered quickly.

"Yes. It has been a long time," he said. Caleb extended his hand. Caught a bit off guard,

Captain Bonèt shook hands with Caleb but avoided eye contact before directing a stern look at Angelina.

Her father was dressed in a gray suit with a deep burgundy vest. His plump stomach stretched the buttons on the vest allowing his white shirt to show. He carried a top hat and a fancy-looking walking stick with a shiny metal tip. His face appeared flushed from his surprise meeting with his daughter...or perhaps from the tightness of the collar around his neck.

"Ahem!" The sound came from a younger man standing slightly behind Captain Bonèt. He didn't greet Angelina nor Miss Nikki, focusing his attention only on Caleb.

Caleb remained standing, waiting on the next display of proper etiquette without knowing exactly what it should be. The man glaring at him was very tall with broad shoulders and several extra pounds around his midsection. His hands looked soft and dimpled, as did his pale, pinkish face. Finally, Captain Bonèt made the introduction.

"Mr. Walters...I would like to present Mr. Maurice Melwood, oldest son of Major Melwood of the Melwood plantation."

Polite nods were made, but neither man maneuvered to a position close enough to shake hands.

Once introductions were made, and everyone was seated, Mr. Melwood was quick to establish a conversation with Caleb.

"May I ask what use you might have for a watercolor," the man asked.

"I'm contemplating making an investment in a new hotel in Ohio and thought some nice art might be a pleasing addition for the lobby," Caleb replied,

The older man looked directly at Caleb for the first time, but did not speak.

"Don't you have any decent artists in the North?" Mr. Melwood said smugly.

"Of course, but times are changing. That's why I'm staying here at the St. Charles. A hotel as fine as this, cannot be found in the North. I'm here to study the finest hotel ever built."

"How are things in Fiddler's Point?" Captain Bonèt asked.

"The town is growing," Caleb answered.

Angelina was amused but listening intently to the interrogation.

"I've been past Fiddler's Point many times piloting the Lucky Lady, but my schedule hasn't allowed me to stop on many occasions.

"I've heard of the Lucky Lady, sir. I came in on the Sister Sue. Are you familiar with that steamer?"

"Of course." He then changed the subject by asking, "Are you enjoying your stay here at maybe the finest hotel in the world?"

"Yes. I've already gotten several ideas that may work with my venture...on a smaller scale, of course."

"How long will you be staying in our fine city?" asked Mr. Melwood.

"For a few days, anyway," Caleb replied, glancing up at the beautiful young woman who brought him to this situation.

The conversation was cordial during the breakfast, but Caleb could sense Mr. Melwood's agitation and concern that Angelina was socializing with a Yankee.

After breakfast, the captain stood.

"Angelina, it's time we finished our business here in New Orleans. Repairs on the Lucky Lady will be finished soon and we'll be on our way back up the Mississippi. Good luck to you, young man. I hope your stay at the St. Charles is fruitful," Captain Bonèt said, gazing at Caleb a long moment before turning away.

With that, and polite smiles from the ladies, Caleb was left standing at the table alone.

***

Around noon the next day, a clerk brought Caleb a sealed note without any suggestion as to whom it was from, but he knew immediately from the fragrance of the stationery. Written in excellent longhand, the note read:

> *If you still wish to purchase my*
> *painting and would like to tour*
> *my home, come aboard the*
> *Lucky Lady at 2:00 p.m. today.*
> *Angelina*

Caleb was a few minutes early and found Angelina and Miss Nikki waiting at the top of the gangplank.

"Good afternoon, Miss Bonèt. Hello Miss Nikki."

"And good afternoon to you, Mr. Walters," Angelina replied as Caleb stepped aboard the small but magnificent steamboat, Lucky Lady. Miss Nikki managed a weak smile but did not speak.

"Everything looks so fresh and new," Caleb said after observing how clean the Lucky Lady was, compared to Sister Sue.

"Yes...we just got her back from dry dock today. They made a few repairs underneath and gave her a fresh coat of paint inside and out. That's why there are no passengers onboard yet. Father must give everything a complete inspection before he'll give orders to load the fuel."

"How long will that take?"

"Several days," she said. "We'll take passengers aboard on Thursday or Friday morning and be on our way back up the Mississippi."

"So...you'll be leaving...that soon?"

"Yes, I told you this was my home."

Angelina took him completely around the bottom deck and then to the second deck where passenger cabins were located. Miss Nikki did not intrude, but stayed within sight. There was a nice dining room and another large room where the men gambled—mostly playing poker. Everything about the Lucky Lady was superior to Sister Sue.

When they came to another staircase, Angelina stopped and turned to speak to Miss Nikki.

"Would you please go back to the dining room and fix my guest and me a glass of sweet tea. There should be a pitcher in the icebox that father just had installed. Fix one for yourself, too."

Miss Nikki looked a little concerned, but followed instructions and soon disappeared back into the dining area.

Angelina smiled as she led Caleb up the stairs to the third deck. She showed him through the pilothouse, explaining that it was where her father stayed most of the time.

"This is the nicest riverboat I've ever seen," Caleb said. "Are most of them built much like this one?"

"Lots of different sizes, but most are similar. But...I doubt that you have ever seen what I'm about to show you."

Angelina moved across a space several yards wide to a door, which she opened with a key and then asked Caleb to step inside. He stopped in his tracks at what he saw.

"I can't believe this! It's absolutely beautiful!"

Angelina smiled broadly with the pleasure of knowing that Caleb liked what he was seeing.

"This is my home," she said with pride.

Behind a locked door on the third deck of a medium sized riverboat was a lovely stateroom that would rival most any home. Windows on both sides and the back provided a panoramic view of both banks of the river. The first room served as a living room with comfortable looking furniture. A small dining area sat off toward the rear. Down a narrow hallway, she led him to two nicely furnished bedrooms.

"That is where Miss Nikki sleeps," she said.

Caleb stood silently staring at the watercolor above the bed. It was the White Bear Inn from the viewpoint of the path leading down to the dock.

"I did that one from memory right after we shared our twelfth birthday in the White Bear Café," Angelina said.

"It's beautiful! How could you remember all the details after only seeing it that one day?"

"I did a quick pencil sketch from the reeds and filled in the details from memory before I ever started painting it. Come on, I'll show you my room."

Above the headboard of Angelina's bed was another watercolor—this one of twelve-year-old-Caleb as he stood in the reeds watching Angelina at her mother's gravesite.

"I'm impressed, but why would you want to paint a rag-tag boy in muddy clothes?"

"I don't know, maybe it was because I thought you were cute."

Caleb smiled as a flush crawled across his face.

"Or, maybe because it was the very first time we ever saw each other and I wondered what your eyes were saying to mine," Angelina said, her lips quivering a bit.

Before Caleb could respond, Angelina smiled and gestured that she wanted to show him something else. She led him out of her living quarters and across to the small room from where her father piloted the Lucky Lady. On the wall beside the large window was another of her watercolors. It was a watercolor of the Bonèt-Phyddle Gardens where her mother was buried. There was no reason to ask her why she painted this one—he already knew the answer.

As they returned to the main deck, Caleb wondered why anyone would ever want to live anyplace else—he was already beginning to love life on a riverboat.

"Ahem!" The loud sound came from behind them.

"Your drinks, ma'am," Miss Nikki said.

"Thank you, Miss Nikki," Angelina responded with a smile as she guided Caleb back to the front room.

"Would you like to join us, Miss Nikki?" Caleb asked.

"No thank you, sir. I have some things to do in my room if nobody minds."

Without waiting for permission, she stepped down the hallway and into her room.

"Well, Mr. Walters, shall we discuss the price of the painting you're interested in?"

Caleb had no idea where to begin a discussion about price. If it would please her, I would pay whatever she asks, he thought.

"Where do we begin? Do you have a price in mind?" he finally managed to say. She looked deeply into his eyes.

"Okay, I'll make you a deal. I'll loan you the painting and you can try it in your hotel. If you like it and want several more, then we can talk about it again. How does that sound?"

"If that pleases you, it pleases me," he replied, knowing that she just provided the opportunity to see her again even after he returned to Ohio.

She put out her hand, "Then we have a deal?"

Caleb took her hand and felt the familiar electricity shoot through his body. Her hand was soft and warm. He wanted to kiss her hand, her cheeks, and her lips. He wanted to hold her in his arms and feel the warmth of her body next to his, but all he could do was smile and say, "Yes, it's a deal."

Caleb had experienced several flirtations in his life, but none of them were serious enough to consider long-term possibilities. This one, if it was indeed a flirtation, was completely different. He had never felt the overwhelming feelings of wanting to be near someone every available moment. But he was well educated and thoroughly aware of the social traditions of the south. He didn't want to say or do anything that would be considered inappropriate to Angelina or her father.

After Angelina and Caleb finished their drink, she called to her chaperone, "Miss Nikki, we're ready to return to shore now."

Moments later, the two departed the Lucky Lady with Miss Nikki a short distance behind. As they stepped onto the gangplank, they could see that the dock had become quite crowded with passengers prepared to board or disembark one of the many riverboats along the shore.

Among the crowd, Caleb noticed Maurice Melwood standing near the edge of the pier staring directly at him and Angelina. The man turned away abruptly, and as he did, he bumped a small black boy standing beside his mother. The boy toppled off the pier into the muddy water between the dock and the riverboat. Melwood glanced down for only a moment, put on his hat, and walked to a waiting carriage.

"Help! My son can't swim!" the boy's mother shouted.

Men and women along the dock watched the boy splash around in the water, but no one came to his aid.

Caleb slipped out of his jacket and tossed his hat aside before he ran to the edge of the dock and dove into the water. He made his way to the boy and pulled him to the edge of the pier where the boy's mother and several men helped drag the child to safety. The boy was soaked and frightened but otherwise okay. The mother thanked Caleb several times before moving away with her son.

Angelina and Miss Nikki rushed to Caleb's side.

"That was the bravest thing I've ever seen," Angelina said, taking his hand.

"Are you okay Mr. Walters?" Miss Nikki asked.

"I'm fine," Caleb replied. "I need to get back to my hotel to get out of these wet clothes, though."

"I have your coat and hat, Mr. Walters," Miss Nikki said. "You can ride to your hotel in our carriage."

The three of them rode back to the St. Charles together. Miss Nikki did not talk to Caleb during the ride back, but she did smile at him often. Something had changed in her demeanor and attitude toward this near stranger who, in Miss Nikki's mind, was a serious suitor of the young woman she had raised from birth.

In front of the St. Charles, the three departed the carriage and walked toward the entrance.

"Well, after the grand tour of the Lucky Lady and the unexpected dip in the Mississippi, I've worked up quite an appetite. Would the two of you consider joining me in the dining room for dinner this evening?

Angelina glanced at Miss Nikki for approval and got it in the form of a genuine smile.

"Yes, Mr. Walters, we would be pleased to join you for dinner. What time shall we meet you there?"

Caleb wondered for a split second if he should ask Angeline for her room number so that he might escort her to the dining room from there, but quickly thought better of it.

"Does six o'clock sound good to both of you?"

"That sounds just right, Mr. Walters. Now, you better get to your room and get out of those wet clothes," Angelina said.

There was something in the tone of her words and the twinkle in her eyes that allowed Caleb's mind to go on a quick journey of possibilities, but he quickly recovered, smiled, and made his exit.

***

Early that evening, Caleb met Angelina and Miss Nikki in the dining room. The mood of the evening was more relaxed than before, due in no small way to Miss Nikki's apparent change of attitude toward Caleb. Just before dinner was over, the mood changed again.

"Well, Angelina...once again I find you in the company of a cowardly Yankee," Maurice Melwood said, with a slurred voice. He was obviously under the influence of too much wine.

Caleb stood to face the aggressor.

"The only display of cowardliness I've witnessed today was watching your actions down at the dock, Mr. Melwood."

Melwood's face grew puckered with anger as he stepped up to Caleb.

"If you are a gentleman, Mr. Walters, you will follow me to the far balcony to discuss this matter privately," Melwood whispered.

Caleb excused himself from the table and followed Melwood to the terrace. Before either person spoke, Mr. Melwood wheeled and smacked Caleb across the face with a glove.

"Let's just see who the coward is on the field of honor, Mr. Walters. My second will contact your second—if you have one—in short order."

"I will be acting as Mr. Walters' second, Mr. Melwood. Your attendant may contact me on the

Lucky Lady whenever he wishes," Captain Bonèt said in a firm voice as he walked onto the balcony.

Melwood looked stunned. He and Captain Bonèt had made several business deals in the past, and Melwood considered him a Southerner or at least a Southern sympathizer.

Puzzled, but determined to maintain his Southern dignity, Melwood nodded with a slight bow, turned, and made his exit.

"Father, why did you exacerbate this situation? Caleb...Mr. Walters didn't accept the challenge. Why would he need a second?" Angelina asked, stepping onto the balcony.

"Because that's the way it's done here in New Orleans. It would be considered impolite for Mr. Walters and Mr. Melwood to discuss any of the details in public," the Captain responded.

"I think it's all a bit uncivilized for two grown men to fight one another for no good reason," Angelina said.

Captain Bonèt looked at his daughter and agreed with her logic, but knew that in the South, a challenge to allow one to protect one's honor was a serious matter.

"Miss Nikki, it's getting rather late. Would you please escort Angelina back to her room," her father said. It was a statement...not a question.

A look of frustration crossed Angelina's face, but she said her goodnights and returned to her room.

Captain Bonèt stared at Caleb for a long moment as if studying every detail of his face.

"Are you familiar with the etiquette involved in being challenged to a duel, Mr. Walters?

"No sir."

"First of all, once the challenge has been made, a note—written by the challenger—must be delivered to your second. It will comment on the nature of the suggested offense and the perceived need to satisfactorily maintain one's honor."

"I see," Caleb responded, seemingly a bit overwhelmed by the situation.

"How are you with a pistol?"

"I am a...a less than average marksman shooting at a target I'll have to admit. Is that what we'll be using?"

Captain Bonèt ignored Caleb's question.

"Mr. Melwood is an expert shot with dueling pistols. He's proven that many times in contests at the shooting range."

Caleb blinked several times. He thought about his mother's warnings to stay out of trouble, and here he was...in a possible duel to the death with a man he hardly knew.

"How about fencing swords? Had any training or experience with them?"

"I watched some students taking fencing lessons at college, but I was never fond of the thought of sticking a sharp instrument into another man's body...nor having one stuck into mine for that matter."

"Please understand, Mr. Walters, this is not a sporting matter, nor something to be taken lightly. Since he challenged you, you have the right to choose the weapon."

Caleb looked down at the tabletop and exhaled heavily.

"Can I just ignore his challenge?"

Bonèt swallowed hard. "That's exactly what you should do if we lived in a truly civilized community, but I'm afraid that refusing Melwood's challenge will result in you being socially disgraced and branded a coward."

"Must I choose only between dueling pistols and swords?"

"Uh...I've heard stories about shotguns being used one time at Dueling Oak in City Park, and a few times the challenged has chosen short knives. But you have to understand that all of these weapons are deadly."

"Must the duel be fought to the death?"

"Not necessarily...if the parties agree that it isn't necessary, but, the only way this happens is if one party is injured in such a way that he cannot continue the duel."

"When must I make a decision?"

"Melwood's second will deliver a note to me in writing perhaps this night or early in the morning. If you accept his challenge, I will send a return note stating such. The seconds will decide on the location in which the duel will take place.

"Then my answer for you...now...is that I will accept the challenge and reveal my choice of weapons on the site and at the specified time of the duel."

Bonèt placed the palm of his hand on his forehead and sighed. "Are you sure?"

"Yes, but I have one last question. Why did you volunteer to be my second?"

Bonèt sighed again. "I'm not really sure myself, but I just had a feeling that it was the proper thing to do."

Caleb stood and thanked Bonèt for his assistance and advice before turning and walking back to his room.

He wanted to get some rest but his night was filled with frightful thoughts...not of being killed by Melwood the next day, but of not seeing Angelina again.

CHAPTER SEVEN

In the half-light before dawn, Caleb was awakened from his restless sleep by a rapping on his door. When he answered, Captain Bonèt was standing there with a note in his hand.

"Melwood wishes to dispense with any additional formalities and meet you at Dueling Oak this very morning at dawn. He has agreed that you have the choice in weapons. You have less than one hour to prepare," Captain Bonèt said, looking nervous for the first time.

"Where is Dueling Oak?" Caleb asked.

"It's just north of here in City Park."

"Can we get coffee downstairs?" Caleb asked.

"Yes. The dining room never closes."

"Then I'll meet you there in about ten minutes. Is that quick enough?"

"Yes, of course...I mean...it isn't far away. We have a little time."

Bonèt went downstairs to the dining room and ordered two coffees. Caleb splashed water on his face, ran his fingers through his hair, slipped into his shirt and coat and headed downstairs. He took a chair at the table with Captain Bonèt.

"When do you need to know the weapon I've chosen," Caleb said calmly.

"As soon as you wish to tell me...I suppose," Captain Bonèt said with an expression of concern sweeping across his brow.

"Good, then I'll give you my handwritten note now if you promise not to open it until we are together at the site," Caleb said without a hint of alarm in his demeanor.

Captain Bonèt nodded his consent and the two began to drink their coffee.

"Captain Bonèt...may I ask you a personal question?" Caleb asked.

"May you ask about what, Mr. Walters?"

"It's about your daughter."

Captain Bonèt did not answer for a long moment. Finally he said, "You may ask, but I won't promise to answer."

"That's fair enough. Does she disapprove of dueling?"

In silence, Captain Bonèt seemed to study Caleb and the question he had asked.

"Mr. Walters...as you have probably already learned, my daughter has opinions of her own that are not based on...or controlled by the usual social norms. She has a deep sense of right from wrong, and I know considers dueling a brutal way of settling simple disputes. However, she believes a person should always stand up for what he...or she...believes. Does that answer your question?"

"Yes...thank you, sir."

Without further conversation, the two men finished their coffee before moving to the front of the St. Charles where Captain Bonèt's carriage was waiting.

***

When they arrived at the park, there were several men gathering into a group—Melwood, his second, and perhaps a dozen others who apparently were there for the show.

Standing alone at a distance from this group was a tall, slim man dressed in leather knee-high boots, brown frock coat, and a soft, wide-brimmed hat to match.

"I must talk with that man for a moment. Is it alright for me to read your note now?"

"Yes."

"Then you stay here until I call you over."

Captain Bonèt walked to the tall stranger and they talked quietly for a moment. Then Captain Bonèt took the note from his vest pocket and turned to allow the rising sun to make it possible to see the writing on the note. Almost instantly, both men turned and looked at Caleb for a long moment before motioning for him to join them.

No introductions were offered, and Caleb stood silently waiting for some comment. Finally the tall man spoke.

"Do you have any experience as a pugilist, young man?"

"I fought on my college team."

"How did you do?"

"Before I learned the skills, I was zero and nine. After I learned the skills, I was 22 and zero."

A slight grin formed at the corners of the man's mouth.

"Do you understand your opponent is at least six inches taller than you and has a weight advantage of probably thirty pounds or more?"

"Yes, but he has soft weight...and I think he's slow."

The man's smile broadened.

"Any other reasons you believe you can defeat this guy?"

"Yes."

"Would you please share them with us?"

"It's the reason we're here fighting this duel in the first place. I called Mr. Melwood a coward and I believe he is."

"That's enough for me, Captain. Take your man's jacket and shirt off to give him some freedom to breath.

The tall man excused himself and approached the crowd of men—calling one by the title, Major. Moments later the man stepped out of the crowd and approached the tall man.

"Mr. Phyddle, I know you're a gambling man, but are you sure you want to wager on the outcome of this duel? My son has challenged a number of men and has always retained his honor."

"I'm quite aware of that, sir, but...as you say...I am a gambling man."

"Then what shall the wager be?" the Major said in a confident tone.

"I never make small bets, Major. I believe that if something is worth betting on...the sky's the limit."

"Then you name the stakes, Mr. Phyddle. I'll match anything you bet."

Mr. Phyddle called for Melwood's second and several other men to join them. He motioned for Captain Bonèt to join them but asked Caleb to remain at a distance.

"Gentlemen, Major Melwood and I are about to make a sizable wager on the outcome of this duel and wish you all, as gentlemen, to act as witnesses. Major Melwood has agreed to match whatever I bet."

Major Melwood looked a bit nervous, but agreed.

"I have, indeed, agreed to put up anything, even my plantation on this wager."

"Then, done, Major...the bet shall be twenty thousand dollars secured by my plantation—lock, stock and barrel—against yours," Mr. Phyddle announced firmly. "This means the loser pays up by noon today, or signs over his working plantation along with his slaves—carrying away only his family and personal clothing within forty-eight hours. Are there any objections to these terms?"

The chins of all the witnesses seemed to drop at the same time. While the terms of the wager seemed a bit harsh, the Major had too much pride to object.

"Then let's get on with it!" the Major said.

"Indeed," Mr. Phyddle said, "But first, Captain Bonèt must announce the chosen weapons.

"Captain Bonèt stepped forward and removed the paper from his waist pocket again and unfolded it slowly.

"Having been challenged by Mr. Melwood, Mr. Walters has the privilege and the right to choose the weapons...and he chooses fists.

"Fists? Outrageous! He can't choose fists!" the major shouted.

Major Melwood was fuming. He looked first to the group of witnesses and then at his son's second. They looked at one another, but none offered an opinion.

"On the contrary, major, fists have been the weapon of choice in duels dating back to ancient times," Phyddle said

"But...but...these are not ancient times...we expect to use modern weapons," the Major said, still looking for support from anyone in the crowd.

"Many kinds of weapons have been used in duels, Major. Shotguns, hammers, sticks, stones, and fists," Mr. Phyddle explained.

"But this is a matter of honor! My son has the right to seriously wound the offender or kill him if it be God's will!"

"Major...your son has the right to do that if he can, but he must do it with fists."

"But...he must choose a deadly weapon. That's how it has always been done in the South," the major said, shouting again.

Mr. Phyddle raised his voice to match the Majors. He made sure that everyone in the still-gathering crowd could hear every word...including Maurice Melwood.

"By all means, major. The fists of German John Vaughanberg killed his opponent in a duel outside Boston some years back. Sean O'Brien killed his opponent with just one punch over in Georgia. Irish James Sweeno knocked out seven men in a bar fight leaving all of them with serious wounds such as broken jaws and noses. One had his left eye knocked nearly completely out of his skull. Fists are serious weapons, major...capable of delivering serious wounds and sometimes deadly wounds."

Maurice's second took the major aside and whispered something into his ear. The major quickly looked at Caleb and sized him up from head to toe. He then looked at his son.

"Mr. Phyddle, my son stands nearly two hands taller than his opponent and outweighs him by maybe fifty pounds. Don't you think...fists...give my son an unfair advantage?"

"If so, then that is his opponent's problem. I have never met the chap, but he has chosen fists, and that is his right. I'm just a gambling man rolling the dice."

The major looked over at Caleb again and back at his son—an air of confidence crossed the major's face.

"Then let's get on with it, gentlemen."

Mr. Phyddle stepped forward.

"Yes...being familiar with the London Prize Ring Rules, I have been asked to state the essence of these rules before we begin."

He walked to a large flat area with no grass and used his boot to draw a three-foot square in the dirt.

"Will the seconds bring the opponents forward," he announced.

Then to the opponents, the witnesses, and all others present, he stated the simple rules.

"One! Neither man shall strike his opponent in any manner until...until..."

Phyddle stopped and looked around. He was unsure for a moment who to pick, then decided on Major Melwood.

"...until Major Melwood utters the word, begin.

Two! If an opponent is knocked down, he will have half a minute to return to his side of this square or he will be deemed a beaten man.

Three! No person is to hit his adversary when he is down, or seize him by the ham, the breeches, or any part below the waist. A man on his knees is to be reckoned down."

Mr. Phyddle stepped back several steps.

"Are we ready, sir?" Melwood's second asked.

"Indeed we are, sir. Will the seconds escort their party to the square and have them place the toe of their boot on either line," Phyddle said.

The seconds moved forward—Caleb without his coat, vest, or hat while Melwood was fully dressed in coat, vest, ruffled shirt, tie, and top hat. As the two opponents neared the line, Caleb kept his eyes on Melwood's eyes at all times. Each time Melwood looked up to see Caleb's icy stare, he quickly looked down or away. As each toed the line, the size difference in the two opponents became even more apparent to the onlookers causing whispers to sweep through the crowd.

While Caleb was shorter and lighter, he nevertheless presented a picture of a strong, healthy specimen of a man. Melwood, on the other hand, appeared soft in face and body and much more nervous.

Caleb placed the toe of his boot on the line first and raised his left arm chin high with his fingers clinched tightly into a fist. His right fist was drawn back near his cheek.

Melwood stepped forward in a slow, awkward movement but finally touched his toe to the line, clinched his fists, and raised them both only waist high and out away from his body as if he were getting ready to hug someone.

Caleb maintained his effort to look his opponent in the eyes, but Melwood would have none of it. Melwood's lips and chin seemed to quiver some as did his knees.

The two seconds stepped back, and total silence swept across Dueling Oak.

As the sound of the first syllable of the word, *begin*, rolled off the Major's lips, Melwood's right hand lashed out in a roundhouse swing toward

Caleb's chin. Caleb pulled his head back just a few inches as Melwood's fist hit only air.

As the last syllable left the Major's lips, Caleb's right fist flashed across the square and hit Melwood on the plump, rounded end of his pink nose. Blood instantly spurted from his nose and mouth. Several teeth dropped out from between his bleeding lips and landed in the dust between his legs. His high hat seemed to jump straight up several inches as his body toppled backwards onto the ground.

Laying flat on his back, blood from Melwood's nose and mouth spread quickly into his eyes as he struggled to clear his head. His second tugged at one of his arms and urged him to his feet. He was only inches away from where he needed to be before half a minute expired, but time was no longer of any importance to Melwood as he raised both hands to his eyes.

"I'm blind! You've knocked out both my eyes!"

As his second tried to console him and explain the situation, Melwood slung him to the ground and began running and staggering, and falling across the field of honor at Dueling Oak.

"This duel is over!" Mr. Phyddle announced.

The witnesses and seconds declared Caleb the winner and openly suggested that Maurice Melwood was a coward for failure to return to the line.

Mr. Phyddle and Major Melwood agreed to meet at a local bank later in the morning to secure the cash to pay the bet. Captain Bonèt helped Caleb into his coat and hat, and together, they took Bonèt's carriage back to the St. Charles where Caleb hoped Angelina might be waiting.

CHAPTER EIGHT

Captain Bonèt dropped Caleb off at the St. Charles before returning to the Lucky Lady to take care of business matters in preparation for the riverboat's departure at the end of the week.

Caleb walked up the marble steps, between the center Corinthian columns, under the projecting portico hoping at each interval to see Angelina standing there waiting for him, but she was not. He walked past the dining room and glanced in before reaching the ornate staircase leading to the second floor and his room around a corner at the end of a hall.

He was disappointed. Had he misread Angelina's warmth and teasing as only friendship? Was she so against duels that she would never want to see him again? He was in the South where a man's honor was everything. Would she have thought him a coward had he refused Melwood's challenge? Should he have fought the duel with pistols or swords? All these questions were rattling around in his mind as he stepped around the corner at the end of the hall to find Angelina sitting with her back against his door. Her face was in her hands and she was sobbing.

"Angi...uh...Miss Bonèt?"

She took her hands down, looked at Caleb, and then sobbed even harder.

"I thought I would never see you again!" she sobbed as Caleb fell to his knees in front of her. He wrapped his arms around her and she buried her face against his chest.

"Mr. Melwood...did you..." She could not complete her question, but she tried again.

"Did you..."

"No." We didn't use pistols or swords. We used fists."

Angelina leaned back to look at Caleb for a long moment.

"Fists? You fought a duel with Maurice Melwood with your fists?" Angelina asked, not believing what she was hearing.

"Well, I figured he would probably kill me if we used pistols or swords, so, I chose fists. I didn't think either one of us would get hurt too badly that way."

"Did you win?"

"I only landed one punch. I never thought he had the heart to stand up to someone who might cause him some pain. Ended up just hurting his pride, I think."

"In the South, hurting one's pride or reputation is probably worse than death. Is Mr. Melwood okay?"

"I'm sure he will be physically, but the last time I saw him, he was running away. I doubt if the social structure here will let him live it down for a long time."

"Would you help me up, please? It's not very lady-like sitting here on the floor in front of a man's hotel room."

"I have the strangest feeling that you're not at all worried what the people of New Orleans think about you."

Angelina smiled as she looked up into Caleb's eyes.

"And, if I'm not mistaken...we are two of a kind," she said.

Caleb smiled. As Angelina rose to her feet, she did not stop her momentum and Caleb did not attempt to stop it for her. Their lips met for the first time and lingered as Caleb's arms wrapped around her small waist and pulled her closer. When their lips parted, Angelina made no effort to move away. Their eyes silently answered the questions that their hearts were asking, and they kissed again.

Suddenly, a thought occurred to Caleb that caused him to relax his embrace and take a small step backwards.

Angelina smiled.

"I asked her to leave me alone awhile...but that was when I thought you might have gotten yourself killed. If she knew what we just..."

"I won't tell if you won't," Caleb said with a broader smile.

Angelina smiled back as she took his hand and led him back down the hall. Near the end of the corridor, a young sophisticated-looking couple passed them. They opened one side of a fancy double door before the groom swept her into his arms and carried her across the threshold. As the door closed behind them, Caleb glanced at a nameplate that read: Cupid's Manor.

"They name their rooms here at the St. Charles?" Caleb asked.

"A few of the special rooms, they do."

Caleb thought about what Angelina said and sighed. The White Bear was so primitive compared to the St. Charles. He felt small.

"Let's invite Miss Nikki to breakfast. What do you say?" Caleb asked to change the subject.

***

At breakfast, Caleb and his two guests were given quick, passing glances by many of the patrons coming in and out of the dining room.

"Gossip spreads fast in New Orleans, Mr. Walters," Angelina said in a low voice.

"What would they be gossiping about?"

"Oh, perhaps the duel you had with Mr. Melwood or maybe about us...if anyone saw us in the hallway."

Miss Nikki looked up from her biscuits and honey by habit, but she did not frown or make any remarks whatsoever. She had already begun to like this young Mr. Walters from Ohio.

"Miss Nikki...while you're finishing your breakfast, I would like to walk around the St.

Charles with Mr. Walters. He is down here to examine the hotel and I believe walking completely around it might help his study."

"Of course," Miss Nikki said, also nodding her approval.

Outside, Angelina put her arm around Caleb's and rested her hand on his forearm.

"I...uh...I have a very important question to ask you," Caleb said, turning slightly toward her.

"Then please do, Mr. Walters."

"When is it considered proper for me to call you Angelina...and when will it be proper for you to call me Caleb?"

"I would say sometime prior to sharing a kiss," she said, grinning.

"Please...I'm serious."

"Okay. If I were a Southern belle, you might call me Miss Angelina by now, but remember what I told you...I'm not a Southern lady...and I make my own decisions. However, I find it wise to follow most of the Southern rules of etiquette when I'm in the south. Makes it easier to move around."

"Then your answer is...I can?"

"Before I answer, let me ask you a question."

"Okay."

"When do you plan on going back to Ohio?"

"Two or three days...maybe," Caleb answered, not wanting to leave while there was still an opportunity to see Angelina.

"Have you finished the work you came down here to do?"

Caleb lowered his eyes, took a deep breath, and exhaled heavily. He spotted a bench under a shade tree and moved in that direction.

"Angelina...I'll call you that now and when we're alone, but Miss Bonèt when anyone else is around. Is that fair?"

"That'll be fine."

"Good. Now, Angelina, I'll answer your question. I'm not just down here to explore the St. Charles for ideas, though that is one reason. I'm a lawyer trying to get a first-hand look at the social processes that perpetuate slavery."

"What kind of law do you practice, Mr. Walters?"

"I just finished my law education this summer and haven't really decided on a specialty. I like being in the courtroom, I like defending the underdog, and I like contract law."

He stopped there in order to study Angelina's face and body reactions prior to her verbal statement. Angelina's eyes lit up when she heard the words contract law, but her only other physical reaction was to smile and pat his hand.

"Do you think that I'm a Southern sympathizer?" she asked.

"You are a very independent woman...but your father...your father moves in the same circles with the gentry society here in New Orleans. And...Mr. Phyddle is a plantation owner, a slave owner, and one of the most notorious gamblers in New Orleans, I suppose. In fact, he won twenty thousand dollars or his plantation from Major Melwood in a wager over who would win my duel with the major's son."

"He won the Melwood plantation?" Angelina said, having to place her hand over her mouth to keep from shouting it out.

"I didn't say he won it, but I guess he would if the major can't pay the twenty thousand dollars by noon today. Am I to understand that this pleases you?"

"Caleb, I must go back to the hotel soon and find my father. There's so much you don't know. This will make a tremendous difference in our return trip up north."

"Angelina, I'm so confused. Please expla..."

Angelina interrupted Caleb with a question of her own that almost floored him.

"Caleb Walters...do you love me?"

Caleb could only stare into her eyes for a long moment. His heart was racing. He could feel it pounding in his chest. Finally, he gathered his thoughts and answered.

"Angelina, I think I fell in...no...I know I fell in love with you the first moment I saw you. You have never left my thoughts since that moment."

"Then your interest is honorable and your intentions are to pursue that love?"

"Over mountains and seas if need be."

"And if I told you that I, also, know that I fell in love with you the first time our eyes met, would that please you?"

Caleb was stunned by what he was hearing. In just three days his mind and heart had filled with great expectations for a future with the first woman in his life that seemed to take his breath away, not only when they were together, but in his thoughts and dreams. Was she now telling him that she felt the same way?

"Of course it would," Caleb replied, answering her direct question with a direct answer because his mind was full of wonder.

"Then you must promise me something very important."

"Anything."

"You must promise to keep our love a secret from my father until I tell you differently. Only Miss Nikki will know. Do you agree?"

"If that's what you wish."

"Good...okay...I've got to go see father..."

Angelina was beside herself as she mentally ran through the events of the past two days.

"What else do you plan on doing before you feel you're ready to return to Ohio?" she asked.

"I wanted to see a slave auction."

Angelina studied Caleb's face and was sure that his interests were honest.

"There are auctions in New Orleans nearly every day, but some of the bidders might be uncomfortable knowing a northerner was observing for reasons other than just bidding...unless you were an invited guest of a bidder."

"I don't know anyone well enough to be invited to such an event."

"Mr. Phyddle attends most of the auctions. Would you consider being his guest?"

Caleb didn't like the thought of associating with a man who would own slaves, but he needed to see an auction to satisfy his curiosity.

"Mr. Phyddle seemed friendly enough when we met at Dueling Oak, but I doubt that he would invite me to attend an auction with him."

"Leave that to me," Angelina said with a sure tone. "After that, are there other things you need to research?"

"My mind is full of questions about the entire slavery issue. I wonder how the slaves are treated on the plantations. Do all slaves wish to escape their plantations, or are some of them happy with their way of life? Who owns the workers on the riverboats? If they can buy their freedom, might I help them, legally? Would they want my help? Those are just some of the things I wanted to learn about."

"Answers to all those questions could take you a very long time to find just walking around observing people. Maybe I can help."

Caleb had no idea what Angelina might be talking about but trusted that she wanted to help him in any way she could.

"I appreciate any help you can offer."

"Then let's go back inside and I'll have Miss Nikki take me to wherever father is at the moment. She keeps track of him about as well as she does me," Angelina said.

Inside, they found Miss Nikki finished with her biscuits and coffee. Angelina spoke to her in whispers and then turned and spoke to Caleb.

"Mr. Walters, it may be several hours before we return from talking with my father. Are you going to be close about for a while?"

"Certainly. Should I be invited to attend an auction would you tell me how I should dress," Caleb responded.

"Most of the bidders make it a social event hoping to show off to others by outbidding them—they'll be dressed in top hats and finery. Whatever you wear will be fine, besides I like you in your wide-brimmed hat."

"Then I'll be bathed, dressed, and ready by noon just in case things work out."

Angelina and Miss Nikki made their exit and Caleb went up to his room to get ready for the auction that he might be attending. Everything was going so fast. Caleb couldn't help but think that there was much more going on than met the eye. He would be correct.

CHAPTER NINE

Shortly after noon, Miss Nikki knocked on Caleb's door and without waiting for him to answer slipped a note under the door.

> *Mr. Walters,*
> *Please join us for wine on*
> *The Lucky Lady at 1:00 o'clock.*
> *Captain Bonèt*

When Caleb arrived at the Lucky Lady, he was greeted by Captain Bonèt and escorted to the dining room where, with the exception of Mr. Phyddle, he found himself in the company of strangers. Caleb nodded his head with respect at Mr. Phyddle.

"Sipping wine at this table is Leah and Jean-Paul. At the other table I'd like you to meet Jorge and Thomas."

Once again, Caleb nodded with a smile.

"Ladies and gentlemen...I'd like you all to meet Mr. Caleb Walters, a lawyer from Ohio."

Everyone sitting around the tables responded with nods of their own. Caleb noticed the positioning of the tables formed somewhat of a semi-circle with Mr. Phyddle sitting alone at the poker table. The other people were sitting in positions that allowed them to be facing an empty table in the center of the room.

"Would you join me here, Mr. Walters?"

Before Caleb could answer, the door opened and Angelina walked in followed by Miss Nikki.

"We apologize for missing the introductions, but we have both already met Mr. Walters."

The group responded with more nods and smiles, the men standing while Captain Bonèt helped seat the two ladies. He left an empty seat between them. Captain Bonèt took the seat on Miss Nikki's left, a maneuver that required Caleb to sit between the two ladies. The rough circle was now complete with all parties facing one another. Mr. Phyddle spoke first.

"Mr. Walters...everyone here wishes to thank you for your heroism in diving into the river and pulling the small child out of the water. He may have drowned had it not been for your actions."

Jean-Paul, a middle-aged man with long, straight, dark hair shifted his position in his chair before speaking with an accent that Caleb did not recognize.

"Mr. Walters, are you familiar with the term, Creole?"

"I know of the word, sir, but I may not understand the exact or correct meaning."

"Slaves born in the Americas as opposed to those brought directly from Africa are often called Creoles. Others think of Creoles as people of French descent who were born in Louisiana regardless of what mixture of blood they may have."

Caleb thought for a moment before responding.

"Does that make a person who was born in Ohio to a Shawnee father and a French mother different from you by blood or simply by your association with being born in the state of Louisiana?"

"I'm not sure I understand your question, Mr. Walters."

"Are you a Creole, Jean-Paul?" Caleb asked hesitantly, but reacting to what he felt was a cross-examination by his new acquaintances.

"Yes," Jean-Paul answered.

"Are you married?"

"Yes."

"Would you be offended if I asked to what race your wife belongs?"

"No, I would not be. She is a mulatto."

"Then let me ask you another question. If your wife got pregnant here in New Orleans but the two of you were traveling by riverboat to say...Pittsburgh, and your child was born there...would your child still be Creole?"

Jean-Paul glanced at the people sitting to his right and to his left before smiling.

"You ask an interesting question. What is your point?"

"Sir, if you and I had passed on the street, I would not know that you are Creole, French, or born in Louisiana. If we talked, I might suppose that you were French by your accent, but you might just as easily be of French descent by way of Canada. In other words, either you choose to be labeled a Creole...or others wish to identify you as such. Either way, the label does not make the man."

"You have an interesting point of view, Mr. Walters. May I ask how you would answer the question you asked me about my child being born in Pittsburgh?"

Again, Caleb thought for a long moment before giving Jean-Paul and the others an answer.

"I would call your child either a little boy or little girl."

Caleb's answer brought another smile to Jean-Paul's lips as he once again glanced at the others.

Leah slowly rose to her feet. She was a thin, attractive, medium complexioned woman perhaps in her mid-to-late-twenties with dark, penetrating eyes. She was dressed in a plain cotton dress much like most other female slaves wore. Caleb's eyes were drawn instantly to her withered and gnarled right hand. It appeared to have been twisted or beaten until all the bones were broken and left to heal on their own. While she prepared herself to speak, Caleb leaned over and whispered to Angelina.

"What is this all about?"

"Just answer their questions honestly and I think you will be pleased when it's over," she whispered back.

"Mr. Walters, I want to thank you personally for saving the boy...his name is Matthew...and he was...I mean...he is my nephew."

"Thank you, ma'am, but I'm sure many others would have done the same had I not been the closest."

"On the contrary, Mr. Walters, there were many men much closer than you who obviously did not value a child's life...especially a slave child...enough to risk their own...especially Mr. Melwood. You didn't hesitate for a moment to consider what the crowd might think of you. In other words, Mr. Walters, you showed great compassion for a fellow human being...a compassion that can only come from the heart."

With tears running down the lady's cheeks, she slowly returned to her seat. Caleb was touched by the woman's words and was surprised but impressed at the gracefulness and clarity of those words. Although he was not at all sure where or how, she was obviously educated. Caleb thought her delivery would have been impressive even in a courtroom.

For whatever reason, the short, dark-complexioned man in his late twenties named Jorge had no questions but did make a short statement.

"My name is Jorge Albanese. I was a slave on a Georgia plantation for twenty years because my mother was a slave...even though my father was a wealthy landowner from Spain. I bought my freedom eight years ago...and now I do all I can to help others."

Thomas, a tall, slim, middle-aged man, had neatly cut hair and a clean shave. He wore a pinstriped dress shirt with what appeared to be a very stiff collar fastened at the neck. He stood before he spoke.

"My first name be Thomas. I've never had no last name like most folks, but sometimes I tell folks my last name be Cutter 'cause I cut hair. Sometimes I say my name be Tom Barber 'cause I be a barber...but I also be a talker. Gotta be a talker if ya wants ta keep on good terms with customers. I ain't no slave, though. Mr. Phyddle saw ta that. I cut hair on the Lucky Lady. Yessiree, I'm a workin' man. You a workin' man, Mr. Walters?"

Caleb liked the man's honesty. He could see the pride in his face as he spoke of being a working man.

"Yes...I mean...I...ah...I just finished law school and I may set up a law practice in Ohio soon. I'm down here looking at the St. Charles Hotel because I'm also interested in the hotel business. My parents own a hotel."

"So...ya not down here doin' no lawyerin' or doin' no lookin' to set up lawyerin' here in New Orleans?"

Angelina's caution to "be honest" returned to Caleb's mind, and he trusted her advice. He decided to lay it all on the line and say exactly why he was there.

"Ladies...and gentlemen...I'm not at all sure why I was asked to join you here this afternoon...or exactly what it is you are searching for with all these questions, but...I've decided to tell you the exact truth. At worse...you may shoot me and toss my body overboard into the river, or you may just tell me why you're so interested in asking me questions."

No one said a word, but everyone's eyes focused on this young, blue-eyed man from Ohio as he glanced into Angelina's eyes for a short moment.

"Continue," she whispered, sending him a message of admiration with her eyes.

"I'm, indeed, here to look at the hotel, but that's not my main reason for traveling down the Ohio and Mississippi on a riverboat. My main reason is to learn how I might help the unfortunate people in my country who have been enslaved like animals!" he exclaimed in a firm voice.

Mr. Phyddle rose to his feet.

"In a sense, you have risked your life three times in the past twenty-four hours." First, you showed great courage in confronting Mr. Melwood on his cowardly act, which left the child struggling in the water.

Second, you proved to be a keen observer of human character by proving Mr. Melwood to be a coward in your duel this morning. Your choice of weapons was excellent strategy in proving your point without taking the man's life unnecessarily.

Third, admitting that you are preparing to fight in a court of law against slavery certainly risked your life since you know that I am a plantation owner. Do you play poker?"

"No, sir...I've never had an interest."

"I've played poker all my life, Mr. Walters, and I've learned to spot a bluff...which is a form of lying...and either you have the best poker face I've ever seen, or you're being entirely honest with us. Which is it, Mr. Walters?"

"I've already answered that question, Mr. Phyddle...I have no interest in poker."

Mr. Phyddle's eyes smiled as he slowly raised his right hand into the air, followed by Leah, Jorge, and Thomas. Suddenly, Caleb became aware that Captain Bonèt, Miss Nikki, and Angelina were also raising their hands. They all began to stand and Caleb hesitantly followed suit. Then, one by one, they walked around their tables and shook hands with Caleb. For whatever reason, it made him feel good...even though he didn't have a clue about the reason he was there, why he was questioned, or why they all shook hands with him. Moreover, he had absolutely no idea what they wanted from him.

□

CHAPTER TEN

Within minutes, only Mr. Phyddle, Angelina, and Caleb remained in the dining room of the Lucky Lady. Even Miss Nikki had excused herself to retire to her quarters.

"Mr. Walters...I know your mind must be full of questions about what this meeting was all about, and I'm going to leave you in the capable hands of Miss Bonèt to answer all your questions. Does that meet with your approval?" Mr. Phyddle asked.

"Yes, of course, sir. I have more than a few questions to ask Miss Bonèt," Caleb said, with an unexpected firmness in his voice that got Angelina's attention and caused Mr. Phyddle to grin.

"Good. Then before I leave, let me say that there will be a slave auction tomorrow at noon. If you are still interested in attending one...meet me in the lobby of the St. Charles around eleven. We will go in my carriage."

"Thank you, sir," Caleb replied, glancing over at Angelina who was pouring two more glasses of wine.

Mr. Phyddle made his exit as Caleb turned to Angelina for some answers.

"Are you suggesting that I needed to pass inspection in front of all of these strangers just to be permitted to attend a slave auction?" Caleb asked.

"Come sit with me and have some wine...it's going to be a long afternoon."

Caleb walked to the table but remained standing directly in front of Angelina.

"So...where do we begin?" he asked.

"We begin with the truth, the whole truth, and nothing but the truth...isn't that the oath people take in the courtroom?"

"Yes...but those words are always followed by, 'so help me God' to make them more powerful."

"Then, that's where we begin," Angelina replied, scooting one of the wine glasses toward Caleb in a gesture for him to sit with her.

Caleb took a seat and picked up the wine glass, lifting it slowly to his lips as his eyes locked onto hers. He wondered what truths she was preparing to tell.

"First of all, I did not add the 'God' thing because I've been angry with God for quite some time. I simply cannot understand why a good God would allow all the pain and suffering that has become a routine part of life in the South.

But those are just my feelings about things...the others may not feel that way."

"I can understand your point. Just before I left Ohio, I witnessed cruelty perpetrated by one human being upon another. There didn't seem to be a God around to help those people."

Angelina stared deeply into Caleb's eyes. She saw his genuine concern for human beings who suffered under the hand of other wealthier or more fortunate people...white people mainly.

"Caleb, if I tell you the whole truth that we spoke of a few moments ago...and you do not like what you hear, then it is unlikely that we will ever see each other again after this day," Angelina said.

She held her wine glass in both hands near her lips so Caleb could not see her chin trembling from her own words.

"That's certainly the most unlikely scenario imaginable."

Angelina continued to study Caleb's eyes, and for a moment, her imagination wandered and she saw herself and Caleb together in Paris...and then on a warm sandy beach on some uncharted island far away from the politically and socially troubled nation that was her reality.

"Okay...let me start by saying that everyone present here this afternoon has abolitionist sympathies."

"Then why are you so worried that I won't like the truth? They are all like me."

"Let me continue by describing each of the people you just met and the role they play in a very dangerous game. I'll start with Leah. Did you find her much more articulate than what you might expect from a slave woman...especially since it's forbidden for slaves to learn how to read?"

"I recognized that she was well educated as soon as I heard her speak."

"I knew you would, but few people ever hear her speak like that. In fact, only the people here today know that she is educated."

"How did this happen? I mean...who...."

"I did! As a child, I was well educated in Paris before coming back to America about three years ago. Leah could not speak a single word of English when Mr. Phyddle bought her at a slave auction. She was my first teaching project that started almost immediately after she arrived on Mr. Phyddle's plantation," Angelina explained.

"That's what has me so confused. How can Mr. Phyddle own a plantation and buy slaves at the auction and still be an abolitionist?" Caleb asked, his face somewhat contorted in his effort to understand the apparent contradiction.

"I'll explain how Mr. Phyddle fits into all of this later. Let me continue about Leah. She's very bright. We began meeting at Magnolia—that's the name of Mr. Phyddle's plantation. I not only taught her how to read, but how to find information, and how to think cautiously without fear. She was my first student and I am very proud of her."

"You should be...she could be a teacher herself."

Angelina smiled with satisfaction.

"Funny, you should say that, because she's been teaching the other residents how to read and write just as I taught her."

"Residents? Why do you call them that?"

"Let me continue and you'll understand," Angelina replied.

Caleb nodded okay but continued with his questions.

"Aren't you worried that she'll get caught and punished?"

"That's always a possibility, but we take every precaution not to let that happen."

Caleb caught the word we and concluded that she must be talking about the group that had questioned him earlier. He sat back, a little more relaxed now, and sipped his wine. Angelina did the same.

"Jean-Paul is the overseer of Mr. Phyddle's plantation. He has a great ability to gain the trust of the residents on Magnolia, and with the help of the others, prepares them for the life of free people.

Caleb just blinked and stared at Angelina for a long moment. He wondered what all this was leading up to, but decided to listen closely to the rest of Angelina's story.

"We begin teaching along the way to Magnolia."

"Along the way to freedom? Is that what you're saying?"

"Yes, Caleb, the Mississippi and the Ohio are rivers to freedom, and the people you met here this afternoon are all part of a systematic effort to help current slaves prepare for that freedom. Reading, writing, bartering, money, and building skills are just a few of the resources they will need in Canada or wherever they eventually settle."

Caleb studied the talented, intelligent, and beautiful lady who just explained how she and a small band of people were now doing what he was hoping to do.

"Thomas...what does Thomas do?"

"Thomas is a skilled barber who teaches his trade to any resident who wishes to train for a future job that is not farm or plantation labor. But he's much more than a barber—he's a perceptive listener and great talker. He's the ears of our entire network. Anyone boarding the Lucky Lady with questionable intentions will be ferreted out by Thomas before the person can cause us any trouble."

"Who might want to cause trouble?"

"Officers of the law, slave hunters, white people who think they are superior...and sometimes other slaves who agree to do it for money or their own freedom. Greed is a characteristic that any human might possess regardless of race."

"Why would anyone care if Mr. Phyddle buys slaves at auction and then frees them?"

"It's the fugitive slaves we worry about most. If a runaway is found aboard without proper papers, Father could get into a lot of trouble."

"Then he needs a bill of sale dated and signed by a slave chaser...or marshal...or whoever it is who puts the fugitive into your father's custody."

"Caleb...sometimes fugitive slaves come to us without papers. In those cases...we choose to take the risk in order to save another human being," Angelina said.

"So, where do I fit into this process?"

"First, you must tell me that you want to fit in. I mean...once you agree to join us...it will be...well...rather difficult if not impossible to drop out."

"I came down here to observe what was really going on and decide how I might help. I never imagined I would become involved in something like this, but before I tell you that I want to join your effort, I have a very important question to ask you. Your answer must be totally honest."

Angelina stood and took their empty wine glasses to the counter. Caleb also stood, thinking the conversation might be coming to an abrupt end.

"A so-help-me-God answer?"

"Yes," Caleb said, hesitating a long moment to get his thoughts and words organized. Finally, he said, "Is my helping your effort the only interest you have in me?"

Angelina, her back still to Caleb, shut her eyes for a moment as a smile formed on her lips. She turned slowly. She could have given him a yes-or-no answer to his question...but she didn't. She walked straight into his arms and kissed him with a truth that he would never doubt. She lingered in his arms until both their bodies trembled for more than a kiss. When their lips finally parted, Angelina took the opportunity to speak.

"Caleb, that's my answer to your question. Now, I must know your answer."

Caleb pulled Angelina back into his arms and kissed her again with his answer.

"Of course I want to join you and the group in doing all I can to help, but I'm not sure what role you wish me to play," he finally said after their lips parted.

"Are you positively sure?"

He kissed her again, sensing the tease in her voice.

"You've made me the happiest woman in the world, Caleb. I want to spend every possible moment with you, but you must leave now to allow the others to return to discuss your answer and the role you'll play."

"When will we see each other again?"

"This evening. If all goes well, I would like you to join me here on the Lucky Lady for dinner. Later this evening, I'll send Miss Nikki with a note telling you what time you should arrive."

Caleb kissed Angelina again...this time a gentle kiss that was returned with promises of an evening filled with an intimacy that Caleb had never shared with anyone before.

CHAPTER ELEVEN

Shortly after Caleb's carriage left the docks, Captain Bonèt and Mr. Phyddle returned to the dining room of the Lucky Lady to receive Mr. Walters' response to Angelina. The others had already expressed their opinion of Caleb Walters and would work with him if instructed. Mr. Phyddle's demeanor expressed an air of confidence.

"Is he coming aboard?"

"Yes, but I haven't explained his role or the process that we use," Angelina answered.

"That's fine," Mr. Phyddle said. "He's a very intelligent lad with a great deal of insight in my opinion. We can all be part of his indoctrination but it will have to be done quickly if he's to make the trip back North with us."

Angelina's face beamed at Mr. Phyddle's words. Having Caleb literally onboard the Lucky Lady the entire trip back to Fiddler's Point would allow them the time and privacy to explore their feelings for one another.

"Maybe he should remain in New Orleans until the last voyage of the season," Captain Bonèt said with a noticeable strain in his voice.

"Father! Stop treating me as if I were still a little girl! I can instruct Ca...I mean...Mr. Walters of his responsibilities. Besides, I'm the one who must help forge the legal documents that he prepares—especially the manumission papers."

"Yes, Angelina, those documents must be perfect and hold up in front of any law officer that challenges them. If necessary, Mr. Walters will have to defend the papers in front of a judge," Mr. Phyddle said.

"He'll have to be ready and willing to travel on the last leg between Cincinnati and Pittsburgh whenever necessary," Angelina's father said, glancing up at his daughter with a heavy sigh.

Angelina could hear the uneasiness in her father's voice. She wondered if his concern was with Caleb joining the group or joining the family. She wondered if her affection for Caleb was showing.

She had had her share of suitors while getting her education in Paris. She and Miss Nikki had traveled to England, Spain, and even Rome, but no one there sparked an interest. After her return to America at age eighteen, the suitors increased, but none of them captured her heart.

She was not interested in marrying into wealth like most of the Southern women. She resented the thought of being reduced to the identity of Mistress of the house even though she wanted a husband and family. She was an activist with independent ideas of her own, but she wouldn't give up her free spirit even for Caleb. She didn't think Caleb would expect her to give up anything. In her mind, he already loved her for what she was and she could feel that love in every fiber of her body and soul.

***

It was nearly nine o'clock before Caleb and Angelina finished a wonderful dinner that Miss Nikki had prepared especially for them. She asked to be excused before the dinner started, but Caleb insisted that she join them. Miss Nikki was delighted and Caleb was finally comfortable with the feeling that he and Miss Nikki had become friends.

"Would you like to take a stroll outside to get some air," Caleb asked Angelina.

"That would be nice, Caleb."

Miss Nikki said she would clean up while they were taking their walk, and informed them that she was tired and would be retiring to her room for the rest of the night.

Outside, the wind had picked up and there was an unmistakable smell of rain on the way.

"Are you looking forward to the slave auction tomorrow?" Angelina asked.

"Not at all...because I find the whole idea of buying and selling humans appalling, but I think it's something I need to see to increase my understanding of the whole process."

"Then I think it's time for me to explain what you are about to get involved in and your role in the operation."

"I think that would be a good idea," Caleb said, taking Angelina's hand in his as they leaned against a railing overlooking the Mississippi River.

"Okay...first of all, don't get upset tomorrow at the auction when you see Mr. Phyddle examining the slaves. It's what all bidders do and if he didn't check them over, the others would soon get suspicious."

"What do you mean...examining the slaves?"

"Sometimes there are men, women, and children put on the auction block. Bidders want to get the healthiest and strongest slaves possible, so they examine them as if they were livestock. Some are quite cruel and examine them, especially the females, in undignified ways. I think they only do it sometimes to get...you know...thrills."

"Has our civilization sunk to that level?" Caleb responded with redness crawling up his neck as his anger grew.

"The examinations are nothing compared to what probably happens to the ones they buy. Legalized rape is what it amounts to," Angelina said.

"Then why does Mr. Phyddle participate in such things?"

"To set as many of them free as he can."

"He buys slaves just to set them free?" Caleb asked with a puzzled look on his face.

"Yes! That's exactly what he does," Angelina replied.

"I think you better explain the whole process," Caleb said.

"It all starts here in New Orleans. My father is wealthy, but Mr. Phyddle is extremely wealthy. It's not because he's an expert gambler, but because he's from a long line of wealth from Europe. He buys slaves at the auction and takes them to Magnolia."

"Are you talking about a working plantation?" Caleb asked, his eyes squinting a bit with wonder.

"Not exactly," Angelina answered.

"What does he raise there?"

"He doesn't raise anything...nothing for sale, anyway."

"No cash crops?"

"No! The slaves he buys down here, he takes to Magnolia where they become what we call residents. He leaves them in the hands of the overseer and the teachers for at least three months. Each lives in a small home sitting on several acres of land. Each is taught several trades such as carpentry, stone masonry, and barbering. Each is also taught to farm the land with crops of their choice. They can also raise whatever kind of livestock they prefer for use at the bartering market each Saturday."

Caleb looked at Angelina with admiration. He was beginning to understand that she was part of a wonderful idea to not only help people escape slavery, but to help prepare them for living in a new world.

"Does someone teach them to read and write?" He asked.

"Oh, yes. In fact, they spend more time learning how to read and write than anything else. Those who fail to attain a minimum level of language skills are not permitted to move on to the second phase."

"I can't wait to hear about phase two," Caleb replied.

"Everyone works on the Lucky Lady as we move north. The men keep the boilers operating and load the cordwood at various stops. The women begin learning to cook and clean as cabin attendants. Each worker is paid a fair wage for his or her labor. The passengers who come onboard mainly to gamble never suspect anything when they see everyone working. Leah begins teaching right from the start, though."

When we reach Magnolia, the teaching continues at a higher level for each trade and language skills but we add basic math skills and money management skills so everyone will be able to survive in a world that exchanges goods and services for currency. Again, each resident must master a minimum level of skills in all areas before moving on."

"Where's Magnolia located?

Angelina blinked several times before saying, "Magnolia is across the river from Cincinnati."

Caleb's mouth dropped open.

"I went to law school in Cincinnati! It's less than a hundred miles from home!" Caleb exclaimed, a look of disbelief on his face.

"You've spent time at Magnolia the past few years?"

"Yes, when necessary to get the teaching done."

"I can't believe I was in Cincinnati for three years and you might have been just across the river! I just can't believe fate sometimes!"

"Fate was good to both of us when you saw me painting on the dock in New Orleans...especially since I don't often find time to paint."

"What do you mean?"

"Well, I only enjoy painting scenes that have some deep personal meaning in my life. I've tried landscapes from time to time, but I rarely finish any of them because my landscapes are always changing as most of my time is spent in motion up or down a river. I'm really not very good."

"I think you're great, and I hope you find many more meaningful scenes to paint.

Caleb spotted a nearby park bench and took Angelina's hand as he guided her to it.

"Angelina, I've lived in southern Ohio all my life and went to school in Cincinnati, but I don't remember ever hearing of a plantation called Magnolia."

"Good. It's best that its location remains inconspicuous to people in the area. Do you understand that the less people know of this farm, the less likely some slave hunters will become suspicious of the activities that might be going on? In other words, we like it that way. Are you ready for phase three?"

Caleb nodded. He was already in awe of what he had learned in just a few minutes.

"Are you saying the slaves...I mean the residents of Magnolia move on?"

Yes, but only when they have the skills to live in a free world? This is the third stage of the system that you have probably heard called...the Underground Railroad. But it's not really part of that system, and it doesn't operate in the same way."

"I've heard of it, but it seems to be more a myth than anything else.

"On the contrary, Caleb, there are stations along the banks of the Ohio that assist runaways on the last portion of a long voyage. Most stations in the Underground Railroad just hide fugitives until they are rested enough to get on their way again. We only have two stations...Magnolia and Wellsville, Ohio."

"I've never heard of Wellsville."

"It's about fifty miles west of Pittsburgh at the end of a railroad line that goes to Cleveland. If things go as planned, we see that our residents have all the necessary skills and papers to make it safely to Cleveland. Some stay there in established communities and others go on to Canada

"It's amazing, but I still don't see where I play a role in the operation."

"A war is coming, Caleb, it's just a matter of time. When it begins, this operation will more than likely cease to exist. If all slaves become free, then they won't be chased down and returned to their masters for punishment. Besides, all steamboats will probably be taken over by one army or another. The rivers won't be safe anymore. Right now, we need manumission papers drawn up with the best legal wording possible to prevent challenges in the courts. Since my father and Mr. Phyddle have legal ownership of our residents as slaves, they are the only ones who can legally free the residents or permit them to buy their freedom."

"And you want me to draw up a manumission document that will hold up in the courts?"

"Yes, that and some kind of reward poster that acts as a legal document permitting someone in our group to buy runaway slaves from the slave hunters...a bill of sale of some sort. That way we can help redirect them on their way to freedom again."

"You buy captured runaways back from slave hunters for a small reward, and then let them join the residents at Magnolia?" Caleb asked, finally seeming to understand the complete picture.

"What a plan! If everyone were as generous and kind as you, your father, and Mr. Phyddle, we wouldn't have all this turmoil in our country. My God, Angelina, it's an honor to be invited to join your movement!"

"Good! Now may I suggest we go inside, have something to drink, and stop talking business for the rest of the evening?"

"That sounds wonderful to me, but may I ask one last question? Are you looking forward to traveling all the way to Fiddler's Point on a riverboat with someone who loves you?

Angelina answered him with a kiss.

"This voyage will give us an opportunity to really get to know each other better."

"I look forward to that," Caleb replied.

***

Mr. Phyddle picked Caleb up at the St. Charles shortly before noon and together they took the short trip to the largest slave pen in New Orleans.

"What you are about to witness will disgust you, but you must not show your concern. I'm here to buy the slaves most likely to be ready and able to succeed in the long process of helping them reach freedom," Mr. Phyddle said.

"I promise to keep my mouth shut and my eyes open," Caleb replied.

"Good. When it comes time to inspect the slaves, you can just stay close behind me. I'll do some inspecting, but will not do any of the invasive inspecting that some bidders do routinely. You'll see what I mean."

When the first slaves stepped onto the block, some of the males were stripped down to their waist, touched all over their bodies, and asked questions about their scars and any illnesses they had suffered. Some bidders inspected teeth for injuries and decay. Several females were stripped to the waist on request by planters who suggested they were looking for house servants as wet nurses. A quiet whisper to the trader and a female slave would be taken to a private room in the slave pen. The captain whispered to Caleb that she would be inspected from head to toe. She might also be ordered to expose her private parts as evidence that she was free of diseases and bugs. These females were often used as breeders not only to produce more laborers, but also to satisfy the bidder's sexual desires.

From noon until 3:00 o'clock, about thirty adult men and more than a dozen women were purchased as field hands. Caleb could hear bidders discussing various positives and negatives about certain slaves. About six lighter-skinned females were purchased as potential house servants.

There was only one family put up for auction. A male with graying hair and his lame daughter got few bids even though the man smiled and bragged of being a strong worker. One of his daughter's legs was shorter than the other. Mr. Phyddle asked her if she was a good cook. She answered him, and added that she was a very good seamstress. The most important factor to Mr. Phyddle was that both could speak and understand English. Mr. Phyddle bought both of them.

After the transactions were finalized, and Mr. Phyddle received his bill of sale for the chattel slaves, Caleb watched as he motioned to someone in the crowd. As the man stepped out into the open, Caleb could see that it was Jean-Paul, Mr. Phyddle's overseer.

"We can leave now," Mr. Phyddle said. "Jean-Paul will escort the two new residents back to the Lucky Lady and get them set up for the voyage north."

"When are you planning on leaving, sir?"

"Friday morning if all goes well."

"I would like to buy passage on the Lucky Lady for the return trip, sir."

"You talk with Angelina about passage. She'll work out whatever arrangements are to be made."

In a matter of minutes, Mr. Phyddle's carriage pulled up in front of the St. Charles.

"I have another matter to talk with you about, Mr. Walters," Mr. Phyddle said, reaching into his pocket and pulling out a leather pouch. "I want you to have this."

"What is it?" Caleb asked.

"It's twenty thousand dollars in gold...my winnings at your duel."

"I can't take that! It was your bet and your money that you risked. I didn't bet anything."

"On the contrary, you bet your life going up against Melwood. You had him all sized up. To me, that bet was a sure thing, and I just bet the money for you in return for your courage."

Mr. Phyddle tossed the pouch toward Caleb causing him to catch it through sheer reflex action.

"But I..." Caleb stuttered, trying to object.

"There won't be any further discussion or I'll consider myself insulted and you'll be looking at another duel," Mr. Phyddle said, a grin crossing his face.

"I don't know what to say."

"You don't have to say anything. You just got out of college, and that money will help you set up your law practice. What we might ask you to do in the future will be well worth that fee."

Caleb got out and Mr. Phyddle motioned for the carriage driver to continue on to another destination. Caleb went to his room, hid his money, and took a bath. He hadn't felt so dirty in his entire life.

☐

CHAPTER TWELVE

The hot and humid dog days of August continued as the Lucky Lady pulled away from the dock in New Orleans. Caleb immediately observed how the secret operation worked. It began by having every potential resident of Magnolia wear one of two uniforms. Those working as attendants, porters, cooks, or servers wore burgundy vests with LUCKY LADY embroidered in large letters on the back. All those working as stokers and loaders wore identically embroidered burgundy shirts. The purpose of the uniforms was to encourage passengers and onlookers at the refueling docks to take for granted that anyone wearing these uniforms were employees of the Lucky Lady.

At the first refueling dock, Angelina and Caleb watched from the deck as workers in uniforms went ashore and carried back cordwood. Runaway slaves often hid in the stacks of wood. If conditions seemed safe, loaders handed the runaways a burgundy shirt. The runaway then carried a load of wood onboard where he would then become part of the crew. At times, there were no runaways at the refueling stops; however, at other times there might be three or four.

"How many refueling stops do we make on our way north?" Caleb asked.

"Between New Orleans and the Ohio River, we have six stops at safe docks."

"What's a safe dock?"

"It's where we have a dock owner who is sympathetic to our cause. Once aboard, the runaway is assigned a new name and identity that match with some paperwork that's already prepared. In other words, in a matter of only a few minutes, a desperate runaway becomes a crewmember."

"What happens when we reach the Ohio?"

"We actually continue the same process. We dock at Louisville where Mr. Phyddle will attend his last auction on our northern voyage. If there are any potential residents, he buys them. Afterwards, we move on to Cincinnati where all passengers depart, leaving us with only the fulltime crew, runaways, and former slaves off the auction blocks. We usually stay moored at Cincinnati for about a week while future residents are quietly taken by canoe up the Licking River to Magnolia."

"How large of a plantation is Magnolia?"

"Not large at all...about a hundred acres, but it serves our needs and still allows for maximum privacy. The land sits in a valley that is surrounded on three sides by tall, rocky hills."

Caleb smiled with satisfaction at the ingenious system.

"So, when do I start doing my job?"

"Today! In fact, we should get started now if you're ready. We'll be working most days in my stateroom. It's the safest place onboard to do the kind of work we'll be doing."

Caleb's eyes lit up as his mind considered the opportunities he might have for some privacy with Angelina. Those thoughts disappeared as they entered her cabin to find Miss Nikki sitting at the dining table.

"Would you two like a cup of tea before we get started," Miss Nikki said without looking up from the table.

"Sure," Angelina replied. "Do you have the sample manumission documents ready?"

"Yes, I'm looking at them now."

"Caleb, have a seat by Miss Nikki and I'll get us all a cup of tea."

Caleb took a seat at the table and Miss Nikki immediately slid a piece of paper toward him.

"Have you ever seen freedom papers before?" she asked.

"I recall seeing a sample in a book at law school, but I haven't seen an actual document."

"That one is written by the former owner of a slave in Georgia."

Caleb examined the document written in longhand and found that it mainly stated names, dates, and a sketchy description of the slave or slaves whom the manumission papers freed. Below the description was a place for the slave owner to sign and place his seal. Below that, was a place for the witness signature and sometimes his seal.

"I can save us some time by writing a standard form that leaves blank spaces for names, dates, and descriptions. As a matter of fact, I have a friend in Cincinnati who can print up as many freedom papers as we want. That'll save us from having to write each one out by hand. Each resident should have their own papers just in case they're separated along the way. Besides, I think separate papers would hold up in court much better should it ever come to that."

"That's what we want you to do. Some of these documents are so poorly written that it's quite possible a judge might misinterpret some important words and disallow the document," Angelina said.

Caleb studied the document for nearly an hour before he began writing notes on what he considered the essential parts of the document. By early afternoon, he had a first draft. With everyone's approval, Caleb finally began feeling part of the team.

***

As the miles passed, Caleb found himself daydreaming about finding time to be alone with Angelina. His love for her seemed to grow stronger with each passing day. One evening when they stepped outside the stateroom to get some fresh air, Miss Nikki remained inside.

"Angelina...you know that I've grown quite fond of Miss Nikki...but...must she be within sight every minute of the day and night?"

His words brought a smile to her lips.

"I'm sorry, but that's part of her job. She's charged with protecting my honor and status as a lady from unprincipled scoundrels like you," she said with an even broader smile.

"Me? As I recall, you were the one sitting in front of my hotel room that morning."

"That was because I was afraid you had gotten yourself killed in a duel."

"I understand that, but when I helped you up, you didn't stop moving forward until you were in my arms...that's where I wish you were right now."

"I wish the same thing, but Miss Nikki...you know...has her job to do."

"I guess we'll just have to get married if we're ever going to share another kiss."

Angelina's eyes lit up for a moment, but it was difficult to tell if she was smiling or about to cry.

"Are you...are you asking me to marry you?"

"I would be honored if you would tell me that you love me and want to spend the rest of your life with me."

This time, she leaned into his arms without hesitation or fear of anyone seeing them. She kissed him long and passionately before speaking again.

"Oh, Caleb...I've already told you that I love you, and yes...I want to spend the rest of my life with you...but you must ask my father for his permission."

"I'll do that, but maybe you could tell me when it would be a good time to approach him."

"Let me think about that. Right now, tell me where we would live," Angelina said.

"Where would you like to live?"

"In a real house on real land where we can get out and touch the trees and the flowers that I usually see only from the river," Angelina replied.

"Do you want to live in a big city like Pittsburgh or New York?"

"Not that big, but big enough for you to establish a law practice," she replied.

"We can decide on that later. The big question on my mind at the moment is when would you like to get married?"

"We can settle that question as soon as you get my father's blessing."

"When should I speak with your father?" Caleb asked again.

"Probably after we relocate our new residents at Magnolia. Father loses a lot of tension once that's done."

"Maybe on our way from Magnolia to Fiddler's Point?"

"Yes, that might be the best time. If it's okay with you, I'll tell Miss Nikki our plans and maybe she'll be a little more flexible in her duties," Angelina said, casting Caleb a look of assurance.

***

Early on the following Monday morning, the riverboat finally docked at Cincinnati. Caleb took the opportunity to show Angelina and Miss Nikki where he attended law school. Miss Nikki rode with them in the carriage, but once they arrived, she chose to remain seated while Caleb and Angelina walked around. She was indeed showing a bit of flexibility.

"It's beautiful here in Cincinnati. Ever think of living here," she asked playfully.

"Not until now...but I get the feeling it might be a good idea to start thinking about it," he said, squeezing Angelina's hand gently.

***

When they all returned to the Lucky Lady, Caleb carried with him printed forms of all the freedom papers and related forms requested by Captain Bonèt.

On the third day, all the new residents were safely relocated at Magnolia. Angelina took Caleb on a horseback tour of the property and facilities, and showed him how encouraged everyone seemed to be. He was impressed with the mood of the new arrivals and those preparing to leave on their journey to freedom.

***

A few days later, the Lucky Lady left Cincinnati with Fiddler's Point being the next stop. Caleb watched until he found the opportunity to catch Angelina's father alone at the helm.

"Captain Bonèt, sir...as you have probably guessed...Angelina and I have grown quite fond of one another. I would like to respectfully ask your blessing and permission to marry your daughter," Caleb said, his voice a bit shaky.

The captain did not look up from his wheel. When he spoke, the tone was firm.

"You haven't yet set up your law practice. Do you intend to do that soon?"

"Yes, but the location should be something that Angelina and I decide on together."

"How soon are you wanting to...to...?"

"To get married," Caleb said, completing the sentence for the captain. We haven't discussed a date, but I think it would be sooner than later."

"Young man...Angelina has important duties on this voyage north. Could we postpone a decision on this until after we return from Pittsburgh in a couple of weeks?"

"Of course, sir, we all need some time to make plans. I look forward to talking with you when you return."

Caleb walked away from the helm in a bit of a daze. He had asked for the hand of Angelina as properly as he knew how, but for some reason felt that Captain Bonèt was a bit apprehensive with his comments. When he arrived back at the riverboat's dining room, Angelina was waiting.

"You look unhappy! What did Father say?"

"He said he would need some time to think about it. Is that what you anticipated?"

"No, I thought he would be happy and give us his blessing immediately."

"He wants to wait until your return from Pittsburgh in a couple of weeks before he discusses it further."

Angelina looked puzzled.

"I didn't think we would be that long. We're only going as far as the railroad station in Wellsville...not Pittsburgh. It shouldn't take but a few days. But don't worry...things will be fine."

When the Lucky Lady finally docked at Fiddler's Point, Caleb became even more disillusioned. Without any fanfare, a porter carried Caleb's bags ashore and set them on the dock. Moments later, the boat pulled away without Angelina even making an appearance.

This was the single most hurtful thing Caleb had ever experienced. He carried his bags up the path to the White Bear Inn as uncertainty filled his mind and his heart.

CHAPTER THIRTEEN

Caleb was surprised and alarmed to find that his father was in bed when he arrived home. Jane hugged Caleb, and told him not to worry because his father's pain was from an old injury that usually went away after a few days of bed rest.

"How was your trip, son?"

"It was very enlightening to say the least. I learned more about slavery than I thought I ever would, I fought a duel, and I almost got engaged to Angelina Bonèt," he said in one breath.

"A duel...engaged?"

"The duel was really nothing because we used fists as weapons and I was much quicker than my opponent. I also helped Captain Bonèt and his associates assist some slaves toward their quest for freedom."

"And the engagement?"

Caleb hung his head. Jane saw his dejection immediately and asked for details.

"Oh, Mother, Angelina and I are in love and she agreed to marry me if her father gave us his blessing, but when I asked for it, he was very elusive in his comments."

Jane closed her eyes and sighed. She had a good idea why Captain Bonèt was vague in his response. She sensed it when he and Angelina last visited Fiddler's Point. He was unsure...she was not. Maybe it was something only mothers could feel, but she knew she had given the wrong child to Nikkipohok that fateful morning. Since that moment, she loved them both. Had she asked him to exchange Angelina for the boy, only mass confusion would have ensued.

"Did he give a reason?"

"No, just that he needed time to think it over."

"Do they plan on stopping here on their return trip?"

"I don't know, Mother, Angelina didn't see me ashore or even say goodbye."

"Jane hurt for her son. She could see the love he had for Angelina. Should she tell him the truth? She decided to wait to see the captain's next move.

***

The following morning after breakfast, Caleb visited with his father. He appeared to be in considerable pain one moment and free of pain the next.

"Dad, how often do you get these attacks?"

"Oh, every week or two. The pain lays me up sometimes for several days. The problem is I can't do much lifting anymore. I couldn't even finish the addition in back."

"How far along are you?"

"Oh, I've framed in several rooms directly behind the café, but there's plenty of space for more rooms," Landon answered.

Ideas immediately began to burst into Caleb's mind.

"Do you mind if I go take a look at the new addition?"

"Not at all. Maybe you can think of some way to finish it up."

***

Landon had described the addition accurately...three rooms on each side of a center hallway were nearly ready to rent on the first and second floors. At the end of the hallway on both floors was one big room that had not yet been divided into hotel rooms.

Caleb's mind drifted back to Cupid's Manor in the St. Charles. He began envisioning a large, fancy room for the White Bear Inn. He walked through the large open area from front to back and found a rough porch for the first floor and an unfinished balcony above. He walked onto the first-floor porch to find that his view of the rivers was blocked by a stand of tall reeds. He went upstairs and walked out onto the balcony. He gazed at the Ohio River and the Soda Creek Valley below. This view was breathtaking.

His plan grew clearer in his mind as he walked back around front to the café. If Jane and Landon approved of his plan, and if Captain

Bonèt offered his blessing, he would immediately begin to turn the upstairs room into a single master bedroom. The name of the room would be Angel's Manor, he thought.

With several new rooming houses already in business, and a new, fancy, six-story hotel in the planning stage for Market Square, expanding the White Bear was no longer a good business decision, but would make a fine residence for he and Angelina should they decide to live in Fiddler's Point.

His parents approved of his plan immediately, and Caleb began putting a crew together that very day. He wanted the room to be ready if and when Angelina became his bride.

***

A week or so later, just after dawn, the Lucky Lady once again docked at Fiddler's Point. A single person left the vessel and made his way slowly to the White Bear Cafe. He stepped up to the front door and saw Jane getting things set up for the business day. He knocked on the door and she let him in.

"Captain Bonèt, what a surprise!"

"Hello, Mrs. Walters. May I talk with you for a moment?"

"Of course. I'll fix us some coffee."

The captain sipped at his coffee for a moment before beginning.

"Mrs. Walters...has Caleb told you about his relationship with Angelina?"

"Yes. He was heartbroken the day you let him off at the dock without allowing so much as a goodbye from Angelina."

"I know...Angelina has hardly stopped crying since we left your dock last week. She won't come out of her stateroom. I don't know what to do."

"Am I to understand that you want the best for Angelina?"

"Yes, of course."

"Then, it's time we both faced the truth."

Captain Bonèt lowered his eyes for a moment before looking back up.

"I suppose it is."

Jane gazed into his eyes. She had no idea how he would take the information she was about to give him, but decided that a straightforward approach would probably be best.

"Lucien...I gave you the wrong child that morning after the storm. When I awoke with two babies on my breasts, I had no idea which child was mine. When I realized that your wife had died giving birth, and the midwife had been killed in the storm...I was devastated. How could I choose? You wanted to hold your child and I had little time to think. I had nursed them both and somehow loved them both. Do you understand?"

"I do, but how can you be sure even now?"

"I was sure the moment your vessel left the dock because of the pain that shot through my heart. I longed for the year to pass when you were supposed to return, but you never came. I had no idea what happened to you or Angelina. Don't think I didn't love Caleb...because I did. I gave him all the love a mother could give, but I never stopped longing for my daughter. When you stopped on her twelfth birthday, I didn't know what to do."

"I thought by then, you would have been convinced that your guess was correct, but when I saw Caleb and his blue eyes, I was filled with indecision. I couldn't see where discussing the matter at their ages would do any good. I decided to go away and stay for the sake of both Angelina and Caleb. When he showed up in New Orleans, I was shocked. When he was challenged to a duel, I felt the overwhelming need to protect my...him...from injury or death."

"Just say it Lucian! You felt the need to protect your son!"

"Yes...that's exactly what I felt, but when he came to ask my permission to marry Angelina, I panicked. It just didn't seem...well moral."

"Oh, Lucien...they are not related in any way. As far as that's concerned, there wouldn't be anything wrong at all. What worries me is how they would feel if we told them what happened. Would Angelina accept that I am her mother and you are Caleb's father?"

"I just don't know. What do you think?" the captain said.

"I don't think we should ever tell them. If they marry...we will have the best of both worlds. We will not only be their in-laws...but also their parents. Both will be back in our lives as much as is humanly possible."

Lucian put his hand on his brow and shook his head.

"I just don't know what decision to make."

"Lucien, let me say this to you...if I give my daughter permission to marry Caleb, would you object?"

The captain finally looked up and grinned.

"Jane...you are wise beyond your years. Let's both give them our blessings and keep our secrets forever, okay?

"Yes. This way, everyone should be happy without so much confusion.

"Good...good! I'm going now to get Angelina and bring her ashore. If Caleb is still sleeping, you might want to get him up."

Caleb was not sleeping. He was standing at the front window of an upstairs hotel room that he was using. He had watched Captain Bonèt walking up the path alone and entering the cafe. If he was going to give his permission for them to marry, she would certainly have been with him, he thought.

When the captain disappeared down the path, Caleb watched for the Lucky Lady to pull away from the dock. He swallowed hard as he fought back tears. He hoped Angelina would be on deck so he could get one last glimpse of the woman he loved.

Moments later, he saw two people appear on the path.

"She's coming back to me!" he mumbled aloud.

By the time Angelina and the captain reached the café, Caleb was there in the doorway. They rushed into each other's arms and they kissed each other with a mutual promise that they would remain together forever.

The great sadness that had earlier accompanied doubt in all their hearts now turned to joy.

"I think we should all go inside and make some preliminary plans," Jane suggested.

Angelina hugged Jane and then took Caleb's hand.

"We can't make any plans without Miss Nikki," Angelina said. "Caleb and I will be back in a few minutes."

On board the Lucky Lady, Miss Nikki sat in her room alone until Angelina knocked.

"Miss Nikki...we need you at the café. There's no way we're going to make our wedding plans without you."

Both women burst into tears as they realized the close relationship they had shared for Angelina's entire life was soon going to change, but it was not going to end.

□

CHAPTER FOURTEEN

An early-October wedding was not the only major decision made that morning. Angelina needed to return to Magnolia to gather all of her possessions that she didn't keep on board the Lucky Lady. Miss Nikki decided that following the wedding, she would take a position as teacher at Magnolia. Caleb agreed he would remain in Fiddler's Point until he and Angelina had time to decide on a permanent location.

"Angelina, before you leave for Magnolia, I want to come aboard and collect two of the watercolors you showed me. I'll leave the one in your father's pilot house for his memories."

"Oh, Caleb, are you sure?"

"Yes, I have a place in mind for them and the landscape from the dock in New Orleans."

Caleb got his watercolors, and around dawn the next morning, the Lucky Lady cast off from the dock. Captain Bonèt wanted to be back at Magnolia before dark.

That afternoon, Caleb and several local craftsmen went back to work on the upstairs and downstairs interior of Angel's Manor. Over the days that followed, the construction and decorating work continued at a rapid pace.

Caleb suggested that several sets of French doors leading out to the balcony be installed across the west wall of Angel's manor. He placed a large oval rug between a tall canopy bed and the French doors. The bed was perfectly placed where they could look out the French doors and see beautiful sunsets in the evening, the moon and stars at night, and the fog lifting from the river and creek shortly after dawn. Above the fireplace mantel on the north wall, Caleb hung all three of Angelina's watercolors mounted in the finest frames.

Landon whittled the name, Angel's Manor, on a plaque and mounted it on one of the double doors facing the hotel hallway. When Jane came upstairs to view the project, she was pleased.

"The room is beautiful, son, and it looks like you decorated it as if you and Angelina were going to make it part of your home."

Caleb looked at his mother with a grin. "I considered both options when I decided to do the room. The rooms downstairs are essentially finished for a residence, but could easily be changed over to hotel rooms. If Angelina and I choose to live in Fiddler's Point, I would like to buy the entire new addition to finish turning into our home."

***

The wedding took place on the first Friday in October onboard the Lucky Lady. Captain Bonèt spared no expense, and the affair was attended by the crew as friends of the bride, and many townspeople as friends of the groom. After the ceremony, food and wine was available for all who attended.

**

Unseen by anyone in the wedding party, Silas DePriest watched the celebration from the shadowy willows along the riverbank next to the dock. He watched the crewmembers as they went about their activities. Two of them looked familiar to him. He finally realized that they were the same two runaways he had delivered to Captain Bonèt for just a ten-dollar reward back in July.

"The bastard cheated me!" he whispered under his breath. "Ten dollars for 'em both and now theys his slaves. Coulda got a hunnert or two at da auction ifin I had a way ta git 'em there! A cheat...that all he be," he mumbled as he moved his canoe away from the bank toward Kentucky.

When he got back to his cabin, he got out his jug of homemade whiskey and began to drink. He removed the rope from the basement door and went downstairs to the basement. Dottie was lying on the dirt floor with her hands tied to a heavy beam supporting the floor above. For a moment, she pretended to be asleep, but she knew that wouldn't do any good. He was drinking again, and she knew what was coming.

"I see'd yur daddy and yur brother today," DePriest said, slobber hanging between the jug and his lips. "They wuz all spruced up after waitin' hand and foot on some rich white folks who got married. I'm agonna git even with that there cap'n someday. God willin' I'm ah gittin' even."

Chills shot through Dottie's body when she realized her father and brother were still alive and maybe just across the river. DePriest walked over to the beam and untied the girl's hands and jerked her to her feet. He pulled her up the stairs and replaced the rope on the doorknob to keep his snakes secure.

"Ya wash that stinkin' body this morning like I taught ya?" he screamed.

"I didn't have time 'fore ya tied me in da basement," she replied.

The bullwhip cracked and she felt the leather wrap around her waist. When he jerked it back, most of her dress went with it. Blood oozed from the welt as she quickly moved to the blue and white pitcher and poured some water in the bowl. She splashed as much between her legs as she could before she felt the next sting of his whip.

"I'm clean, suh. I'm clean jist like ya say God wants me ta be."

"Git on that bed on yur hands and knees like I taught ya," he said, taking another long drink before setting the jug on the wash table and staggering back over to the bed.

When she finally felt him slowing down inside her, she prepared herself for his collapse. At the last moment, she managed to get most of her body from under his weight before he passed out. She waited to get off the bed until he was snoring loudly. The young girl picked up her torn dress and slipped it over her naked body. She tied several ripped pieces together so it would hang over one shoulder and at least cover some of her nakedness. She was afraid DePriest might have the front door rigged to jingle bells or to set some snakes free, so she pushed open a small window on the back wall and crawled out headfirst.

***

The child hadn't been outside since July and the evening air was cool against her skin as she made her way down the rocky hillside toward the river. The jagged stones along the footpath stabbed at her bare feet but she continued to move forward. Finally, she reached the river's edge where DePriest kept two canoes, a small one for fishing, and a larger one to transport his runaways. She pulled the small canoe into the water, got in, and began to paddle. About half way across, she wished she had taken a jagged rock and punched a hole in the big canoe, but it was too late for that. Knowing nothing about a river's current, the small canoe drifted downstream past the Lucky Lady and into the mouth of the narrow Soda Creek.

She saw the lights on the riverboat as she floated by in the darkness, and she saw other lights on the hill above the dock. She paddled the canoe into the willows, got out, and began wading back across the Creek toward the lights.

Soda Creek was not deep this time of year. The long, hot summer had reduced it to not much more than a knee-deep stream running across a sandbar. She waded across the chilly water and climbed through the reeds to the top of the hill. Straight ahead, hazy candlelight came from the master bedroom of Angel's Manor.

Dottie wanted to walk through the reeds to the path leading down to the dock to her father and brother, but she was afraid DePriest might be after her by now.

The moon was nearly full and Dottie thought she saw something moving in and out of the reeds near the side of the White Bear. She worried that it was DePriest, but she moved a little closer and could tell that there were two people; neither nearly as big as her captor.

As a cloud passed in front of the moon, Dottie watched closely as one of the shadowy forms crawled on his belly into the lean-to woodshed along the rear of the building. The second person started to follow, but the moon reappeared causing him to scamper back into the reeds. It was a long wait before another cloud hid the moon and allowed the second person to crawl into the shed.

Dottie moved up to where the last man had been and waited for a cloud to bring darkness. When it did, she just lay there too frightened to move. The way the men hid and crawled in the darkness reminded her of when she, her father, and her brother did much the same thing trying to avoid the slave chasers before DePriest caught them hiding in a barn.

They must be runaways, she thought. She was wet, cold, hungry, and frightened. Her welts were stinging and her feet were bleeding. It had to be warmer in that woodshed, she thought. Maybe they would let her join them.

She watched for the next cloud, and when it brought darkness, she slithered across the opening to the shed and disappeared inside.

Among the reeds along the ridge, other eyes were watching what the clouds and the moon allowed.

"Is anybody here?" she whispered just loud enough for someone to hear, but got no reply. She moved around the lean-to feeling her way along in the darkness. No one else was in the shed. Suddenly, she heard a muffled sound coming from some place behind a small but heavy wooden door. She tapped lightly on the wood. Moments later, Landon Walters opened the secret trapdoor partially hidden behind some lumber.

"Do you need some help?" he whispered.

"Yessuh! Oh God...yessuh!" the girl said as tears burst from her eyes.

Landon helped her inside before pulling several pieces of lumber over the opening as he backed into the basement on his hands and knees. He bolted the thick door from the inside while the two young teenage boys huddled together a short distance away.

"You'll all be safe in here if you follow my instructions. You'll have to crawl on your knees until we reach the center room. There, we'll be able to stand."

The large cut stone used for the foundation of the building was more than two feet thick and supported every upstairs wall. There were openings in the stone that corresponded to doors on the first floor. There were even windows in several places that had vertical metal bars like a jail cell. Perhaps these windows were used at one time to keep out hostile Indians.

The group crawled through several of the openings until they arrived at a long but narrow passageway—one of two secret safe rooms in the basement that Landon had built as part of the new addition. This one was directly behind the café's kitchen and the second one was located under the hallway near the entrance doors to Angel's Manor.

Each room had a heavy door that could be locked from either side depending on the situation. After locking the wooden door to this safe room, Landon lit several small candles. He showed the three runaways a bucket of water and a cup beside a platter of bread. He encouraged each of them to eat and drink, and wrap themselves in available blankets while he got them some hot food. They followed his instructions and a moment later, Landon climbed a homemade ladder and pushed open a trapdoor to the first floor. From there, he pushed open another hidden door and entered the café's kitchen where he found Jane heating a pot of vegetable soup.

"How many this time?" she asked.

"Two young boys and an even younger girl."

"Brothers and sisters?"

"I don't think so. She was the last to come to the shed, and she keeps her distance from them. She's in pretty bad shape."

"How so?" Jane asked, looking up as she stirred the soup.

"She appears to have recently been flogged with a bullwhip, she's wearing a rag for a dress, and she has no shoes. The two boys are dressed warmly at least. Probably haven't been on the run too long, maybe coming from Kentucky."

"How big is she?"

"Little smaller than Angelina, maybe," Landon replied.

"Take some soup down to them and I'll get her some warm clothes and shoes."

"I doubt if she can wear shoes. Her feet are bleeding pretty bad. Musta been walkin' on some sharp rocks somewhere."

Landon wrapped a heavy cloth around the kettle of soup and opened the secret door. Jane got some clean bandages and some whiskey and waited for Landon to return. When he did, she headed for the basement to help the girl. She was shocked when she arrived. She recognized the young girl as the same person who took a beating from Silas DePriest back in the summer.

"Hi, my name's Jane...what's your name?"

"Dottie. I ain't got no second name."

"Okay...Dottie, I've got some salve for the welts on your back, but I'll have to wash it first. Then I'll have to pour on a little whiskey to disinfect the wounds. It'll hurt a bit."

"I feel like I be hurtin' my whole life, ma'am. My momma used to bandage me up when I be hurt, but my momma be dead now."

"Turn around, child, and eat some of this hot soup while I wash your back."

The girl followed instructions and hardly moved as Jane washed the newest welts on her back. She moaned just a bit as the whiskey was poured on, but the salve seemed to sooth her pain. After the bandages were placed on the wounds, Jane pulled up the blanket around her shoulders.

"Now, let's take a look at those feet!" Jane said, moving around in front of her.

Jane washed the girl's feet, and then poured on what was left of the whiskey.

"Looks like you have a small cut or two on the edges of both feet, but the bottoms look okay. Feet tend to bleed heavy, but you'll be up walking in no time," Jane said before wrapping both feet in cloth to help stop the bleeding.

"I brought you a pair of my very special shoes just like the ones I wore when I was a young girl like you."

Jane slipped the moccasins over the bandages.

"Now, let's see if you can stand on those feet."

The girl stood and smiled for the first time.

"They don't hurt much," she said.

"You boys turn around while I get her into this dress," Jane ordered.

The boys seemed more interested in the vegetable soup than anything else. Jane slipped the dress over the girl's head and then handed her a pair of pantalets.

"I ain't never seen nothin' like these 'afore. They soft and warm, though."

"Good. Now it's time for you all to try to get some sleep. You two boys stay on your side of the room."

Jane went back up the ladder to the kitchen. Landon was there drinking coffee. He fixed Jane a cup and they sat down at a table.

"I didn't think this day would ever get over!" Landon said, showing signs of weariness.

"I know, the wedding went fine, but I didn't expect so many people to hang around so long. Caleb and Angelina are finally upstairs in Angel's Manor, and most of the lights are off down at the Lucky Lady. Everyone needs a good night's sleep. How's your back?"

"It's doin' better. Otherwise, I wouldn't have been able to make my way through the basement and climb that ladder."

"Before we go to bed, Landon, I need to tell you something very important...the young runaway in the basement is the same girl that Silas DePriest took a bullwhip to last summer.

Remember? I could hardly keep Caleb from interfering."

"Are you thinking she ran away again and he's after her?"

"No...it's unlikely a runaway would get caught by the same slave chaser twice. He must have been keeping her captive all this time for his own needs."

They looked at one another for a moment and worry spread across both of their faces.

"Let's look up the café and turn the outside lamp off. Anybody watchin' will think we're goin' to bed," Landon said.

They followed the same closing routine as always by turning off the lamp to let any runaways know that they could no longer find help at the White Bear the rest of the night. They never really knew if it did any good, though.

To be effective and safe, everything about the station had to be kept secret from everyone. Yet, word somehow got back to runaways that if they made it across the Ohio, they could find help at the White Bear if the lamp was on.

Fugitive slaves didn't come to the White Bear in great numbers—maybe ten or twelve a year, but if they somehow made it into the shed, they could find help. Landon and Jane never asked any of the runaways how they learned of the station.

Tonight, Landon was glad that he built in several new safe rooms and escape routes in and out of the White Bear. In their bedroom, Landon moved a rug and opened a trapdoor to the basement. He went to the safe room and gently shook Dottie out of her sleep.

"Who were you running from when you came here?" he whispered.

She didn't answer, but he could see her shrug her shoulders that she didn't know.

"Where were you running from?"

"Across the river," she replied in her own whisper.

"The slave chaser's cabin?"

"Yessuh."

Landon immediately woke up the two boys.

"Listen closely! Do you see this ladder?" he said, pointing to the homemade ladder leaning against the foundation stone. "If any of you hear someone tryin' to get in the basement from the shed, all of you get ready to climb this ladder into the kitchen above. Either me or Jane will open the trapdoor so you can come up."

There were no lights on inside or outside the White Bear now. The only light outside came from the moon. Nearly an hour went by before Landon heard the sound of someone apparently trying to kick in the small door to the shed. It wasn't likely that the strong, heavy door would give in, but Landon didn't want to take any chances. He opened the trapdoor and told the three runaways to climb the ladder to the floor above. Once there, Landon bolted the trapdoor before opening a secret panel and leading the three young people into the café's kitchen.

Landon had seen Silas DePriest in town from time to time. The slave chaser was a very large, stout-looking man. His head appeared to sit squarely on his broad shoulders. What neck he might have had was covered with a course, ragged beard.

"Bring them all over here," Jane whispered from the secret door leading out of the kitchen into a hallway.

Landon ushered the three runaways over to the door. He picked up a boning knife from the kitchen counter. No one saw Dottie hide the empty whiskey bottle inside the pleats of her dress.

"I went up to the manor and warned Caleb and Angelina about what was going on," Jane said. "I told them that we might have to bring the runaways through their room if it was the only safe route to safety. Angelina seemed to understand the situation much better than Caleb."

"I'm sure DePriest suspects the White Bear is being used as an Underground Railroad station. If he contacts the authorities, we may all go to jail," Landon said quietly, but with urgency in his voice.

"Right now, we need to get everyone upstairs. There will be some safety in numbers even if he breaks into the building somewhere," Jane said.

The thumping on the trapdoor stopped soon after Landon led the group upstairs to Angel's Manor. There were stairs from the balcony down to the back porch, and there was no way of knowing exactly where DePriest might be at any moment. He could still be in the woodshed in back, or outside hiding in the darkness.

The seven of them stood in a tight group near the fireplace mantle with their eyes riveted to the double doors to the hallway. If DePriest managed to get into the building and came that way, it would be a simple thing for him to kick the doors open.

The only intrusion into the silence within the master bedroom was the panicked breathing of seven frightened people. The full moon once again escaped from behind passing clouds revealing a blurry shadow moving on the balcony.

"That's him outside! Caleb, escort all the ladies and the runaways out the café front door and down to the Lucky Lady. DePriest won't be able to see you leave from the balcony. You'll all be safe there," Landon whispered.

"What about you?"

Landon patted the revolver in his belt.

"I won't let him get close enough to hurt me. Now go on."

Moments later, Caleb led the ladies and the runaways down the path through the reeds to the Lucky Lady. Angelina explained what was going on to Captain Bonèt and he immediately barked orders to crewmembers to secure the runaways. He then stuck a revolver into his belt and handed one to Caleb.

"Angelina, see that our new residents have everything they need. Stop and tell Mr. Phyddle to join us immediately at the café."

Angelina started to object because she wanted to join the men but knew it would do no good.

"That's DePriest's canoe down in the reeds!" Caleb said as he and the captain stepped off the Lucky Lady onto the dock.

The two men hurried up the path leading to the café with Mr. Phyddle just a few steps behind. They made their way into the White Bear without being seen.

The only light inside the bedroom was coming from the fireplace. Landon stood in the shadows near the secret panel he had recently installed. The other three men joined him there but none could see DePriest on the balcony any longer, but they could hear his drunken tirade.

"I know ya be in dare li'l Dot. Ya be my propity cause the law sez so and I'm gittin ya back right now."

Suddenly, the French doors exploded inward, followed by the rushing, ominous form of a hulking, no-neck brute with his bullwhip raised high above his head. But, as he staggered through the door, his foot tripped on the doorframe sending him sprawling onto the floor. He screamed in pain as shards of broken glass pierced his skin in various places—one slicing into his right hand, causing him to drop his bullwhip.

"Gad dammit, Dottie, where ya be hidin?" he shouted, struggling to his feet, his arms flailing as he whirled in a circle searching for any sign of his prey.

His spinning motion sent drops of blood flying through the air and splattering the three watercolors over the mantle. Once again, DePriest lost his balance sending him crashing to the floor again. This time, a sliver of glass penetrated the area of his left eye. He managed to get to his feet again while mumbling more cuss words as he staggered back onto the balcony. He turned toward the broken door and peered inside as if pondering whether to try one more time to reclaim what he called his propity.

As the moon passed behind large, thick clouds again, Silas DePriest staggered down the balcony steps into the darkness.

Landon, Caleb, Captain Bonèt, and Mr. Phyddle walked through the glass and blood to the railing and looked over. DePriest was nowhere to be seen.

"We need to go after DePriest now!" the captain said. "If he gets away, he'll be a continuous threat to all of us. Nobody wants him lurking in the shadows from now on. It's hard to tell when he might try to get his revenge if we leave him out there."

"It's pitch dark out there, Captain. Depriest probably knows the woods around his cabin like the back of his hand. He could pick us off one by one." Mr. Phyddle said.

"I think the best idea is to get the ladies down river as far away from this beast as possible." Landon suggested.

"Dad's right! It's too dark to do anything right now," Caleb added.

"You all need to get on board the Lady now. I'll be here to protect Jane. Come daylight, I'll do whatever's necessary to end this thing."

The other three men agreed and the Lucky Lady was soon steaming toward Cincinnati.

CHAPTER FIFTEEN

Jane and Landon stayed awake all night in one of the safe rooms. Shortly after dawn the next morning, Landon escorted Jane to the general store where she would be safe while he went looking for DePriest. He returned to the café and stuck two pistols in his belt along with his Bowie knife. He walked to the dock where he found that DePriest's canoe was gone. His eyes scanned the river in all directions as far as he could see but found no activity this early in the morning. Landon walked to the far side of the dock, climbed into his own canoe, and quietly began paddling upstream along the shoreline. After a while, he pointed the canoe toward Kentucky and paddled hard against the current.

Minutes later, Landon pulled his canoe into the willows a short distance from a dirt path leading up to DePriest's log cabin. As he walked along the path, he observed drops of blood, especially near a large oak tree where the slave chaser had apparently stopped to rest.

"Silas DePriest!" Landon yelled from behind the oak at the edge of the thick forest surrounding the cabin. "This is Landon Walters, the owner of the White Bear Inn that you broke into last night. I've come to take you into custody or kill ya...your choice!"

A warmer-than-normal October breeze whistled through a nearby stand of Birch trees before a weak voice came from the cabin.

"I'm 'bout half kilt already, so it won't be much of an undertakin'. I ain't got but one good eye now that I pulled the sliver of glass out of the stabbed one. I ain't gonna make it easy on ya, though," DePriest said, shooting several times from somewhere inside the cabin.

Landon returned the fire, his slugs shattering a small front window. Moments later, smoke began to roll out of the broken window followed moments later by DePriest's cussing and screaming.

"Ya done set my cabin on fire! Guess I'll be feelin' the torture of Hell afore I ever git thar! Damn ya and all the other thieves who stole my propity. Y'all gonna burn in Hell, too!"

Landon guessed one of his bullets had hit an oil lantern that set the fire. It didn't really matter. He would wait until the cabin burned to the ground to be sure DePriest would never threaten his family again. That didn't take long as the flames quickly burned through the roof just before the back wall caved in sending a cloud of orange cinders into the air.

For just a moment, Landon thought he heard another explosion from inside the cabin before he realized it was a clap of thunder. The first large drops of rain to hit the logs sizzled and turned to steam as the rest of the cabin's walls collapsed inwardly. He thought he caught the unmistakable stench of burning flesh just before the downpour quenched the flames and left nothing but a layer of smoldering embers.

Landon waited and watched for more than an hour as the heavy rain finished extinguishing the hot embers until even the smallest ribbons of smoke were gone. He finally walked back down the path to his canoe and started to get in before he took a second look at DePriest's canoe. He picked up a jagged rock and smashed it into the side of the canoe leaving a gaping hole.

"That's just for good measure," he said to himself before heading back to Ohio.

***

Shortly after noon, echoes of hammer on nail bounced back from the Kentucky hills and across the river valley. Thick, roughhewn boards were soon nailed across all of the downstairs doors and windows of the new addition to the White Bear Inn. All of the French doors to the upstairs balcony were boarded up. The heavy velvet drapes on all the side windows were closed, shutting out nearly all outside light.

Inside, shards of broken glass and splintered pieces of wood were cleaned up. The new rug that had been between the foot of the bed and the French doors was gone. Angelina's three watercolors remained on the wall above the mantel. The bloodstains had already dried and would be nearly impossible to remove. That would be up to Caleb and Angelina to decide someday. They were safe now in Cincinnati and Angelina had already indicated to Jane the night before that she wanted nothing from the room that would remind her of the savagery that occurred there on her honeymoon night.

At precisely seven o'clock Monday morning, Landon unlocked the front door and the café was open for business as usual. The lantern near the front door of the café would be lit again that very evening. Landon had eliminated the threat of the slave chaser, Silas DePriest, but there were still many threats from the law and those who still believed strongly in slavery. However, he and Jane were determined to help runaways in any way they could—they had strong beliefs of their own.

***

Shortly after the Lucky Lady anchored near the Cincinnati riverfront, Angelina and Caleb got a room in a nice hotel where they located a telegraph and sent a message to Landon at the general store. Jane and Landon listened in amazement as the general store owner read their message.

All aboard are safe and well. How are things there? Respond.

Landon and Jane hesitated for a long moment before answering. Landon finally spoke up.

The White Bear Inn is open for business as usual.

The storekeeper did as instructed as Jane and Landon left the store talking about the wonders of the new technology that had recently strung wires along the street in front of the café and down the river road to Cincinnati. Times were changing.

***

Over the days that followed, Dottie and the two teenage runaways were moved to Magnolia where they became residents and began their training on the path to freedom. Her father and brother elected to stay at Magnolia until Dottie finished her training so they could go on to Canada as a family.

Caleb established a one-room law office near the docks in Cincinnati, but spent most of his time on board the Lucky Lady with Angelina doing whatever legal work that needed to be done to best insure that the residents were safe as they moved from Magnolia to the final trip aboard the Lucky Lady to Wellsville and on to Canada. This allowed Landon and Jane to visit with their family at least every few months.

***

The Lucky Lady's first visit to Fiddler's Point since the DePriest incident came in late

December. Jane and Miss Nikki prepared a hot, hearty breakfast of eggs, bacon, biscuits, and gravy. Everyone sat around a large table and talked about many things, but the fact that Angel's Manor was boarded up from the inside and outside was never mentioned. The terrorizing incident a few months earlier with the slave chaser, Silas DePriest, was never mentioned. The conversation seemed to be much about a group of twenty-two residents who had successfully completed their program at Magnolia—a group who would soon be in Canada to start a new life of freedom.

"How is the young girl, Dottie, doing?" Jane asked, directing her question toward Angelina.

"She's doing great! She's back with her father and brother and that alone gives her confidence that things are getting better in her life. Miss Nikki and I both work with her on reading and writing and she is an aggressive learner. She'll do well in the program and be on her way to freedom come next spring," Angelina replied, an air of pride in her tone.

Even though Christmas was several days away, everyone agreed to exchange small gifts at breakfast. When that was completed, Angelina and Caleb announced to everyone that their main Christmas gift would have to wait until the following summer to be born. Everyone was elated with the announcement that a new generation of Walters was on its way.

As usual, Captain Bonèt was antsy about weather conditions. It had been a cold December and he had noticed small pockets of thin ice along the calmer waters near the shore. It would likely be even colder as the Lucky Lady turned north towards Wellsville. He told everyone about his observations and plans to leave soon. He, Mr. Phyddle, and Angelina did have Caleb take them in a carriage to visit family gravesites, but shortly afterwards, everyone said their goodbyes and boarded the Lady for their final trip upstream until spring. They would stop at the White Bear dock for refueling, but the visit would be short before continuing on to Cincinnati. Once there, Captain Bonèt and Mr. Phyddle would decide if they should take the Lucky Lady south for the winter. Caleb and Angelina had already decided to spend the winter at Magnolia. Angelina would continue teaching the new residents while Caleb easily traveled back and forth across the river to his office in Cincinnati. He not only wanted to establish his law practice there, but he also needed to find the kind of home Angelina always wanted before their baby arrived.

What no one knew at the time was that another child would also be born in the spring.

CHAPTER SIXTEEN

After wintering in New Orleans, the Lucky Lady made its way north to Cincinnati soon after large chunks of ice had finally melted and disappeared from the Ohio River. Mr. Phyddle's gambling skills had won him enough money to buy seven slaves at the New Orleans auction. The Lucky Lady would pick up six more runaways at several friendly fuel stops along the way back. Thirteen new residents would be going to Magnolia and about the same number would be leaving Magnolia for Wellsville soon; however, Dottie and her family would not be making the trip this spring because she had just delivered a baby girl. She named her Janie.

No one asked about the baby's father and Dottie never mentioned him. Those horrors were all in her past and she had no place to look but to the future.

***

By mid-June, that future began as Dottie and her family, along with other residents, boarded the Lucky Lady for a voyage up the Ohio to Wellsville and freedom. As usual, the Lucky Lady would stop for fuel in Fiddler's Point giving Caleb and Angelina the opportunity to visit with Jane and Landon.

It was late evening when the Lady moored. Angelina and Caleb went directly to the White Bear while Captain Bonèt and Mr. Fiddle informed the passengers and crew that they would be spending the night at the dock. A short time later, the two made their way to the café to visit with the Walters.

Dottie stood against the railings on the deck staring at the Kentucky hills where she had been held captive for months. Then, she turned her back to the hills and walked around to the dockside of the Lucky Lady where she once again stared at the path through the reeds that led to the White Bear. Miss Nikki came out on deck and put her arm around Dottie's shoulders.

"You know that this will likely be the last time you ever see this part of your past," Miss Nikki said, patting her lightly on the shoulder.

"Yes! I just looked at the hills across the river where we all suffered more cruelty than we ever did on the plantation. Then on this side of the river, I found the most kindness that helped me survive. Mr. Walters led me to shelter and safety and Miss Jane doctored my wounds with gentleness. Then they all risked their lives when that monster came looking for me. I wouldn't have survived without their help."

"I'll watch the baby if you want to go up to the café and pay your respects," Miss Nikki said, patting her on the back again.

"Thanks, Miss Nikki. I think I will."

"Don't stay too long. It'll be getting dark soon and I don't want you coming back through the reeds in the dark. Besides, little Janie is sleeping right now, but she'll be hungry when she wakes up," Miss Nikki said as she headed back to Dottie's cabin to watch the baby.

The first day of summer was only a few days away and the reeds were already tall, thick, and full of leaves. Dottie stared up and down the riverbank for a long moment watching the reed tops sway in a gentle breeze. She could see birds flying in and out of the dense willow trees with their leafy branches hanging only inches from the water. She could see the sun beginning to hide itself behind the smoky hills on the horizon as it cast long shadows across the landscape. What she could not see was the no-neck slave chaser, Silas DePriest, lurking in the reeds along the path to the café.

Dottie checked her burgundy vest, white blouse, and white ruffled skirt to be sure they were clean. She loved wearing clean clothes. She smiled when she recalled the pantalets and dress Jane had given her the night she escaped. She suddenly realized that it would be dark soon and she wanted to be back on board while there was still some light. She hurried down the gangplank and across the dock to the dirt path running through the tall reeds. Moments later, Silas DePriest's large, heavy fist struck Dottie behind her right ear and knocked her unconscious. When she finally came to, she found her hands were tied behind her back with a coarse rope that also bound her ankles. She was hog-tied. DePriest lifted her from the canoe and sat her on the muddy bank. He then shoved the canoe with his foot and sent it into the swift current where it would quickly disappear far downriver.

"Good to see ya still be alive. Thought for a while I might ov kilt ya," he said.

Dottie wanted to scream, but DePriest had stuffed something in her mouth. The last remnants of sunlight bounced off the surface of the river allowing Dottie to see the disfigured face of her captor. He wore a leather patch over his left eye that had been pierced by a sliver of glass from the balcony of Angel's Manor. There were reddish patchy scars on his right cheek, and his right ear appeared to be nearly gone.

DePriest removed the coarse rope from around Dottie's ankles and looped it around his left wrist.

"Ya be too heavy to tote to the top of the hill, so I'll keep hold of ya while you walk in front of me," he said, pushing her along what Dottie recognized as the rocky path to his cabin. When they finally arrived, DePriest kept her away from what was once a small clearing in front of his cabin. He didn't want to leave a trail in case someone tried to follow them. In the last glimmer of twilight, Dottie could see that the cabin where she was once held captive had burned to the ground.

"Mr. Walters from the White Bear across the river burned my cabin down and he thought I was still in it. Got burned some, but I crawled out the same window you used to make yur getaway. Found a cave on top the hill. That be where we be livin'," he said, nudging Dottie around the burned cabin and up the hillside.

"You're taking me to a cave?" Dottie asked, speaking for the first time.

"Ya talk differnt now, Dottie."

"That's because I can read and write now, and I can speak up for myself. I've read the whole Bible now and what you're doing to me is a sin!

"The Bible don't say nothin' 'bout sinin' with your own propity!

"I'm not your property! I'm not anybody's property anymore! I have legal papers now and I'm on my way with my baby to freedom in Canada," Dottie said in a firm tone.

DePriest stopped and turned Dottie around to face him. For the first time, he was looking into Dottie's eyes. His one eye blinked rapidly for a brief moment as if he might be feeling the tiniest bit of compassion.

"What baby ya be talkin' 'bout?"

Dottie looked away for a moment before speaking.

"You're the only man I've ever been with, so you are her father."

Once again, Dottie saw something different in his facial expression as if he was in deep thought—but she quickly learned it was not compassion that she was seeing.

"Then that baby be my propity, too!"

Tears burst from Dottie's eyes as the stark truth settled into her mind—she would never be free of this insane man until he was dead. But, he had shown a remarkable ability to survive. She also realized that he would now be a threat to her daughter if he could find a way to capture her. All she could think about as they trudged through the trees was how she could prevent any chance that this brute might hurt her child.

With only the full moon to light the way, DePriest finally took the lead and more or less dragged Dottie the rest of the way up the thickly forested hillside until the trees suddenly ended and layers of shale rock began. The rocky cliffs formed a dome as high as the tallest pine trees.

"That be the cave straight ahead. The Shawnee call it Devil's Den 'cause of findin' so many human bones in and 'round the cave. Musta been a bear's den at one time or maybe a mountain lion's. Don't make me no nevermind—it's mine now."

Dottie was bruised and exhausted by the time DePriest untied her hands and warned her not to try to escape. He built a small fire at the mouth of the cave that provided some light and warmth.

"Ya smell mighty good now, Dottie. Must be wearin' some of that store-bought toilet water or somethin'," DePriest said as he took his whip off a makeshift hook on his belt. "I see yur wearin' fancy cloths and underwear, too. Take 'em off!"

Dottie knew what was coming. She also knew that there was no use in trying to resist without feeling the ripping sting of this heartless man's whip. She followed his instructions and removed her vest, blouse, and skirt first.

"Ya lookin' more like a full-grown woman now, Little Dot. Yessir, nursin' that baby is makin' a woman out of ya," he said. "Now, take off those long panties. Ya been keepin' your private parts clean like the Bible sez?"

"I told you I read the whole Bible and it doesn't say anything about a woman keeping her private parts clean, but I've been taking a bath every day where I've been living."

The crack of his whip just inches away from her nearly naked body startled Dottie and she knew what he expected her to do next. She removed her pantalets and stood there quietly as he walked up close to her and began exploring her body with his rough hands. She cringed inside but did not move.

"The Bible don't make me no nevermind nomore anyways! Git over there on my pallet on your hands and knees like I taught ya!"

When he was finished grunting and moaning, he collapsed on top of her. After a while, he re-tied her hands and feet and looped one end of the rope around his thick wrists. Dottie would not escape him again this night while he slept.

CHAPTER SEVENTEEN

When baby Janie woke up crying just after dark, Miss Nikki became worried that Dottie had not yet returned to the Lucky Lady. She cuddled the baby in her arms and walked to Mr. Fiddle's cabin to have him go check on Dottie. He soon returned to report that Dottie never came to the café at all. No one there had seen her, and after talking with every crewmember and some of the passengers, Mr. Phyddle could only report that none of them had seen Dottie depart the Lucky Lady. In a matter of minutes, Caleb, Angelina, Landon, Jane, and Captain Bonèt were on the dock discussing the possibilities of what could have happened to Dottie. No one even mentioned the name DePriest because to everyone concerned, he was long dead. In the end, common sense prevailed, and they all agreed that it was too dark to do any searching until morning. If the worst thing had happened and Dottie fell off the gangplank into the river, she may have been knocked unconscious and carried into the current. Everyone knew that bodies of people who drown in the river were rarely found. What no one seemed to consider was that drowning was not necessarily the worst thing that could have happened to Dottie.

***

At dawn, everyone from the night before returned to the dock, but could find no clues as to Dottie's disappearance. If she didn't drown, she might still show up sometime, somewhere. If she drowned, she would never be seen again. Captain Bonèt knew that there was nothing more he could do moored at the dock. He decided to set out for Wellsville and hope that Dottie showed up at the café where she would be safe until the Lucky Lady returned.

Jane quickly found a young Shawnee girl who had recently lost a child to act as a wet nurse for the baby. Miss Nikki and the wet nurse would take care of the baby together—on board the Lucky Lady.

As Landon and Jane stood on the dock alone waving farewell to their family and friends, Landon began to stare at the hills across the river.

"Could it be possible that Silas DePriest escaped the fire?" he asked Jane.

"You said you could smell burning flesh. Flesh has a distinct odor that no one is likely to ever forget," Jane replied.

"Yes, but what if it was the scent of burning snakes?" Landon whispered almost to himself as he turned and led Jane back up the path to the café.

***

Across the river in a cave known as Devil's Den, Dottie and Silas DePriest sat near the opening eating nuts and some fresh berries that DePriest had just gathered near the tree line that marked the beginning of a large, bald dome of rock. The fire had long burned itself out sometime during the night. DePriest had untied Dottie to allow her to eat, but he never took his one eye off of her for more than a second or two. He knew, as did Dottie, that if she made a break for it, his long bullwhip would find her ankles long before she made it into the trees and bushes.

"I'm still hungry!" DePriest huffed as he stood up. "I'm goin' over to those bushes to pick more berries. You sit still, now, or my whip will find ya and strip some hide ofen yur bones."

Dottie sat still at the mouth of the cave as instructed. She longed to hold her baby against her swollen breasts and wondered what Miss Nikki was doing to feed her child. Then, her heart began to race as she caught just a glimpse of what appeared to be a small bear cub moving silently behind its mother in the direction of the berry bushes where DePriest was busy gathering more food.

Dottie had heard the men at Magnolia talking about the dangers of bear and cougar attacks while they were out hunting. She also remembered that the most dangerous of all were the mothers when they thought their cubs might be harmed.

The idea came quickly and before she could give it more thought, she picked up several stones, stood, and charged directly at the bear cub. She threw a stone and missed, but the second stone hit the cub on the rump and made it yelp. The mother bear immediately charged at Dottie and slapped her across the face with its huge paw and sharp claws. Dottie's head turned nearly backwards as her bloody face and body flew several feet in the air before landing in a heap—dead.

Silas DePriest took several steps toward the bear and let his whip crack across the bear's face. By the time he drew his whip back for a second try, the mother bear was mauling DePriest's body, ripping one arm completely off before biting his face and shaking him savagely until he stopped screaming and his limp, dead body stopped struggling. The mother bear finally gathered up its cub and disappeared into the berry bushes.

Scavengers would eventually pick their bodies clean and the hot summer sun would bleach whatever bones were left. Over the years, the bones would simply become part of the Devil's Den folklore. Their remains would never be buried and no headstones would ever bear their names.

But, if the truth were ever told, it would be said that Silas DePriest was a cruel, savage animal who died as a result of a mother's love.

Dottie—with no second name—would be that loving mother.

CHAPTER EIGHTEEN

In late June, the Lucky Lady once again returned to Fiddler's Point and all hands were on deck scurrying around to get the Lady tied off and the gangplank secured. Caleb carried one end of a stretcher and Captain Bonèt carried the other end. Miss Nikki and Mr. Phyddle were at the sides making sure Angelina was as safe as possible along the path to the White Bear. Each time she screamed, Caleb's face would wince with concern while the captain's face became pale. Miss Nikki held Angelina's hand and kept assuring her that everything would be okay.

Immediately after the group burst into the cafe, Jane realized what was going on and directed the men to carry Angelina upstairs to the anteroom. She put a large pot of water on the stove and had Miss Nikki get a whole bolt of white cotton cloth from a cabinet. Within minutes, the women were carrying everything they needed to the anteroom to assist in the birth of Angelina's child. The men were ordered to go downstairs with Landon.

As Angelina's son was born, all present were aware of the role they had played more than two decades earlier when Angelina and Caleb were born in the same anteroom of the White Bear Inn.

***

Early the next year, Mr. Phyddle and Miss Nikki were married. They raised Janie and a son on the farm at Magnolia.

Caleb launched a successful law practice in Cincinnati and eventually became a judge. Angelina continued to teach residents of Magnolia until the war began.

Captain Bonèt carried on with his freedom journeys, but only along the Ohio River from Cincinnati to Wellsville. Caleb, Angelina, and their four sons often made the voyage with the captain in order to spend time in Fiddler's Point with Jane and Landon. However, not one time did anyone ever reenter the boarded up part of the building.

In the early spring of 1861, the Lucky Lady was appropriated by the Union Army for the transportation of troops. It was sunk by Confederate troops less than a year later. All aboard were lost.

Landon Walters died in April 1865—one week after the assassination of President Lincoln. It is claimed that he helped load a dozen cords of firewood onto a Union riverboat the day before his death. Jane died in her apartment next to her café in the autumn of 1901 surrounded by two children, four grandchildren, and eighteen great-grandchildren.

After the funeral, the family collected Jane's personal items from the building. What they did not find were her journals that began in August 1828. They remained hidden within the walls of the White Bear Inn for more than a century.

As per Landon and Jane's request, the White Bear Inn could never be sold, but could be leased from time to time if necessary. Caleb drew up an ironclad lease agreement for the property. A clause in the lease set one absolute restriction; the back rooms of the inn, both upstairs and downstairs would remain boarded up without the expressed, written consent of the owners.

With the opening of several modern hotels in Fiddler's Point, the White Bear Inn was soon closed and never reopened as a hotel. In the years that followed, the café was leased to a number of different people who left no significant record of their occupancy.

It was not until the mid-1930s that Garret Walters and his wife, Rosie, leased the building and returned the Walters name to the White Bear Inn.

PART TWO

WATERCOLORS
(NOT FOR SALE)

CHAPTER NINETEEN

FIDDLER'S POINT, OHIO—1945

The eighth day of May came on a Tuesday in 1945. The morning began routinely at Rosie's Diner, but it would not end the same way.

Inside the diner, the aroma of fresh ground coffee beans lingered in the air and mingled with a whiff of bacon grease, salt, pepper, and flour browning in a cast-iron skillet. Rosie Walters stirred the mixture slowly until the scent told her the exact moment to pour in the fresh milk.

Outside, thunder cracked in the distance as heavy storm clouds moved up the Ohio River Valley. All the signs were there as the wind whipped through the trees and cornfields. So far this spring, four severe storm warnings had been issued on radio, but no tornados developed. Today would be no different, but the Captain of the tugboat, Lady Lexi, could not know this. Around eight o'clock that morning, his vessel, towing only another disabled tugboat, docked just east of the Court Street landing, and the small crew of five men headed for a safe place to have some hot breakfast. Rosie's Diner was the closest spot.

Hannah Frazey, just over five feet tall, could carry seven breakfast plates on one arm at the same time. Being the only waitress at the diner, this talent came in quite handy during rush hour. While Rosie cooked, Hannah served mainly biscuits, gravy, fried eggs, and bacon to mostly the same regulars nearly every morning.

The Captain and most of his crew sat around a large center table. They ordered what everyone else was eating. One crewmember sat alone on a swivel stool at the front end of the coffee bar.

Bing Crosby and the Andrew Sisters, singing A Hot Time in the Town of Berlin, kept playing repeatedly on the jukebox until Rosie turned it off about five minutes before nine. She clicked on the radio sitting near the coffee grinder, and the diner became quiet.

As anticipated, at exactly nine o'clock, President Harry S. Truman came on the air and announced the unconditional surrender of Germany. World War II in Europe was over!

The full house at Rosie's immediately burst into a roar. Men shook hands, patted each other on the back, and made loud whooping sounds. Hannah was the only woman in the diner other than Rosie, who was being embraced by her husband, Garret. He had come over from his barbershop next door to join everyone in the celebration.

The mechanic from the Lady Lexi, a tall, stoutly built young man, spotted Hannah standing near the jukebox. Spontaneously, and without asking, he put his large hands around her waist, picked her up, and held her in the air like a father playing with his infant child. His friendly gesture was certainly innocent enough considering Truman's announcement. He slowly lowered her back toward the floor, stopping the descent only when her eyes were level with his. At that exact moment, something unexpected and magical happened when he looked into Hannah's dancing eyes. The shouting and whooping continued around the young couple, but they didn't seem to hear it.

Neither he nor Hannah were experienced with romantic encounters, but human instincts seemed to replace their awkwardness as he pulled her closer and she responded by sliding her arms around his neck. As their lips met, they were no longer just celebrating the end of the war. They were sampling the first intoxicating splendor of a love that would seed itself at that very moment and continue to grow like a field of wild flowers in the spring.

Hannah was not beautiful by any means. She was rather short, but well proportioned, with light brown hair that turned nearly blond with the summer sun. For the most part, the twenty-five-year-old waitress was average looking with the exception of her eyes. They were light blue most of the time, but in certain light, they were nearly violet. The color was not the outstanding feature of her eyes, though. They seemed to sparkle as if they were reflecting all the starlight from a clear, night sky.

The mechanic looked to be about the same age as Hannah. He stood nearly six-feet-four. His hands were large and his arms strong looking. He worked primarily as a mechanic on the Lady Lexi, but also doubled as a cook when the engine was running smoothly. His hair was dark brown and he wore it short. His broad smile revealed a nearly perfect set of pearly white teeth. He often allowed his beard to grow during the long, boring trips between the two major port cities of Pittsburgh and Cincinnati, but this morning, for some unknown reason, he shaved and splashed on a little Bay Rum.

When their lips finally parted, their eyes remained locked as the young man gently lowered Hannah to the floor.

"My name's Hannah...what's yours?"

"Patrick Phoot, but everyone just calls me Paddy."

"Irish, huh?" Hannah responded with a grin.

"Yes...and proud of it."

"Does your last name start with the letter "F" like it sounds?" she asked.

"No. It starts with "Ph" but it sounds like the thing with toes on it," Paddy replied with his own big grin—having been asked the same question many times in his life.

"Nice meeting you, Paddy."

The magic continued for a long moment until Hannah suddenly blinked several times, turned away, and hurried back behind the breakfast bar and on into the diner's kitchen.

Crewmember, Roe Cagney, remained seated during the entire celebration. He did not shake any hands, pat any backs, or kiss any girls. His eyes remained glued on Paddy and Hannah from the time Paddy picked her up until she stepped away to go to the kitchen. On his swivel stool, Roe turned slowly, allowing his eyes to follow every movement of Hannah's body as her hips moved from side to side beneath her thin, pale-yellow, summer uniform.

Rosie watched everything that was going on as her hands removed dishes and silverware from the tables. Most of her customers had already poured out of the diner and into the streets to celebrate the war's end.

In her early-thirties and the mother of two sons, ten and three, Rosie glanced first at Paddy and then at Roe before taking the stack of dirty dishes to the kitchen. She had never seen Paddy before, but recognized the shy, naïve expression of wonderment on his face. That pleased her.

As for Roe Cagney, Rosie had seen him riding his bicycle around town since he was a kid. His father died in prison but his mother still lived in a trailer just outside of town on the west side of Soda Creek. She heard about him getting a job on the tugboats and was glad that he now spent much of his time away from Fiddler's Point. Roe had been in and out of trouble with the law most of his youth. Now, the undisguised lust Rosie had just seen in his eyes made her edgy.

Nearly all of the local businesses, except for the taverns, closed up for the rest of the day following Truman's announcement. All the town's schools closed while most of the churches opened up for those who wanted to give thanks for the end of hostilities in Europe. Rosie locked her doors and walked across the street to her sister's house to collect her kids. She and her family would enjoy the rest of the day together.

Hannah left the diner and walked around the corner to a small porch leading up to her two-room apartment behind the diner's kitchen. She washed her face, changed clothes, brushed her hair, and put on a thin layer of pink lipstick. She slipped a clean, white apron with a large patch pocket over her head and tied the strings behind her back. She then stuck several drawing pencils into the patch pocket and picked up a sketchpad from a shelf on her way out her front door.

She walked south a block to the River Street opening of the floodwall. The brick street turned into gravel as it snaked along the river-side of the wall. The Lady Lexi was still moored at the dock a short distance away. Hannah found a place to sit where the sun was just right and began sketching the Lady Lexi. Although it looked much like the other tugboats she had drawn over the years, this one was different now—not because of its construction, but because Paddy Phoot spent much of his time on board.

Afternoon turned to early evening before she spotted Paddy, Roe, and the other three crewmembers approaching the riverbank from the Court-Street entrance. Her heart beat faster in her chest as she flipped to a clean sheet of paper and began drawing as the men stopped to observe a wall of tall, dark, storm clouds moving slowly up the river valley.

Paddy raised his right arm above shoulder level and pointed in the direction of the approaching storm. Hannah couldn't hear the Captain's words, but in a matter of minutes, the men began securing both tugboats with additional ropes. It appeared the Lady Lexi would not continue her voyage to Cincinnati until the storm passed.

Hannah collected her pencils and paper and began walking along the gravel road toward Court Street. It was a bold move on her part, but she just didn't care. Memories of Paddy's morning kiss lingered on her lips. If she could put herself in a position to talk with him again, it would be worth the effort, she thought. This time, luck was with her as Paddy spotted her from the dock and met her near the Court Street entrance.

"Still celebrating?" he asked.

"I'm not much of a party person. I just came over to draw whatever I could find of interest."

"What did you find?"

"Your boat!" Hannah said, nervously gesturing with her closed drawing pad by holding it up so Paddy could see that she was telling the truth even if it wasn't her main reason for walking along the riverbank.

"You're an artist, then?"

"Oh, I don't know about that...I just like to draw."

"May I see your work?"

"I...uh...I don't have any finished work with me," Hannah said, suddenly worrying that her sketches might not meet with his approval, and not knowing what else to say.

Crazy thoughts ran through her mind. Did he think she was an easy touch? Was he like so many of the diner's customers who thought waitresses were their captive audiences? Was he only interested in one thing?

She looked down at her sketchpad, then raised her face slowly until their eyes met again, silently asking so many what-if questions. She could see that he was also nervous as his broad smile changed to a slight tremble in his chin.

"I can show you what I did today," she said.

Hannah opened her tablet to the picture of the Lady Lexi that she had just finished sketching.

"Wow! That's fantastic! You are an artist!"

Hannah felt good inside about Paddy's praise of her work, but wasn't sure if she wanted him to see her second sketch that included him. Paddy took that decision out of her hands when he lifted the front page to reveal that sketch.

"That's me!"

"Yes, I just finished it before we saw each other."

"How did you draw so many details so quickly?"

"I've been sketching for as far back as I can remember. You get faster with practice. Besides, there are not really that many details there now...I mean...I'll add many more details before I paint them with watercolors."

"May I see it when it's finished?"

Hannah wasn't sure how to answer him. She had no idea if he would ever be around again once he continued his trip down river.

"I suppose...if you're around when I finish it."

"How long will that take?"

"Hard to say...maybe a week or two."

"I finish up my thirty as soon as I get back to Cincy. That means I'll be off for the next month. If I come up sometime...do you think I could see it if you're finished?"

"Sure...if you want to. Do you really get a whole month's vacation?"

"In a way...I guess. On the tugs, you work thirty days on and then get thirty days off. When you're on, you work six hours on and six hours off...day and night."

"Then...what are you all doing off today?"

"Cause of the storm that's supposed to be comin'. Normally, we don't stop rain or shine, but the Captain doesn't like goin' through tornadoes. They can throw barges and tugs around like toys...and ya can't see a twister comin' after dark."

"So, you'll be here until tomorrow morning?"

"Yeah, Captain was in the last war and I think he wants to do a little celebratin' like the rest of America."

"Where will you sleep?" Hannah said with some alarm in the tone of her voice because she knew the closest hotel was within two blocks.

"Oh, we all have to sleep on board if possible. We'll know soon if that storm is goin' to pass north of us."

"Speaking of storms, I just felt a drop or two of rain. I'd better be getting home before I get sopped."

"Can I walk you home? It's getting dark, and lots of people are getting' drunk and actin' crazy because the war is finally over. It might not be safe to be out alone."

Neither he nor Hannah had any idea of just how prophetic his words of caution would become.

□

CHAPTER TWENTY

Paddy walked Hannah the three blocks back to the diner and they watched as the dark clouds spread across the valley, broke apart, and then reformed on the horizon to the west. There was even a small slice of sun from time to time until it finally disappeared. The storm threat seemed over one minute and again threatening the next.

"The sky has cleared for a while at least...would you like to continue our walk. Maybe you could show me your town."

"Okay. Wait here on the porch while I put my sketchpad away."

Hannah thought about asking Paddy in, but her apartment was only one big room with a small kitchen. She slept on a pull-down Murphy bed. She just didn't know him well enough to get that familiar, but she wanted to...and taking a long walk would give her plenty of time to get to know him better. While she was inside, she brushed her teeth, combed her hair, touched up her lipstick, and picked up an umbrella.

"I'm ready if you are," she said.

"Okay. Where shall we start?"

"Let's go over to the half-park. We can walk the levee and see lots of the town."

"What's the half-park?"

"Oh, it's where young people from this end of town go to play softball. It's so small that it only has an infield and half an outfield."

A few minutes later, they were walking along the levee overlooking the halfpark. From there, they could see all the way to Tenth Street.

"I see lights on at Morgan's. Would you like to walk there and get a cup of coffee or a sandwich...or something?"

"Sounds great. I haven't eaten since breakfast at your diner this morning."

"Oh, that's not my diner...I only work there for Rosie."

"Really? How long have you worked there?"

"Almost ten years. I started when I was sixteen. Rosie has been like a mother...or sister to me."

"It's nice to have someone that close, isn't it?"

Hannah smiled, but did not answer. They continued walking along the levee that snaked around the outskirts of town.

"Is that another river," Paddy asked as he glanced at the stream of water flowing through the beautiful valley spreading northward as far as they could see.

"No, that's Soda Creek. Can you see the sandbars?"

"Yes...they're as white as lots of the beaches I've seen on the ocean," Paddy replied.

"Have you been to the ocean? Which one?"

"Both. I was in the Navy before I got hurt."

Hannah stopped in her tracks, turned, and looked at Paddy. She felt a little queasy and sad at the thought of him ever being hurt. She didn't understand it all, but for some reason, she wanted to hug him...and she did.

"What was that for?" he asked, a little surprised.

"I don't know...I just felt...you know...funny when you told me you'd been hurt in the war. What happened?"

"Oh, it's been a couple of years ago. I was one of the engineers in charge of keeping our ship in the best possible operating condition. We came under attack by a Japanese sub and all hell broke loose. I ended up losing two toes on each foot. That's why I got sent home before the war ended."

"So, do you do the same job now on the tugboat?"

"Yep. Pays pretty good money, but the hours stink."

"Where do you live during your thirty days off?"

"Cincinnati...now. I tried Pittsburgh, but didn't like it too much. Same as Cincy...too big for my tastes. But I don't have a wife or kids, so I can move around all I want. How 'bout you?"

"How about me...what?"

"You got any kids?"

"Oh...uh...no, I've never been married."

They both seemed pleased with the conversation. Paddy took Hannah's hand and they continued their walk along the top of the levee. To the west and across Soda Creek, Paddy noticed a string of headlights moving through the cornfields towards the white sandbars.

"Is that part of Fiddler's Point?"

"No, the other side of the creek is out of the city limits. Farmers own those cornfields, but they allow some teenagers to drive across their land to get to Popcorn Beach. That's what the teens call that beach over there."

"So you think they're celebrating the end of the war?"

"Oh, I'd like to think so, but the seniors just recently graduated. I'm guessing they're still celebrating that with another beer party," Hannah said.

Hannah led Paddy down the levee and across Waverly Street to Morgan's Restaurant. It was much larger than Rosie's and the neon sign in front below the name read in all capital letters, WE NEVER CLOSE! They found a small booth near the back. All the waitresses wore black and white uniforms with nametags on the lapels.

"Hello, my name's Gina and I'll be your server tonight," the attractive young server said with a friendly smile.

Hannah returned a pleasant greeting and Paddy nodded.

"May I get you something to drink while you're looking at the menu?" Gina said.

"We'll have two coffees...cream and sugar...and what's your best sandwich?" Paddy asked.

"Oh, Jacklyn, our cook, just started making a new sandwich! It's called the All American Burger! Would you like to try one?"

Paddy looked at Hannah for a hint. She just smiled because she wanted Paddy to decide.

"Sure, they sound great. We'll each have one.

While they were eating, the wind began blowing a light rain against the large plate glass window beside them. Thunder rumbled and lightning flashed to the west. A short time later, the wind died down but the light rain turned into a downpour.

Nearly all the customers in Morgan's decided to stay inside and ride out the storm. A young man made a mad dash for his car. He was soaked before he got his door open.

The conversation between Hannah and Paddy grew easier as they drank free refills of coffee. When they finished bringing each other up to date on pasts, they began touching upon each other's dreams and aspirations. It was past midnight before the rain stopped long enough for them to walk back to Hannah's apartment.

"Well, we've spent nearly the whole day together on our first date. Can we do it again sometime?" Paddy said,

"Do you consider this our first date?" Hannah asked, fishing for some evidence that he wanted to see her again.

"I'm not sure, really. We kind of got things out of order by having our first kiss this morning and our first unofficial date this evening. Now it's tomorrow already and I'm not sure if I should kiss you goodnight or..."

Hannah smiled with her eyes and gave Paddy a quick kiss on the cheek.

"I guess that will have to do until we have our next date whenever that might be."

Paddy looked at Hannah as if he knew what she was wondering. Would he ever be back to Fiddler's Point? Was he just an ex-sailor with a girl in every port? There was no way of knowing through talk. Proof of his interest would have to come another day. Hannah said goodnight, turned, walked into her apartment, and closed the door.

Paddy was the last crewmember to return to the Lady Lexi that night. Everyone appeared to be asleep, so he quietly undressed and got ready for bed. Barefooted, he stepped into the bathroom where he felt something gritty beneath his feet. He glanced down to find white sand on the floor.

□

CHAPTER TWENTY-ONE

The sound of distant sirens roused Hannah from a dreamy sleep shortly before her alarm went off at 5:00 a.m. She quickly got ready for work and hurried to the floodwall entrance while a misty dawn spread across the valley.

Her heart beat rapidly as she stepped onto the gravel road leading to the boat dock. From there, she saw that the Lady Lexi, her cargo, and Paddy Phoot were gone. A few minutes later, she was in the diner waiting for the first customers to arrive.

Rosie turned the radio on and selected a station with the local morning news. What they heard shocked them both. According to the county sheriff, a recent high school graduate attending a party on Popcorn Beach the night before had disappeared. Deputies and volunteers were combing the cornfield surrounding the west bank of Soda Creek. The city and county firemen were dragging the creek's deeper areas in case she had drowned.

"So, that's why there were so many sirens earlier this morning," Hannah said.

"My goodness, I hope they find her safe," Rosie replied, shaking her head as if the opposite were going to be true.

Witnesses provided some information. They claimed the girl, Clara Lowe, only had two or three beers at the party. She danced with several of the guys that were there, but wasn't with a date. She excused herself to go into the cornrows to pee but never came back.

When asked the approximate time the party ended, all the kids at the party agreed that it began to break up when the rains began. Until then, nobody seemed to realize that Clara Lowe had not yet returned. The girl she came with and several of the guys at the party walked along the bank and the cornrows calling out to her, but got no response. When the rains got heavier, everyone left the beach and contacted the sheriff's office soon afterwards.

However, the strong storm made it impossible for authorities and rescue workers to get across the muddy cornfields that night. By dawn, Soda Creek was several feet out of her banks and all evidence that may have been on the beach or in the cornrows was washed away.

Speculation among Rosie's regulars at the diner began immediately. Some suggested Clara Lowe may have sneaked away with a boy and would show up safely at home when she was ready. Some guessed that she eloped with her high-school sweetheart.

Deep down inside; however, everyone knew what the three worst-case scenarios were, and each was spoken only in whispers. One theory was that the young girl might have fallen into Soda Creek and drowned. Another suggested she had been abducted and carried off. A few mentioned that foul play had left her lifeless body somewhere along the banks of Soda Creek or buried somewhere in the sprawling acres of muddy cornrows.

The search for the young girl's body on land would continue for only a couple of days. After that, it would be assumed that her body had somehow gotten into Soda Creek and drifted into the Ohio. If so, it could now be anywhere between Fiddler's Point and Cincinnati.

Hannah's mind drifted back to last evening when she and Paddy were walking along the levee overlooking Popcorn Beach. They had seen the string of headlights as the teens were arriving. Sometime in the hours that followed, something dreadful happened to one of them.

***

On Thursday afternoon, a Harley Motorcycle with a sidecar passed by the diner while Hannah was cleaning the front-door window. She only got a quick glimpse of the rider from behind, but thought for a moment that it might be Paddy. She hadn't seen his face, but the rider had broad shoulders and sat high on the seat. She sloughed it off as wishful thinking and went back to her chores.

Shortly before closing, the motorcycle returned to the diner parking lot. Rosie was at the register counting cash. She recognized the rider as Paddy Phoot.

"Hannah! I think there's someone here to see you," she said, calling back to the kitchen where Hannah was washing the coffee pots.

Hannah dried her hands on her apron as she walked out into the dining room. She was excited, but didn't know what to do. She wanted to hug him, she wanted to kiss him, she wanted to run into his strong arms, but her feet would not move as she tried to catch her breath. But Paddy didn't hesitate. He walked up to her, lifted her high into the air, and then lowered her slowly until their eyes met. Then, he kissed her just as he did the day the war ended. Rosie smiled and went back to balancing her cash register receipts. Moments later, Hannah took Paddy by the hand and led him up front to meet Rosie.

"Paddy, I want you to meet my boss and best friend, Rosie Walters. Rosie, I think Paddy and I are officially dating now," Hannah continued, clinging to his arm.

"Well, Paddy, Hannah has mentioned you more than a few times. It's good to meet you finally. Would you like me to fix you something to eat...since you're here...before closing time?"

All three looked up at the Pepsi clock on the wall and laughed—it was one minute until closing time.

"Thank you, ma'am, but I'm hoping to take Hannah on a ride around town on my new motorcycle. Well, it's really a '34 model that I got for a great price. I just bought it so I'd have transportation up here from Cincy."

"That sounds like a fun way to spend the afternoon," Rosie replied.

She watched as the couple walked across the lot to Paddy's bike. She could see that he limped slightly and his toes turned out some as he walked. She wondered if this was a condition caused by the war injuries Hannah had mentioned.

Paddy and Hannah drove slowly along the major streets of Fiddler's Point. After a while, Paddy pulled over and stopped at the edge of a large paved parking lot.

"What is this place?" he asked Hannah as he slid off the bike.

"It's the local stadium."

"This is the perfect place to teach you to ride the Harley."

"Me?" Hannah managed to say, totally surprised at his suggestion.

Paddy moved around to the sidecar and helped Hannah out. He had her sit on the bike while he explained how it operated. Finally, he slid in behind her and wrapped his arms around her waist.

"Now, just let the bike idle in gear and it will start moving along slowly. When you're ready, give it a little gas to go faster."

An hour later, Hannah was doing quite well and had a smile of satisfaction on her face. Paddy, too, had a pleased look, but it was from being snuggled tightly against Hannah's soft body. When he decided that she had practiced enough for one day, they changed places and continued their tour of the area.

Finally, they crossed the Kentucky Bridge and disappeared into the hilly countryside. It was nearly twilight before they returned to town.

"Where to next?" Paddy asked.

"Before you stopped by today, I had planned on visiting my father to make sure he had plenty of food in the ice box."

"Would you like for me to take you there?" Paddy offered

Hannah thought about it for only a second and decided she wanted her dad to meet Paddy. She had never brought a man home to meet her father before...but Paddy was different.

When they arrived, Mr. Frazey was sitting on the front porch of his modest clapboard house. A frown crossed his face when the cycle backfired. He did stand when Hannah and Paddy arrived on the porch.

"Dad, I want you to meet my friend, Patrick Phoot...he prefers to be called Paddy."

Mr. Frazey nodded once, but did not offer to shake hands.

"Dad, I stopped by to see if you've been eating decent food and taking care of yourself."

"I'm doin' okay."

Hannah turned and walked into the house and straight back to the kitchen. She opened the icebox door and stared in disbelief at a half stick of butter and a partial loaf of bread. She knew her father didn't cook much, but this was ridiculous, she thought. She stormed out of the house and straight to Paddy's cycle.

"Come on, Paddy, we've got work to do!"

Paddy followed instructions and the two drove away without another word to Mr. Frazey. This was not the first time she had visited him to find nothing to eat in the house. Ever since Hannah's mother died and her only brother, Jimmy, ran off to join the Army, her father seemed to have lost interest in nearly everything. Hannah, though, simply would not let him sink to the bottom.

Thirty minutes later, Hannah and Paddy returned with several sacks of groceries. Paddy carried them to the porch.

"Dad, would you sit here and talk with Paddy while I go in and fix you something to eat?"

"Oh...that won't be necessary. I'll eat something later."

Paddy sensed that Mr. Frazey might feel uncomfortable sitting there talking to a stranger, so he offered a different plan.

"I'll tell you what, why don't you sit down and talk with your father while I fix supper for all of us?"

"You don't have to do..."

"I insist. You already worked a full shift at the diner today. It's time you got some rest."

Hannah didn't know what to say and neither did her father.

"I know my way around a kitchen. Just relax until I call you to the table."

Paddy knew what he was doing. He cooked on the tug whenever needed and everybody seemed to enjoy the meals he prepared. In less than an hour, Paddy had fixed a giant tossed salad, hot rolls, and a bowl of the tastiest stroganoff Hannah had ever eaten. She was sure the same was true for her father.

The conversation around the kitchen table was slow until Hannah mentioned the injury Paddy received in the war. Mr. Frazey rolled up his sleeve and showed Paddy his Semper Fi tattoo.

"Hannah's sixteen-year-old brother lied about his age and enlisted three months ago. Sure glad the war ended before he got shipped off," Mr. Frazey said.

The ice had been broken. After dinner, the three moved onto the front porch and continued their friendly conversation until late evening. When Mr. Frazey mentioned the missing Clara Lowe, Paddy reacted with surprise as his mind drifted back to the moment he and Hannah watched the headlights coming through the cornrows on their way to a beach party. Other thoughts...grim thoughts...bounced around in his mind but he was unable to put his finger on the uneasy feelings that concerned him most.

As the couple prepared to leave, Mr. Frazey hugged Hannah and then insisted that Paddy stop by anytime he was in the neighborhood.

On the way back to Hannah's apartment, Paddy pulled over in front of a tourist home.

"There's my home for the next thirty days," Paddy said.

"What do you mean?"

"I rented a room there so I could visit with you as often as you wanted."

Hannah was thrilled with Paddy's announcement and the entire afternoon she had spent with him. When they arrived at her apartment, she invited him in for iced tea. It was time, Hannah thought, that they make some ground rules for their budding relationship.

"Paddy, are things going too fast for us?"

"What do you mean?"

"Uh...not what we've done, but uh...what it seems like we want to do."

"Oh, you mean..."

"Yes!"

"That's not why I'm up here. I just enjoy being with you, and it seems like that feeling grows every day."

"I feel the same way, but some guys expect a girl to go all the way if they kiss...you know...the way we do."

Paddy sighed and hesitated a long moment before he replied.

"I can't help what happens when we kiss. I think it's natural, but if it bothers you..."

"No...no...it doesn't bother me...I mean...it bothers me just like it does you, but I just think we need to take our time and learn all we can about each other before we do something we can't take back," Hannah said, placing her hand on Paddy's shoulder.

"Me too! I mean...I...I...don't want to do anything that you don't want to do."

"Okay, let's make a deal. How often do you want to go out while you're here on vacation?"

"Every day after you get off work...and of course, I can stop in the diner for breakfast and lunch...if you want."

Hannah smiled because she felt the same way. It was the first time she had ever wanted to be with someone all the time. But...there were things she needed to talk with him about before she made love with him—things that might just change his mind about entering into a serious relationship—things that might change any guy's mind.

CHAPTER TWENTY-TWO

Hannah and Paddy spent nearly every free moment with one another over the days that followed. Paddy was at the diner for biscuits and gravy every morning and sampled a different plate lunch each day at noon. Most evenings, they would spend time taking long motorcycle rides that usually ended up with Paddy in the sidecar. They often stopped at Mr. Frazey's house for supper. Paddy did most of the cooking, of course.

***

When Hannah went to work, Paddy often walked through the floodgates and across Soda Creek Sand and Gravel Company's field of giant sand piles and gravel hills. Behind the field were several paths leading through a stand of horseweeds to the river below. He enjoyed exploring the riverbank looking for the best fishing holes.

On a Thursday afternoon near the end of May, Paddy found something much more exciting. He could hardly wait to tell Hannah. When the diner closed at two o'clock, he was waiting on his Harley with the motor running.

"Come on, honey, I want to show you something."

"Okay, but I need to run in and change into some slacks first."

"Just hurry. Bring your sketchpad and some pencils, too. I want you to draw something for me."

Even though the object Paddy wanted to show Hannah was within walking distance of Rosie's, he took her on the bike. They weaved between giant piles of sand and gravel taller than many of the trees at the edge of the bottoms. He parked his bike and took Hannah's hand.

"Shut your eyes for a minute."

Hannah followed instructions as Paddy led her into a stand of tall reeds.

"Okay, open your eyes and tell me what you think?" he said, standing in front of a burned out boat of some kind.

Hannah was puzzled but answered the best she could.

"Well...it's the burned out houseboat that used to belong to Sherman Braggs."

"Oh! So, you knew that this boat was here?"

"I knew that it was somewhere around here, but I had forgotten exactly where. The night it burned, we could see the cinders and smell the smoke at the diner. Mr. Braggs fell asleep with a cigarette in his hand. He woke up and managed to get out without being injured, but by the time the fire department got to the boat, it was...well, you see what's left of it."

"Yes, and I wonder why it's so far from the water. Was it in the creek when it burned?"

"No, I remember people making fun of Mr. Bragg for having a houseboat stuck up on land. That happened one spring when the Ohio floodwaters backed up Soda Creek and left his houseboat stranded up here on this bank when the water went down quickly. He apparently didn't care if he lived on land or water."

"Where's Mr. Bragg now?"

"He was over eighty years old when the fire happened. One of his kids took him down to Florida to live. That's been a couple of years ago."

"So, who owns this boat now?" Paddy asked, losing a little of his exuberance.

"No one, probably. It was just abandoned after the fire...and eventually just disappeared in the reeds and was forgotten. Rosie might know who to talk to about it. Why?"

"Because, I know how to fix lots of things, especially boats and engines. This one has a concrete hull and an engine, you know."

Hannah was now getting excited for Paddy. She had never seen him like this before.

"So, why did you have me bring my pencils and sketch pad...exactly?"

"I want you to sketch this boat the way it is now. Then, I want you to sketch it after I'm through with it."

"Sounds like you plan on spending most of your thirty-day vacations here in Fiddler's Point, huh?"

"I want to do more than that—I want to move here permanently to be near you."

Hannah felt butterflies swirl through her midsection but she hoped Paddy couldn't tell how excited she was. First, she wanted to find out his plans for after he moved to Fiddler's Point. She began to sketch as if she didn't hear his last comment. Paddy was so absorbed with exploring the boat that he didn't notice.

Hannah continued sketching while Paddy inspected the vessel inch by inch. As he moved around the stern, he noticed a small johnboat strapped to the starboard side that seemed undamaged by the previous fire.

"Can we go back to the diner and ask Rosie about these boats now? I just can't wait to find out," Paddy called out as he made his way back to Hannah.

Hannah smiled, put her pencils and pad away, and mounted the sidecar. When they got back to the floodgate, a large steam shovel was blocking the opening. A man was in the driver's seat trying to get the machine started while another man wearing a white shirt and tie looked on.

"Good afternoon, Miss Frazey," the middle-aged man said, rubbing his graying goatee.

"Hi, Mr. Sizemore."

Paddy got off his bike and walked over to the man in the white shirt.

"Having problems?"

"Yeah, this damn thing is more stubborn than my wife. It only works when it wants to," the potbellied man said.

"I know a little bit about fixin' engines. Want me to take a look at it?"

"Sure, if you think you can fix it, go right ahead."

Paddy listened for only a moment to the noise the starter made. He then opened a panel to the engine and studied it, touching one part and then another.

"Got an adjustable wrench and screwdriver handy?"

The driver reached into a side compartment and pulled out the tools. He tossed them down to Paddy. A few minutes later, Paddy yelled up to the driver, "Crank it up."

The engine started immediately. Paddy handed the tools to the man in the tie.

"I can't believe you fixed it so quickly. My name's Benny Sizemore. I own this place. If you ever need a job...or I can help you some way, just come see me."

"Thank you, sir. I'm Patrick Phoot...I may do that someday. You might be able to help me a little now, though. Do you happen to know who I could talk with about that burned out boat back in the reeds?"

"You're looking at him. It was abandoned back there on my land nearly three years ago. Old Mr. Braggs built that houseboat from the ground up. Never had a title or nothin'. I got ownership 'cause of back rent he owed me for letting him keep it on my land. Don't think he ever had it in the water except when it flooded around here. It's worthless now."

"I'd sure like to have it to tinker with. How much you take?"

The man rubbed his goatee and spit in the sand.

"You helped me out of a big mess today. I tell you what...I'll give it to you if you haul it away."

"How much rent did you charge Mr. Bragg for keeping it in the reeds?"

"Oh, old Sherm was a fisherman. He brought me a couple of nice catfish ever month for his rent. You fish?"

Paddy grinned. I'll make you the same deal if you let me keep the houseboat where it is until I make the necessary repairs. Then, if you want me to move it, I will."

"Sounds like a deal to me," Benny said.

The two shook hands and Paddy headed back to his bike and Hannah.

"Hey!" Benny called out...I'll have some kind of paper signed giving you ownership. I'll drop it off at the diner sometime tomorrow."

The next morning, Mr. Sizemore brought a handwritten piece of paper to the diner. Just to make it official, he had Rosie and Hannah sign the paper as witnesses to the transfer of ownership. When Paddy came in later that morning, Hannah gave him the paper and a big hug. Paddy was the new owner of what appeared to be a piece of junk.

Within two weeks, Paddy had the vessel stripped down to the hull. To him, the motor and the hull were the most important parts; he had plans to replace everything else in time. Paddy even had plans for his johnboat that was now moored at the small dock beneath Soda Creek Bridge. However, unforeseen events would soon send his plans into a tailspin.

☐

CHAPTER TWENTY-THREE

On Friday evening, Paddy took Hannah to a movie at the Royal Theater. Like two teenagers, they sat in the balcony and had popcorn, candy, and soft drinks. Afterwards, they walked up Waverly Street to Morgan's Restaurant for coffee and a sandwich.

"Thanks for the movie. I like Gary Cooper. Do you know if they really had a war in Spain?" Hannah asked.

"They probably did, but this was just a movie. I like Hemingway's books," Paddy replied, sipping his coffee and staring out the window as heavy clouds slowly moved across the sky.

"You read a lot, don't you?"

"If everything goes smoothly on the Lady Lexi, I get in a little reading from time to time," Paddy replied.

"Looks like we might get some rain, doesn't it?"

"I hope not. I was hoping you'd go fishing with me in the morning since it's my last weekend in Fiddler's Point. I've got the johnboat all cleaned up...and we could even take a picnic lunch if you want to."

Hannah felt a trembling inside as she realized Paddy's thirty-day furlough would soon end.

"I'd love to, but I've never fished before. Can you show me how?"

"Sure. Are you afraid of worms?"

"How big are they?"

"Night crawlers are pretty big...why?"

"Not as big as a snake are they?"

"No."

"Do they bite?"

"No...I don't think they have mouths. If they do...they're so small you can't see them."

"Good. I don't like things that bite. What time do you want to start?"

"Right before daylight would be good if you don't mind getting up that early."

"That's fine...I'm used to getting up early."

**

Hannah and Paddy were already in the old johnboat when the night brightened into day. Paddy gave Hannah some quick instructions on how to slip a hook through a night crawler so it couldn't wiggle off. They fished the east bank of Soda Creek for a short time and neither of them got a nibble. He paddled the boat over near the west bank for a while but they met with the same fate.

"Looks like we're gonna have to move to deeper water if we're gonna catch anything."

"Where does it start getting deeper," Hannah asked.

"I'll take us over to one of the bridge piers and tie off. We might hook a big catfish around there if we fish the bottom."

Paddy let the boat drift with the current until he got near the pier. It wasn't hard to find something to tie the boat to because of all the trotlines that had drifted away over the years and wound themselves around the piers.

"Don't even have to cast here...just drop your line in the water and the sinker will take it to the bottom."

Hannah was the first to catch a fish. It wasn't a catfish though. She reeled it in close to the boat and Paddy put a net under it and brought it aboard.

"What kind is that?" She asked.

"It's just a carp...not worth keepin'" Paddy huffed.

Moments later, Paddy got a hit on his line and began reeling it in. He felt his line stiffen and realized that he was hung up on something other than a fish. He didn't want to break his line, so he worked it gently back and forth trying to free the hook. Suddenly, he felt it partially loosen and he reeled in some line.

"Shit! What the hell is that?" he shouted as Hannah looked over to see what was on Paddy's line.

Paddy put his net under the object.

"Don't look, Honey!" he cautioned as he realized what was in the net. We've got to get to shore and find a phone! We've got to call the police!"

Hannah did not respond. She just sat there staring at the object in Paddy's net. Her mouth dropped open and she began to pull on her right ear lobe.

"Hannah...Hannah...can you hear me?"

Again, she didn't respond. Paddy wasn't sure what to do. Finally, after she hadn't moved for several minutes, he untied the boat from the pier and paddled back to the dock. He managed getting her out of the boat and onto the wooden dock. He picked her up in his arms and carried her up the winding path to Soda Creek Carryout. There, he had the owner call the police. Before they arrived, Hannah recovered from her trance.

"Paddy, what am I doing here?"

"I think what I found back there scared you, and you just kinda froze in one spot. I couldn't get you to answer me."

"I remember seeing them...the bones, but I can't remember how I got here in the carryout," Hannah said, her lower lip quivering as she rubbed her forehead.

"The police are on their way."

The owner brought Hannah a drink of water. When the police arrived, Paddy went with them to show them the arm bone that was in his net. Within minutes, there were several other city vehicles on the scene and Paddy escorted several policemen to the exact spot where his fishing line had gotten tangled up. Some expert swimmers from the Fire Department arrived and went into the water around the pier. It wasn't long until they managed to cut the rest of the body free from the tangled trotlines. The body soon proved to be the badly decomposed remains of Clara Lowe, the recent high-school graduate who disappeared three weeks earlier on the night World War II ended.

The officers questioned Paddy on the scene and then escorted him and Hannah back to the diner where they briefly questioned Hannah. Both were told to remain available for further questioning while they checked out Paddy's alibi for the night Clara Lowe disappeared. It didn't take long for the police to confirm through a server named Gina that Paddy was with Hannah at Morgan's Restaurant well past the time of the victim's disappearance.

Rosie, Hannah, and Paddy sat in the front booth drinking coffee for a while and talking about the harrowing events of the day until Rosie finally excused herself to go fix her family's lunch.

"Thanks for the coffee, Rosie. Hope we didn't hold you up too long," Paddy said, standing and moving toward the front door.

"Ross is probably still at the halfpark and Gib is over in the barbershop waiting until closing time so he can get his hair cut. It's well past lunch time...I'm sure they'll all be hungry," Rosie said as Hannah and Paddy left the diner.

***

Once alone in Hannah's apartment, Paddy took Hannah's hand and searched her eyes for a long moment.

"What happened out there today, honey?"

Hannah knew that he was not asking about the body or the frenzy of police activity around them. He wanted to know about the trance she had fallen into when she saw the girl's decomposed arm. She sighed deeply, closed her eyes, and rubbed her forehead for a long moment before opening her eyes and gazing into his.

"Paddy, I have a mild case of epilepsy. Doctors think it was caused from a bump on the head when I was a child," she said, without lowering her eyes from his.

He blinked several times and squeezed her hand a little tighter, but didn't show any signs of alarm.

"I've heard of that, but I had no idea that it caused...uh...what happened to you."

"I read up on epilepsy over the years, and no one knows much about it. What happened to me today is called a seizure. Some people call them spells or trances. They just happen sometimes, but I have no control over them."

"Do you know what causes them?" Paddy asked, but not sure he wanted to hear her answer.

"When I was a kid, my doctor told me that the seizures were probably brought on by stress. The one I had today was the first I've had in a couple of years...I think."

"What do you mean...you think?"

Hannah finally broke her gaze and stared at the ceiling for a moment.

"Okay...you saw everything that happened today. What did you see me do?"

Paddy's eyebrows rose as he exhaled loudly.

"Let's see...I asked you not to look at the...you know...the bones, but it was too late. All of a sudden, your body kind of stiffened and your eyes sorta glazed over. I think your mouth dropped open...yes...and uh...you kept tugging on your ear."

"How long did you watch me just sitting there?"

"I don't know for sure...maybe a minute or two. I tried to talk to you, but you wouldn't answer. I finally got a little scared, and paddled back to the dock. I picked you up and carried you to the carryout. I didn't know what else to do."

"When did I start talking to you?"

"Right after I sat you down."

"That's what my biggest concern is...I never remember a single moment of what happens during a seizure. It's as if time stands still. And...uh...when I'm in the trance...I can't protect myself. What's worse than that, I couldn't protect anyone else even if I needed to.

"Then let me protect you!"

Hannah seemed taken back for a moment.

"What do you mean?"

"I mean...I'm in love with you and I promise I'll take care of you for the rest of our lives if you'll have me."

Hannah could only blink as her chin trembled and she fought back tears.

"Oh, Paddy, are you asking me to marry you?"

"Well...yes. I mean...you don't have to decide now...I mean, would you consider it sometime?"

Hannah took a deep breath and shook her head yes.

She looked at Paddy and knew that she would never love anyone else...now or ever, so, she saw no reason in waiting a long time to get married.

"When?" She looked directly into his eyes.

"Today, tomorrow, yesterday if we could. You decide."

"You have to go back to work next week and won't be back until the ninth of July. We'll do it then...the very first day you get back. I want a whole month with you after we get married."

"Great! I won't be able to think of anything or anyone but you while I'm gone. I can hardly wait."

"Me either, but we'll have to go to the court house tomorrow morning to get a marriage license and a blood test if they say we need one. Then there'll be no waiting after you get back in July."

***

During the last days of Paddy's thirty-day break, he and Hannah were nearly inseparable. The night before Paddy was to return to Cincinnati, the passion and desire that had been building in their relationship simply became overwhelming.

They had visited with Hannah's father during the early afternoon and got his tacit approval of their plans to marry. They spent the late afternoon at a secluded spot along the Ohio River where they enjoyed a picnic dinner that Hannah had prepared for the occasion. When everything was cleaned up and put away, they sat, cuddled in each other's arms, watching the barges moving slowly up and down the river.

"Paddy, I want to tell you that I love you and have loved you since you picked me up and kissed me the day the war ended...I'm sure of it. When did you begin to have those feelings for me?"

Paddy didn't answer immediately. He seemed to be slowly tracing back the days and evaluating each one, but when he was ready, he smiled at Hannah and hugged her tightly.

"I felt that invasion of butterflies as I lowered you down to where our eyes met that first day. There was something in the way your eyes twinkled that allowed me to see your deepest feelings. I've felt the same about you every day since. Of course, I very much enjoyed our first kiss that day, too, but it's a fact that I've loved you a few seconds longer than you've loved me," he kidded.

Paddy leaned back on the checkered tablecloth and Hannah followed until their bodies were together in a passionate kiss and embrace. All of Hannah's concerns about what

Paddy might think of her ailment were gone. She loved him and believed with all her heart that he loved her. They made love there on the riverbank as the sun hid behind the darkening horizon far downriver. They made love again as heavy clouds spread across the river valley.

The first raindrops were large and noisy as they splattered against the dense summer foliage. A gentle breeze strengthened and began to move the treetops in one direction and then another.

"Looks like a summer storm moving up the river," Paddy said, standing up and extending a large hand to help Hannah to her feet.

"We had better get back to my apartment," Hannah said as she began putting things away.

Moments later, they were racing up the riverbank. As they ran across River Street, warm, fat raindrops smacked against the paving bricks behind them. They reached Hannah's apartment as the first sign of lightning was followed almost immediately by a rumbling of thunder. Shortly after Hannah switched on the lamp in her apartment, nearly all of the lights in the neighborhood went out.

"That happens all the time during electrical storms. I'll get some candles. You'll find some matches on the kitchen range."

Paddy found the range and the matches where Hannah said they would be. Hannah opened a kitchen cabinet and got out three candles and three coffee cups.

"Light this one first and drop some wax onto the bottom of the cups. That'll hold the candles up," Hannah said.

Paddy followed instructions and after he lit the last candle, he stuck the book of matches into his shirt pocket. The small apartment was suddenly filled with soft, shimmering candle light.

Hannah and Paddy made love until the storm passed, and the candles burned out, and the dawn relit their world. They showered together before getting dressed and walking to the Greyhound Bus Station.

"Paddy, are you sure you want to leave your bike at my place while you're away?"

"Yes. I live in a furnished room in Cincy, but I have clothes and too many personal items of my own that I couldn't carry all of them in the sidecar. I'll pack them up and bring them here on a bus."

They kissed until the bus driver spoke up.

"You goin' to Cincy with us or stayin' here?"

Paddy smiled, stepped aboard, and then turned and gave Hannah another quick kiss as the door closed slowly between them. Paddy moved to the back windows and waved at Hannah until the bus pulled out of sight.

Somewhere between Fiddler's Point and Cincinnati, Paddy touched something in his shirt pocket. He slipped two of his large fingers into the pocket and pulled out a book of matches. He smiled as he read the bold red words embossed in all capital letters: ROSIE'S DINER at the top and FIDDLER'S POINT, OHIO on the bottom. He shut his eyes and slept the rest of the way to Cincinnati.

□

CHAPTER TWENTY-FOUR

When Hannah didn't receive a letter or even a postcard from Paddy after a week, she began to worry a little, but when she missed her period that was due in the middle of June, she began to panic. She hadn't been more than a day late in her life.

The first day of summer arrived and passed without a word from Paddy or the arrival of her period. The same for the Fourth of July, that came on Wednesday this year.

After work each day, Hannah walked down to the river and sketched whatever she found of interest while keeping a close eye on the tugboats pushing barges up and down the river. She always took her sketch of the Lady Lexi that she had drawn the first day she met Paddy. Over the past three weeks, she had seen the Lady Lexi on four occasions—each time hoping that Paddy would come out on deck and wave to her. It never happened. Each time, though, she made some excuse for him—he was busy below deck doing his job, or he was sleeping when the boat passed Fiddler's Point. Whatever doubts she allowed to creep into her thoughts would be answered in a few days when he finished his thirty days onboard.

When July 9th finally rolled around, Hannah kept her eyes on the corner across the street from the diner. She knew that a Greyhound bus arrived in town from Cincinnati around 9 a.m. The second bus came by around 3 p.m. The last one was at midnight.

She sat on the front steps of the diner and watched as the last Greyhound of the day made its way across Soda Creek Bridge. She stood with anticipation as the bus moved towards her on River Street. Tears rolled down her cheeks as it passed without stopping.

The following days turned into weeks until Hannah finally had to admit two realities—Paddy was not coming back to her, and she was indeed pregnant.

Rosie sensed that Paddy's failure to return was not the only thing on Hannah's mind. Shortly after closing one day in late August, Rosie came out of the Kitchen and walked to the cash register to balance the day's receipts. She saw that Hannah was staring out the front door at the empty parking lot.

"Did you have a good day for tips?" she asked, but Hannah didn't respond or turn around—she just continued pulling on her right ear lobe.

"Hannah? Are you okay?"

Again, Hannah did not respond. Rosie locked the register and walked to the end of the breakfast bar where she could see Hannah's face. Her mouth had dropped open and her eyes seemed glazed over. Rosie walked back to the pay phone on the back wall and began searching for the phone number of her doctor. Before she could find the number, Hannah turned and began talking.

"Wow! You can almost see the heat rising off the concrete pavement. Must be over a hundred degrees out there," Hannah said without a hint of the condition she had been in a moment earlier.

Rosie returned the receiver to its hook and sighed.

"How were tips today?"

"About the same as usual...steady."

"Hannah...do you remember me asking you that same question a few minutes ago when you were staring out the front door?"

Hannah's face drew serious as she considered Rosie's question for a long moment.

"No," she finally replied. "When was I doing that?"

"I saw you just standing there like you were in a trance while I finished washing up the coffee pots. Maybe five minutes later, I noticed you were still standing there. When I walked to the register, I saw that you were tugging at your ear repeatedly. I asked if you were okay and you didn't respond—that's when I saw a glazed look across your eyes and your mouth was hanging wide open. You were drooling."

Hannah slowly moved to the front booth and sat down. She began crying. Rosie took a seat across from her.

"If something's wrong, Hannah, I'll do anything I can to help you...you know that, but you must tell me what it is."

"I'm pregnant!"

"You're pregnant by Paddy Phoot and you believe he's abandoned you?"

"It sure looks that way, and he's broken my heart, but I have another problem much worse than my own heartache."

Rosie patted Hannah's hand but waited silently for Hannah to continue her story.

"What you saw at the front door was probably a mild seizure—I have epilepsy."

"Hannah...you've been working for me since you were sixteen years old. That's nearly ten years, and I have never seen you have a seizure before."

"It's supposedly caused from a childhood head injury. Years ago, my doctor said it could eventually go away completely, stay very mild with infrequent seizures, or...get much worse as I grow older."

"Have you had other seizures since you started working for me?"

"That's the problem...I can't answer your question because I can't remember anything that happens during the seizures. Unless someone sees me while it's happening...and tells me about it, they just go away unnoticed."

"So, it may have been years since your last one?"

Hannah hung her head as she thought back to the day under the bridge.

"No. I had one just over a month ago when Paddy found that girl's dead body tangled in those fishhooks. My doctor told me my seizures could be brought on by stress...and that was certainly a stressful moment in my life...you know...seeing part of a decomposed body like that."

"Did Paddy tell you that he saw your seizure?"

"Yes. He described what I did much the same as you just did. I didn't remember anything."

"Do you think this one today was brought on by Paddy not showing up or by learning that you're pregnant?"

"Both...probably, but I'll be able to get over Paddy someday...I guess...but I can't take a chance with a baby."

"What do you mean you can't take a chance?"

"You saw what happens to me when I have a seizure. What if I was giving my baby a bath and I had one of those things? During the minutes I'm frozen in a trance, my baby could...you know...."

Rosie knew. Without someone else's presence at all times, her child's life would be in constant jeopardy. Hannah had no money to pay someone to help her raise a child.

"Do you have any ideas on how to work this thing out?" Rosie asked.

"Adoption! That's the only thing I can think of that I could live with. Half the doctors in town are rumored to do secret abortions, but I could never do that to my child.

"Do you still have a doctor you see here in town?"

"No, I haven't seen a doctor since I quit school and came to work for you. I just can't afford it."

"Okay! First things first," Rosie said, getting up and walking behind the breakfast bar.

She picked up a note pad and pencil and returned to the table.

"First, you'll have to see my doctor from time to time to make sure you and the baby stay in good health. As far as saving the delivery expenses and a stay at the hospital, I know a mid-wife who does as good a job as any doctor could do. Then, you'll probably have to sign some kind of paper to arrange for an adoption if that's what you still want to do when the time comes."

"I can't see any other way," Hanna said, tears swelling in her eyes.

"Okay, but you still have to earn some kind of living while you're pregnant. I could teach you to cook and let you work in the kitchen when it gets to the point that you can't get around well enough to wait tables. Of course, I would pay you a little higher wages as a cook. The less stress you have...the better."

Over the weeks that followed, Rosie and Hannah put their plan into motion, and things eventually settled into a routine as the distinct aroma of autumn filled the air. Hannah became the cook and Rosie the waitress.

When the diner closed in the afternoon, Hannah would walk the gravel road behind the floodwall. She usually found something to sketch while she daydreamed of her lost love.

Later in the evening, she spent time with her father. She eventually covered Paddy's Harley with a tarp and chained it to a post on her porch. In time, falling leaves from the maple trees covered the tarp and nearly hid it from view. She never rode it one time.

Her two-room apartment began to look like an art studio. She left most of her pencil sketches in the pad for easy storage. The only one she completed as a watercolor was of Paddy standing with his shipmates on the first day they met. It was framed behind glass and hanging on the wall opposite her Murphy bed...the same bed where she and Paddy had made love the night before he left town...the exact same Murphy bed that accidentally knocked a large hole in the plastered back wall of the closet when they put the bed away the next morning. Paddy promised to repair the hole when he returned in July. Hannah hung a flat picture over the hole and forgot about it for a while, but it would not stay forgotten long.

***

One weekend in mid-October, Hannah began her fall housecleaning. When she removed the picture in the closet, she instantly thought about Paddy and the wonderful evening they had spent together. He had put the Murphy bed up for her the next morning, but had pushed too hard. A bedpost pierced the plaster all the way through the partition at the back of her closet.

Using a flashlight, she looked into the hole. She could see what appeared to be a dark passageway of some sort, but the flashlight took up so much room that it was difficult to get a good look. She decided to tell Rosie about the hole, not knowing at the time that what was on the other side of the wall would change many lives forever.

◻

CHAPTER TWENTY-FIVE

After the lunch rush the next Monday, Hannah brought up the topic of why all the windows and doors on the back section of the building were boarded up. Rosie had told the story shortly after Hannah came to work for her, but that was ten years ago.

"Were they all boarded up when you got here?" Hannah asked.

"Yes, and I have no idea how long before that. All I know is that my lease has a short paragraph stating that none of the boards on the back half of Angel's Manor may ever be removed to attain access to that part of the building. I've never broken that agreement."

"But, haven't you ever been curious about what's in the back and upstairs...and why it was boarded up?"

"In the early years, I was very curious, but as time passed, I guess I just got used to the old place looking the way it does."

"What would happen if you tore some boards off and looked inside?" Hannah asked.

"Probably nothing. The roughhewn boards were supposedly put up way back around the Civil War. Ownership of this place has been in my distant family since it was built. I've never seen the current owner, but I understand it's a distant uncle or aunt living in Europe," Rosie explained.

Hannah went behind the bar and brought the coffee pot out to fill their cups. She was trying to find the right words to tell Rosie that she had a hole in the closet behind her Murphy bed.

"What if you could see what's in the back and upstairs without pulling off any of those timbers?" she finally just blurted out.

"What do you mean?"

"I mean, what if there was another way in...a secret way?"

"Hannah...what are you holding back from me?"

"I...uh...I had an accident a while back when I shut my bed and it knocked a big hole in the closet wall behind it. I covered it with a picture, but I can't stop thinking about what I can see through the hole."

***

Immediately after closing the diner, Rosie and Hannah walked around to Hannah's apartment and pulled down her Murphy bed. They took their shoes off so they could stand on the bed and look into the hole behind a curtain that Hannah had recently installed.

"Oh my God almighty...it is a hidden passageway!" Rosie nearly shouted.

"Yes...but if you use this mirror, you can see further back where the ladder is."

"Ladder? There's a hidden passageway running between your apartment and the boarded up part of the building and it has a ladder? Where do you suppose the ladder leads? I can't believe this!" Rosie said, her voice growing more excited.

"I didn't know whether to tell you or not...but isn't it exciting?" Hannah said, a smile of satisfaction creeping across her face.

"Let's go back to the diner...I need more coffee," Rosie suggested.

Rosie poured then both a mug of coffee and they took seats in the front booth near the jukebox.

"Oh, Hannah...I can't believe you've found a hidden room. I've heard rumors over the years that this old building was once used as part of the Underground Railroad. You don't suppose we found where they hid the runaway slaves, do you?"

"Are we going to find out?"

"My lease says we can't pull off any of the timbers to gain entrance. We're not going to do that. Let me get a couple of flashlights and a hammer!"

The two women went back into Hannah's apartment and began removing enough plaster and lathing until the opening was large enough to walk through. Each held a flashlight in one hand and a rolled piece of newspaper in the other to clear the cobwebs that hung like moss from the ceiling. They moved along slowly until they reached the homemade ladder.

Rosie led the way. After she reached the ceiling and cleared the cobwebs, she pushed up on the ceiling. A trap door opened into another narrow passageway. She pulled herself inside, and then gave a hand to Hannah.

They quickly discovered the musty corridor apparently had no doors.

"I think this whole back half of the building must be full of secret trap doors and hidden panels," Rosie said, beginning to push on the walls.

Hannah also pushed and pulled until she felt part of the wall slide slightly to her right.

"This wall just moved a little bit!" she said.

Together, they pushed harder on the panel until it slid between two stud walls like a pocket door. They found themselves inside another small room that had a door and appeared to be used as a linen closet. Slowly, Rosie opened the door to find herself looking at a large bedroom. Hannah and Rosie shined their flashlights around and were surprised that the bed had been used and not remade. Other than dust and cobwebs, the rest of the room seemed undisturbed and in excellent condition.

The floor was covered with a thick layer of dust, but hints of a beautiful parquet floor were revealed in each footprint they made.

"Rosie, this place doesn't look like it's ever been lived in."

"These side windows are not boarded up, are they?" Hannah asked as she moved over to a pair of heavy velvet drapes covering what appeared to be a window.

"No, I guess someone figured the windows were too high for anyone to break in without a ladder."

Hannah pulled back one panel that allowed a little more light into the room, but the windows were so dirty and stained that the extra light was minimal.

"This room is huge!" Rosie said.

It ran the entire width of the building with matching draped windows on the left and the right. In the center of the room sat a beautiful French-style canopy bed facing a bank of French doors.

"Look, Rosie, most of the glass panes are broken out and some of the framing is broken!"

"There's no glass or splinters on the floor. Someone must have cleaned it up. Maybe the same people nailed up the boards until they could replace the broken French doors."

All of the furniture appeared to be expensive. Matching walk-in closets were on the wall opposite the French doors. In one corner, behind a silk folding divider they found a beautiful, freestanding, ceramic bathtub.

"Have you noticed that there's no bathroom?" Hannah asked.

"Yes, unless it's behind those two double doors," Rosie answered.

They moved together to the doors. Rosie pushed down on what appeared to be a set of brass door handles. The doors creaked open to a wide hallway leading to a carpeted stairway to the first floor. The floors downstairs were also parquet. Plastered walls divided the space into what appeared to be a large reception room, kitchen, dining room, and three small rooms that might have been planned for future children.

"Someone built a partition here and boarded up the entrances to keep anyone from entering this entire brick section of the building. It appears to be designed as a residence and not more hotel rooms," Hannah said.

"This is more than I can take today," Rosie said. "Let's go down to the diner and think this thing through."

They made their way back upstairs to the passageway and then down the ladder to the opening in Hannah's bed closet. It was past 6 p.m. and Garret had already closed his barbershop. Rosie went directly into the diner's kitchen and whipped up a quick supper for her family while Hannah sat in the front booth staring blankly into a hot mug of coffee.

What she and Rosie had seen swirled around in her mind, but an unanswered question remained—why would someone board up such a beautiful suite?

**

Rosie and Hannah were glad when the business week was over and the diner was closed. It was Gib and Ross's weekend to sleep over with their cousins across the street, and Garret would be busy cutting hair all day Saturday.

Rosie bought new batteries for the flashlights, wore an old apron with patch pockets, and carried a short-handled broom to fight off the heavy cobwebs. Hannah also wore an apron and carried a flashlight. In her apron pocket, she carried a box of matches just in case the oil lamps she had spotted earlier in the week still worked.

It was shortly past dawn when Rosie knocked on Hannah's door. Hannah had a pot of coffee ready and a couple of fresh doughnuts waiting. A bite or two of doughnut and a sip of coffee is all they had the patience for in anticipation of their second venture into Angel's Manor. Ten minutes later, they were back in the room.

"There's an oil lamp on that table," Rosie said.

"Think it will light?"

Rosie picked it up and looked at it closely.

"No, the oil must have evaporated...if there was ever any in it, but the wick isn't hard or gummy."

Rosie picked it up and smelled the wick.

"There's no scent at all or any smoke stains. I don't think this lamp has ever been used."

They checked several more lamps and all looked unused.

"We'll get some new wicks and oil the next time we come up, and that will provide more light," Rosie said.

"Can you imagine how beautiful this room was when it was first decorated?" Hannah said.

"Yes, but it's so dusty after sitting empty so long that it just has a gray look to it."

"You're right; this place should be cleaned up and kept beautiful."

"Let me show you something, Rosie. I don't think you noticed them," Hannah said, flashing her light onto the north wall.

Rosie followed the light to three paintings hanging above the mantel.

"Those are watercolors with the initials, A B, in the lower right corner. Do you know anyone with those initials?"

"Not to my knowledge."

"Now look at these walls."

"What do you see, Rosie?"

"The hooks! Three of the walls have hooks placed exactly where a person would probably want a piece of art hung...but there's no more artwork anywhere."

"You're right, but there should be. Whoever lived here wasn't finished decorating."

The two intrigued ladies returned to the diner and spent hours discussing what they had discovered. Hannah offered to spend her afternoons cleaning the place from top to bottom and maintaining the premises in good condition for as long as she lived in her apartment. Rosie gratefully accepted her offer and Hannah started cleaning the entire suite the next day.

***

The Thanksgiving holidays rolled around before Hannah finished her project. When Rosie went up to see the place, she was amazed. Each month thereafter, Hannah dusted every room and then returned to her apartment through the hidden passageway.

Eventually, the novelty of what they had discovered wore off and the place was only visited by Hannah about once a month. It would not always remain that way.

CHAPTER TWENTY-SIX

Only a few people commented to Rosie about how much weight Hannah was gaining. She would simply stare them down for a long moment before saying, "I gained more than she has when I was cooking. Are you saying I was fat?"

Generally, that question stopped the topic of conversation flat. It simply wasn't anyone else's business if Hannah was pregnant, and it wasn't necessary for people to second-guess her decision to give her baby up for adoption had they guessed her secret. She got the necessary papers from the midwife to handle the birthing and the adoption shortly after her second epileptic seizure, but she didn't sign them until the day she went into labor. She also gave Rosie her power of attorney in case the worst happened. Hannah was expecting to give birth sometime in early-March, but she went into labor on the twelfth day of February 1946. It was late evening when Rosie took Hannah to the midwife's facility in a taxi and was surprised to find another expectant mother already in delivery, and one waiting in the outer room expecting her water to break at any moment.

Problem was, Hannah's water had already broken in the taxi, and she needed help immediately. An assistant informed the midwife and Hannah was placed in a bed in the delivery room directly beside the other woman. Rosie waited outside.

For the next ten minutes, there was moaning, screaming, and a little cussing coming from the delivery room. Then as suddenly as it had all started, there was stone silence for a long moment before Rosie heard the cry of a newborn baby. An assistant hurried in and out of the room several times before the midwife came out and called Rosie to the side.

"Mrs. Walters, I'm so sorry to tell you that Hannah's little baby girl died shortly after birth."

Rosie hung her head as the tears began to flow. She and Hannah were like sisters and she felt all the hurt as if losing her own child. After a long moment, Rosie looked up to find the midwife still standing in front of her.

"There's more. Hannah had some kind of stroke during delivery. I had my assistant call an ambulance to take her to the hospital. I'm not qualified to treat her for that, you see."

"Yes...I know. You did the right thing. Can I go in to see her?"

"I suppose it'll be okay for a moment. I see the ambulance pulling up right now."

Rosie stepped into the delivery room and walked to Hannah's bedside. The young woman in the bed appeared to be only semi-conscious as her right eye opened and closed from time to time, but her left eye remained shut and appeared drawn down and somewhat withered. Her left arm and hand looked like they were twisted unnaturally.

"Oh, Hannah..."

Before she could say more, the team from the ambulance entered the room and ordered Rosie out.

"Can I ride to the hospital with her?"

"Sure, but we must hurry. It looks like she's had a major stroke. Her life's in danger."

Rosie stepped into the waiting room only to find as much commotion going on there as in the delivery room. The lady who had been waiting outside was now in full labor. The midwife and her assistant were helping her control her pain as the ambulance team wheeled Hannah through the room and out the front door. Rosie followed behind, and then got into the ambulance when told. Moments later, the vehicle pulled away with sirens blaring.

At the hospital, Rosie waited as emergency room nurses and doctors rushed in and out of a treatment room. Several hours later, a doctor came out and briefed Rosie on Hannah's condition.

"She's a lucky woman. She appeared to have had an epileptic seizure that resulted in a stroke...or vice-versa," the doctor advised.

"Is she out of danger?" Rosie asked maintaining eye contact with the doctor.

"She has a strong heart...and that helped her survive the stroke. The downside is that she will probably have a permanent facial distortion that could influence her speech. She may also suffer some possible limitations on the use of her left hand and arm.

"How long do you expect her to be in the hospital?"

"At least a couple of days. She's sleeping now, so why don't you come back tomorrow and see how things are going."

"She lost her baby tonight. When should she be told?"

"Wow...I...uh...I really don't know for sure. Stress brings on seizures and that would be stressful. We don't want another stroke, do we?"

Rosie got the hint. The doctor wanted Hannah to have as much rest and recuperation as possible. She thanked him for all his help and concern.

***

Outside the hospital, she thought about calling a taxi, but decided to walk home. On the way, she stopped at the midwife's house to talk about the arrangements for Hannah's child. She had no idea what the procedure was.

The midwife's name was Nellie Claypoole. She had been serving as a midwife for more than twenty years. Her husband had been a doctor before he died and Nellie assisted him when he delivered babies. She was a very experienced and respected midwife, but her assistant, Flo Brooks, left a little to be desired. Rosie felt that the assistant was extremely nervous and seemed quite disorganized during the time she helped attend Hannah and the other two women.

"Mrs. Claypoole, Hannah may be in the hospital for several days and I need to know what to do to help her."

"Are you talking about the final arrangements?"

"Yes."

"Well...we work very closely with Goodman's Funeral Home. Frank Goodman can provide the death certificate and other necessary papers that need to be signed. He donates the coffin and other services so she won't have any costs. Park Lawn Cemetery also provides a free plot for babies who die at birth."

"I see, but what if Hannah is unable to sign any of the papers? How soon will these final arrangements need to be made?"

"Soon! I mean...right away if possible. I've already had Goodman's pick up the child. Of course, if Hannah prefers to make other arrangements, they should be made soon...I mean...by tomorrow if possible. Otherwise, you'll have to sigh off as her power of attorney."

Rosie thanked the lady and walked out onto the front porch. A light drizzle had begun, and the cold mixture of rain changing to snow felt good on her face. She needed to clear her mind and figure out how she was going to manage.

When Rosie arrived home, she immediately entered the diner and got out a piece of paper and a pen. She wrote the words, "CLOSED DUE TO ILLNESS" across the paper and taped it to the inside of the front door. She woke Garret and informed him that Hannah's baby had died and that she would be busy helping with the arrangements. Rosie walked across the street and got her sister out of bed. She arranged for Gib and Ross to stay there over the weekend.

It was nearly midnight when she thought of Hannah's father. Mr. Frazey would need to be told, so she put her coat back on and headed for his house. He lived in a small frame house next to the Cutter Elementary School playground. As the school's janitor, he needed only to walk out his back door and across an asphalt basketball court to the entrance to the basement and boiler room.

As Rosie neared his house, she recalled how she and other students used to make fun of Mr. Frazey's little house because it was crooked. Something had happened to the foundation that caused one corner to dip down more than a foot. It made the whole building crooked. All the windows sagged one way or the other and the front and back doors were tilted. It was painted lime green. In the spring, blooming zinnias and daffodils made the house look like it was straight out of a fairytale.

Rosie had to knock on the door several times before Mr. Frazey answered.

"Hello, Mrs. Walters. What are you doing out at this hour in this kind of weather?"

Rosie didn't know Mr. Frazey well, but he was a regular customer at Garret's barbershop. To her knowledge, he had never eaten at the diner.

"I have bad news. Hannah lost her baby."

"What baby?"

His answer stunned Rosie for a long moment before she finally realized that Hannah had succeeded in hiding her pregnancy even from her father. Rosie instantly wished she hadn't spoken those words, but she could not pull them back. Hannah would need support over the next days and weeks perhaps, and her father was her only relative in town.

Rosie proceeded to tell Hannah's father the entire story and hoped he would understand and be sympathetic.

Rosie agreed to keep Mr. Frazey informed. Early the next morning, she gave Mr. Goodman permission to bury Hannah's child without any services. She would find some way of telling Hannah...when the time was right.

□

CHAPTER TWENTY-SEVEN

During three days of visits to the hospital, Hannah made no effort to talk even though Rosie sat by her side most of the time. On the morning Hannah was to be released, Rosie decided it was the best time to tell Hannah that her child had died. Should the stress of such news cause another seizure, there would be doctors there immediately to take care of her, but no seizure came. Hannah's eyes filled with tears and she nodded her head to indicate she understood, but she never spoke a word.

***

In the days and weeks that followed, Hannah regained her strength, but her left arm remained slightly withered and her speech impediment prevented clear articulation. She went back to work cooking at the diner where she didn't need to talk unless she wanted to...and the only person she ever wanted to talk with was Rosie. By early April, the daily routine returned to normal with one exception—Hannah no longer carried her sketchpad around with her. Rosie finally asked why she wasn't sketching any more.

"Nothing interesting to sketch!" Hannah replied without hesitation.

Rosie didn't push for more information. She could see that Hannah's fire had gone out...the twinkle in her eyes that once defined her was replaced with sadness and longing. When the diner was not busy, Hannah often stood near the front window staring at the street outside for long moments—not as if she was expecting someone but like she was trying to keep fond memories alive.

In mid-April, around closing time a Greyhound Bus stopped at the corner across the street from the diner. Hannah was in her usual position at the front window next to the jukebox. As the bus pulled away, Hannah's eyes began to blink rapidly. Her chin quivered as she inhaled deeply. She knew instantly that the man now walking across the street toward the diner was Paddy Phoot.

"Rosie!" she shouted.

"What is it, Hannah?"

"Look who's coming across the street!"

"Do you want to see him?" Rosie asked.

"Not now. I'm going back to the kitchen. You talk to him and find out what he wants."

Hannah moved quickly away from the window and disappeared into the kitchen. Rosie watched Paddy as he walked toward the diner. He seemed slower now and not as tall and strong looking. Somehow, he looked much older and unsure of himself.

Rosie looked up at the Pepsi clock on the back wall. It was only a few minutes before closing time and she thought about locking the door and turning the closed sign around, but she didn't. She was curious to find out what he was doing there after leaving Hannah alone and pregnant nearly a year earlier. She opened the door as he stepped up onto the concrete walk in front of the diner. She could see across his eyes that he was unsure of himself as he hesitated there for a long moment as if he were searching somewhere in the deep corners of his mind for the name of the woman standing in front of him.

"Paddy?" Rosie said when he didn't make any effort to enter the diner. His chin began to tremble and he could not speak as tears burst from his eyes and ran down his cheeks.

"Paddy...are you okay?"

Still trembling, the man reached into his shirt pocket and pulled out what appeared to be a letter. He handed it to Rosie. She looked at the front of the envelope and read the return address. It was from a Dr. Kantor in East Liverpool, Ohio. There was no other writing on the envelope and it did not have a stamp.

Paddy nodded for Rosie to open the letter.

As she did, she glanced back towards the kitchen, trying to imagine what poor Hannah might be thinking. She finally unfolded the one-page letter and began to read:

Gene McSweeney

To Whom It May Concern:

Nearly a year ago, an Amish family found a young man along the banks of the Ohio River near East Liverpool. The man had no identification so they brought him to me for treatment. He had suffered a severe head injury that left him in a semi coma for several months. He eventually regained most of his strength but refused to talk with anyone, although he was physically able to do so. He was suffering from partial amnesia and apparently a deep depression.

The Amish family continued to provide nourishment and moral support to the young man. While searching his clothes for any hint that might provide his identity, in his watch pocket, I found a book of matches tightly wrapped in some sort of waxy paper. When I showed him, he smiled for the first time. I asked him if he wished me to buy him a bus ticket to the town embossed on the matches. His eyes lit up and I knew that was where he wanted to go.

If you are reading this, he has perhaps found his way to Rosie's Diner...and to Hannah...the only word he has ever uttered, and the only name that has ever brought joy to his eyes.

Respectfully,
Dr. Z.M. Kantor

Rosie was stunned. She didn't know what to do, so she took his hand and guided him into the diner and over to the front booth.

"Let me get you a cup of coffee, Paddy," she said, seeing a look of recognition when she said his name.

She took him a mug of coffee and asked if he was hungry. He nodded that he was.

"I'll fix you some soup and a sandwich," she said as she walked away toward the kitchen.

When she got there, Hannah was waiting for some kind of explanation. Rosie simply handed her the doctor's letter. As Hannah read, her facial expressions seemed to change from anger to fear to concern to joy as she read each line. Finally, she burst into tears and rushed out of the kitchen to the front booth. Paddy immediately stood, wrapped his large hands around her waist, and lifted her high into the air before lowering her slowly until their eyes met.

"Hannah...Hannah...I've missed you so!"

He seemed to be reliving the moment when he and Hannah shared their first kiss. As their lips met and parted, there was joy in his eyes and in her eyes for the first time in nearly a year.

After encouraging the young couple to remain in the diner as long as they wished, Rosie locked the front door and went back to her own apartment. Hannah and Paddy sat in the front booth becoming reacquainted until late evening.

That night, Hannah's father offered to let Paddy stay at his house until he found work. The following morning, Hannah gave him a lead for a job.

"Paddy, do you remember Mr. Sizemore at the Sand and Gravel up the street?"

Paddy's eyelids began to blink; he seemed to be putting some memories together.

"Yes, didn't I fix his steam shovel a long time ago?"

"It was just last summer. Do you remember anything else?"

"Uh...my boat! Did he keep my boat?"

"Yes. You were supposed to take him a fish or two each month for rent while the boat was on his property. I was worried that he might sell it to someone while you were gone, so I made another deal with him."

"Another deal...what do you mean?"

"Instead of a fish each month, I gave him a free fish sandwich every Friday. He was more than satisfied."

"Thanks, Hannah. I'm sure glad I didn't lose my boat."

"Paddy...I hear Mr. Sizemore is looking for a mechanic to work on his equipment. Why don't you go see about getting a job there? He told you to stop by if he could ever do anything for you."

Paddy got the job at the Soda Sand and Gravel the next day. His job duties included keeping the heavy equipment running efficiently and delivering small loads of sand or gravel to area customers. When Paddy wasn't working or being with Hannah, he fished for pleasure and relaxation off the banks of Soda Creek.

When he discovered that there was a big demand for fresh-water fish at local restaurants, grocers, and butcher shops in the area, he found that he could earn extra money catching and selling fish from Soda Creek.

But fishing with a rod and reel sometimes took hours to catch one fish. Paddy was determined to do better. With his johnboat, he was able to rig up a trotline just upstream from the bridge where the river deepened just before emptying into the Ohio River.

Each morning and evening, he checked his trotline. Success came immediately. He kept the fish his customers preferred and tossed the rest back. Soon, Paddy could be seen riding around the neighborhood with his catch of the day swimming around in a makeshift container of water sitting on the seat of his sidecar.

In mid-June, Paddy snagged a four-foot paddlefish on his trotline. He immediately sold it to the local butcher shop. Before cutting it into steaks, they hung it on an awning in front of their store for all to see. A reporter took Paddy's picture standing alongside his rare catch and published it in the local newspaper. Soon afterwards, customers along Market Square began to call Paddy...Paddlephoot. He was becoming part of the neighborhood.

□

CHAPTER TWENTY-EIGHT

Illness, injuries, and fate had left both Paddy and Hannah with partially broken bodies, minds, and spirits, but spending some of every day together seemed the only medicine they needed. In the summer of 1946, they shared new hopes and dreams of making a life together.

As Hannah and Paddy watched the Independence Day celebration, Paddy asked Hannah why she seemed rather sad in recent days.

"Don't you enjoy watching the fireworks?" he asked.

"Yes, of course I do, but...." She didn't finish her sentence.

"Please tell me what's wrong," he asked.

"Paddy...do you know what's coming up next week?"

"No." Hannah wasn't sure if he had just forgotten or if it was due to his injuries, but she needed to talk about it.

"One year ago next week, we were supposed to get married. Do you remember that?"

Paddy lowered his head as the memories returned.

"We got licenses at the courthouse...didn't we?"

"Yes. We planned to get married the first day you came back from Cincinnati."

Hannah could see that Paddy was remembering things.

"I worked on the tugboats...I fixed the engines and cooked sometimes!"

"Yes. Do you remember thirty days on and thirty days off?"

"I do. My tug was named...uh...Lady Lexi. We pushed barges from Cincinnati to Pittsburgh, and...and we were gonna get married when I finished my thirty."

"That would have been on the 9th of July...that's next week."

Paddy took Hannah's hands and gazed into her eyes as if he were searching for her answer before he asked the question.

"Do you still want to get married?" he finally asked.

"Paddy...so much has happened since you left last year. I haven't told you because...you may not want to marry me when you know."

"Nothing will make me not want to marry you!"

Hannah looked down at her left hand that was being held.

"My hand is deformed now, and my face is not the bright pretty face that you knew last year."

"Hannah...your eyes are the same. They twinkle like the stars and when they do, I can see all the honesty and goodness inside you, but I fell in love with all of you...and I still want to marry all of you."

Hannah began to cry.

"There's something else," she said, choking up as her body trembled.

She was about to reveal the most stressful experience she had ever had. Would it cause another seizure...another stroke? She could never be sure, but she needed to get it out.

"Do you remember that we made love on the riverbank that evening after our picnic...and uh...racing the storm back to my apartment where we made love by candlelight all night long?"

She could see in his eyes that he remembered.

"I got pregnant that evening..."

"Pregnant? You mean...we...you and me...?"

"I lost the baby," Hannah blurted out.

Paddy burst into tears and buried his face against her breasts. He sobbed as she sobbed and they caressed each other to sooth each other's pain. Finally, Paddy leaned back and again gazed into Hannah's eyes.

"Was it a...a...?"

"It was a little girl."

"Was she beautiful like her mother?"

Tears once again burst from Hannah's eyes.

"I never saw her...Paddy...I...I...had a stroke and almost died. By the time I regained consciousness enough to understand anything, she had already been buried."

Paddy slumped into her arms again. They sat there in each other's embrace for a long time mourning the loss of their child until Paddy finally spoke again.

"Then, we'll start all over again. We'll get married next week and just start all over again. We'll have dozens of kids!"

"Paddy...Paddy...I can't have any more children. The doctor said another child would surely cause another stroke that would probably kill me. So...I agreed to being sterilized."

"We'll have each other, Hannah. Is that enough for you?"

Hannah didn't answer, but she pulled him close and again they cried together.

***

The next day, Hannah and Paddy went to Goodman's Funeral Home on his motorcycle and got the location of their child's grave. A few of the graves had ornate headstones, but most had small markers that lay flat on the ground. Others had only plot and section markers that indicated the location of the coffin according to the cemetery's numerical system.

The young couple—still in their mid-twenties—walked with unsure steps as they followed the printed map through the damp grass. She, with her arm in his for support, and Paddy, with his slight limp, looked much older than they were.

When they finally located the section and plot, a small, flat, stone marker read: Infant Frazey – 2-12-1946. Without tears, they stood there in silence for several minutes before Hannah placed a small bouquet of flowers near the marker. Hannah had never mentioned a possible name for her child because of her plans to give it up for adoption, so, Rosie had the stone engraved according to the funeral director's advice.

"Didn't you have a first name picked out for the baby?" Paddy asked.

"No," Hannah said, turning away from the grave and Paddy.

"I'm sorry, Hannah, I just thought you might have given her a name."

"I don't want to talk about it right now. Let's go to Morgan's and have a cup of coffee."

At Morgan's, they sat in a booth drinking coffee without speaking. The silence lasted long enough for Paddy to get nervous and uncomfortable.

"Is something wrong, Hannah?"

"Yes, everything seems wrong. I can't explain it, but something's wrong."

"Then I'll just sit here until you feel like talking about it," Paddy said in a child-like tone, stirring more cream into his coffee.

Finally, Hannah placed her hand on his and began to talk.

"First, let me explain why there is no first name on the marker. You were gone and I didn't know if you would ever be back. I had another seizure and Rosie saw it. She and I talked about things, and I explained that I would be too scared to try to care for my child because of the danger of passing out. Do you understand?"

Paddy exhaled heavily. He didn't seem sure of what Hannah was talking about, but he began to figure out that his absence during Hannah's pregnancy complicated matters.

"I'm not sure if I understand...exactly," he said.

"I...uh...I signed papers to give my child...our child... up for adoption. I didn't want to think of her in terms of a first name because I was afraid I might love her too much to give her up."

Hannah fought back tears.

"Would you have done the same thing if I had not been injured and we had gotten married last year?"

"I don't know, Paddy...if you thought we could have managed...you know...together. But you weren't there and I did what I thought was best for our child."

"I think you did the right thing, honey. Can you ever forgive me for not being there for you?"

"I've already forgiven you. It wasn't your fault. You were injured and unable to get in touch with me. We need to move on with our life. Do you agree?"

"Yes...I promise I'll never leave you again."

"Good! Now...I have something else to talk with you about. You have to promise me first that you won't think I'm crazy...and that you won't do anything about it unless we both agree."

"Of course I promise you that. I think we should always agree on things before we do anything that's important to both of us."

"Paddy, that isn't our baby in that grave. I don't know how to explain it, but I know."

"But...Hannah...how can you know this?"

"Because! I never felt anything inside my heart when we were standing over the grave. I warned you that you might think I'm crazy."

"No, it's not that...I think you can usually trust your feelings, but shouldn't we try to find proof?"

Hannah sighed again.

"Paddy, there were three babies born that night at about the same time. My baby was to be taken away without me seeing her at my request. Then, the awful pains came and sometime during delivery, I had the seizure and stroke. In all the confusion, it's possible the babies might have gotten mixed up. I don't know...but...something happened and I think our little girl is alive."

"What do you want me to do," Paddy asked, looking a bit bewildered.

"Nothing, I think the baby is with someone who can give her a good home...someone who doesn't have epilepsy and won't put the child in danger."

They gazed at each other in silence for a long moment. Paddy nodded his understanding and Hannah took his hand. They had just decided that their happiness would have to come from each other without the joy of having children...an agreement that would not last long.

□

CHAPTER TWENTY-NINE

On Tuesday, the ninth day of July 1946, Hannah Frazey became Hannah Phoot exactly one year later than originally planned. Rosie and Garret Walters were witnesses for the bride and groom as they took their vows in front of a justice of the peace. Afterwards, Paddy and Hannah got on their motorcycle and drove off into the hills of Kentucky for a one-night honeymoon. On Wednesday morning, Hannah was back at Rosie's Diner cooking breakfast as usual while Paddy was fishing on Soda Creek.

Time brought strength back into Paddy's body and mind. While he still drifted away from time to time as if he were searching for answers to unasked questions, much of his memory and skills had returned—as well as some dreams. Restoring the burned out houseboat was just one of them. By mid-August, Paddy had the repairs on the hull completed and had given it several coats of paint. Reconstruction was a slow project as he could only do what he could afford from his earnings at the Sand and Gravel and his side business of selling fresh fish.

Gradually, over the summer and fall of '46, Paddy worked on framing the houseboat and completing the exterior before winter set in. Hannah sketched each phase of the project as Paddy had requested. Nearly a year passed before the exterior was completed to Paddy's satisfaction, and another year before the interior was finished.

Finally, in late September, Paddy brought Hannah aboard for her first look at the inside.

"Wow, I didn't realize how much room there was going to be inside," Hannah said, stepping from the front deck into what Paddy described as a lounge.

On the starboard side of the room was a small kitchen counter with storage cabinets above and below and a full-size booth for dining. The range was fueled by propane and was also rigged and vented for use as a heating stove. On the portside, there was an L-shaped couch directly behind the helm. Paddy opened a door toward the stern and allowed Hannah to enter first. She stopped two steps inside and began to cry.

"Oh, Paddy, this bedroom is absolutely beautiful," she said, looking at the complete bedroom suite—clean and shining like it had just come from a furniture-store showroom. He opened another door to show her a full-size bathroom.

"I painted all the walls off-white so they'd go with anything. If you don't like it...I'll change it to whatever you want."

"It's lovely, Paddy," Hannah said, walking into his arms. "I wouldn't change a thing."

Hannah didn't bother pulling the curtains on the window opposite the bed. She kissed Paddy passionately; they undressed each other, and made love in their new bed.

Paddy never mentioned that his original plan—when he first discovered the burned-out boat—was to have a second bedroom with bunk beds for their future children. That reality was gone now, but his dream of being a father remained.

Paddy wanted Hannah to move into the houseboat as their fulltime home, but Hannah objected.

"I'm not sure that would be a good idea, Paddy. We can have terrible winters here and I don't think I would feel safe when the river freezes over. Going up and down that steep bank after a snow would be difficult. We can't afford to risk missing any work because of where we live."

Paddy lowered his head and sighed.

"Do you mean you'll never live on the Hannah's Gaze?"

"Hannah's Gaze?" she said, as her eyes twinkled and her smile broadened with the realization that Paddy had named the houseboat after her.

"Yes! I named her after your eyes."

"That's got to be the nicest thing anyone has ever done for me. Thank you, Paddy. "

"So you still won't live on her?"

"Oh, yes...Paddy...only I was thinking we would keep my apartment for the winter and live on Hannah's Gaze from early spring to fall. Wouldn't that be the smart thing to do?"

Paddy smiled. He knew she was right.

Winter was on its way so there was no reason to launch the houseboat until spring. Hannah added feminine touches to the decorating while Paddy prepared her for winter. During the last mild days and nights, they often slept on the houseboat, pretending it was the honeymoon they never had.

Rosie was pleased that they were going to keep the apartment. She didn't want to rent it to anyone else for fear the secret entrance into the back half of the building might be discovered. She allowed Hannah and Paddy to stay in the apartment free during the winter in return for Hannah keeping Angel's Manor clean.

What Rosie didn't know was that Paddy had removed the closet wall behind the Murphy bed and added a fake panel that was nearly impossible to detect. Only Paddy and Hannah knew how to open the panel. While curious, Paddy never entered the secret passageway because he promised Hannah that he would never do it without Rosie's permission. That permission never came.

□

CHAPTER THIRTY

The decade of the '50s brought many changes to the neighborhood and to the people who lived there. Rosie's husband, Garret, was diagnosed with cancer. His radiation treatments left him progressively weaker until he died in 1951.

The United States allowed itself to be pulled into another war—this time in Korea. Young men from Fiddler's Point and surrounding areas joined the armed forces with the goal of stopping communist aggression in that part of Asia. Among them were Rosie's oldest son, Ross, and Hannah's younger brother, Jimmy, who reenlisted with the Marines.

Many changes were also in store for Hannah and Paddy as they settled into their married life. They spent most of their free time during the warm months on their houseboat. In November, Paddy pulled the vessel back to its land location where he winterized it and made any needed repairs. Paddy settled into his job at the Sand

and Gravel and continued fishing Soda Creek to earn extra money.

Hannah's job at the diner was perfect for her. The diner opened at six in the morning and closed at two in the afternoon. It was closed on the weekends. This schedule allowed Hannah plenty of time in the evenings and on weekends to do her sketching.

Over time, the couple became somewhat of an anomaly in the neighborhood. Every afternoon after work, Hannah could be seen sketching one thing or another at various locations around town. Paddy would join her in the evening, and together, they would frequent many of the local neighborhood taverns. Paddy would have a beer or two while Hannah had a glass of buttermilk. She simply didn't like the taste of beer, wine, or whiskey.

"Hannah," the bald bartender said as he set down a bottle of Burger Beer and a glass of buttermilk, "could you sketch that Red Top Ale sign hanging above the cash register?"

Hannah glanced at the sign and answered, "Sure."

The sign had a picture of an attractive woman with red hair behind a bottle of Red Top Ale. The ad read, Meet Miss Red Top.

"Good!" When my boss comes in, he always sits on the stool under that sign. Could you do a drawing of him under the sign...and make his hair red...and write, 'Meet Mr. Red Top' at the bottom."

"Cost ya a dodder," Hannah said, causing the bartender to grin before turning away quickly. He didn't want Paddy to think he was making fun of Hannah's speech impediment. It wasn't a severe impediment, but certain words were difficult for Hannah to pronounce and dollar was one of them.

Hannah opened her sketchbook and quickly drew the sign, the cash register, the end of the bar, and the single barstool. She left white space in the appropriate spot to add the bartender's boss whenever he came in.

In the meantime, Hannah spotted two men playing pool near the back. One man was middle-aged, of average height and weight, and smoked a fat cigar. His opponent was a midget. Only his head could be seen when he was on the backside of the pool table.

Hannah watched while the small person looked at the eight ball from several angles, and then got into a most unusual stance before taking the shot. He rested the heavy end of his cue stick on his right shoulder, steadied it by hooking the index finger of his left hand around the small end of the cue, and then smoothly cut the eight ball expertly into the side pocket. Ten minutes later, Hannah had a sketch of the shot on paper.

Walking up to the winner, she said, "You like it? One dodder."

The man looked at the picture and smiled broadly before taking a dollar bill from his winnings and handing it to Hannah.

In just over an hour, Hannah sold four more sketches. Her last one was of the redheaded owner of the tavern sitting under the Red Top Ale sign.

On an average, Hannah would sell four or five sketches in the time it took Paddy to drink two beers. That was his limit. When he was done, they would leave the tavern, mount Paddy's Harley, and head home.

***

In early February, Paddy returned home from dropping off a sack of groceries on Mr. Frazey's back porch that overlooked Cutter Elementary School's playground.

"You look pale as a ghost, Paddy. Is something wrong?" Hannah said, pouring him a mug of coffee to warm him up from the cold trip to Market Square.

Paddy just stood there staring at Hannah's eyes. She sat down across from him and held his hand.

"It was her...I'm sure of it!"

"Who was it, Paddy? Who are you talking about?"

Once again, he gazed deeply into Hannah's eyes. His thoughts drifted back to the first day he met her the morning the war ended. He remembered how her eyes sparkled like diamonds in the sun. He remembered falling in love with her during those first moments together—not because of their first kiss, or her warm smile, but because her eyes captured his heart. He took a deep breath and searched for the right words.

"My God, Hannah...you...were right...our daughter is alive!

Hannah's eyes blinked rapidly.

"What? Paddy, why are you saying this?"

"I saw her...just a few minutes ago after I dropped off some groceries at your dad's place. A black panel truck pulled up beside the playground and Mr. Kessler from the butcher shop got out with a little girl. He walked her over to the jungle gym and let her play on it a few minutes. Since he buys some of my fish, I thought it would be polite if I stopped and said hello. We talked for a few minutes until the little girl slipped and fell. Mr. Kessler ran to her and picked her up. I offered to help if I could..."

"Was she hurt?"

"No, it just scared her, but as he held her in his arms, she looked straight at me. She had big tears in her eyes—your eyes. I swear, Hannah...her eyes were exactly like yours."

"Oh, Paddy...I doubt that she was our daughter...what would the chances be? How old did she look?"

"Five...maybe six...blondish hair."

"Paddy, I'm not so sure that we should be talking about this. If it is her...it'll break our hearts...if it's not...it'll break our hearts."

"But Hannah..."

"Let's not talk anymore about it today. Let's sleep on it, and tomorrow, we'll decide what we should do. if it is our daughter."

***

The next day was Monday and 6 a.m. found Hannah in the diner's kitchen preparing breakfasts for the regulars. Paddy went to work at nine o'clock and didn't get off until six. Maybe Hannah planned it that way and maybe not, but shortly after 2 p.m., she was sitting on her father's back porch watching for a black panel truck to appear near the playground. None did that day, but Hannah was persistent, getting to the back porch each school day shortly before the children were dismissed. If the little girl went to school at Cutter, she was determined to get a look at her...especially her eyes.

It was not until late in the afternoon on Valentine's Day that her luck changed. Cutter students were dismissed at 3 p.m. and once again, she saw no one who matched Paddy's description of the little girl. Half an hour later, she folded her sketchpad and prepared to leave.

Suddenly, a black panel truck pulled up near the playground and a thin man got out. KESSLER'S PROVISION was written in large orange letters across the side of the vehicle. The driver opened the back door of the truck and collected several large packages into his arms. He carried them across the street and disappeared into the side door of Saint Joseph's Elementary School. Hannah's attention quickly returned to the panel truck and the small passenger sitting in the front seat.

Hannah began to sketch the entire scene in front of her to put the truck in perspective. This included part of the school, the playground that showed the jungle gym, Fifth Street, and the exact location of the panel truck. She flipped that page over and did a larger sketch of the panel truck on another sheet of paper. She was now ready to sketch the little girl behind the fogged up passenger window. She waited patiently hoping the child would roll the window down.

Moments later, a back door at Cutter opened up and Hannah was surprised to see Rosie's youngest son, Gib, leaving the school. He was carrying a small brown paper bag. She watched as he peeked around the corner down spouting at several older boys loafing around the outside basketball court. The boy abruptly turned and walked in the other direction, bringing him to the concrete sidewalk just in front of the panel truck. He looked nervously over his shoulder several times before the first ice ball hit him behind his right ear. Hannah drew a quick partial sketch of the event while her eyes darted frequently back to the fogged up window.

A second ice ball hit Gib in the shoulder and a third smacked loudly behind his right leg causing him to fall to his knees. Three older boys from the Catholic school approached him and began pushing him around. A tall kid grabbed the brown paper bag from Gib's hands.

As the bullying continued, Hannah decided Gib needed some help. She slipped her sketchbook into the wide, front pocket of her apron and walked across the playground to Cutter's furnace room where she knew her father would be working. As she made her way across the asphalt, the window on the panel truck rolled down a few inches, but she was still too far away to get a good look at the little girl's eyes.

She saw one of the Catholic boys turn the brown sack upside down. All of Gib's valentines landed in the gutter's runoff water that carried them just past the front of the panel truck and down through the street grate to the sewers below.

As the taunting and shoving continued, Hannah entered the basement where she found her father and sent him to Gib's rescue. She followed at a distance.

"Hey! Leave him alone, ya hear me!" the janitor shouted.

The Catholic boys ran and quickly disappeared behind their school.

"Thanks, Mr. Frazey," Gib said, picking up the empty paper bag.

Moments later, the ex-marine returned to the boiler room and Hannah took a seat on a bench near the sliding board just a few feet away from the panel truck. Once again, she saw the passenger's window go down several inches. She could see bright, shiny, blond hair fixed up in two ponytails. As the child moved closer to the window, Hannah got a good look at the little girl's sparkling blue eyes. Without a single doubt in her mind and her heart, Hannah knew. Tears burst from her eyes as she sketched an event that would remain in her memory forever.

The little girl's small finger motioned for Gib to come closer. As he neared the passenger door, the little girl slid a torn piece of pink construction paper out of the window.

Hannah could see that it was some kind of valentine that the little girl probably made in school earlier that day. On it were many cut paper hearts pasted to form the shape of a person. In one of the heart-person's outstretched hands was the word "MINE" printed in large letters. The other half of the homemade valentine had been torn away and remained in the truck.

Hannah's hands shook as she attempted to capture the scene on her sketchbook. When she saw the thin man returning to the truck, she pretended to be sketching the steeple with the large clock.

"Okay, Josie, that's my last delivery. We can go home now."

"Josie! Her name is Josie!" Hannah said to herself.

As the panel truck pulled away, Hannah stopped sketching and walked back across the schoolyard to her father's house. She needed a warm place to cry.

□

CHAPTER THIRTY-ONE

When Hannah finally confided in Rosie about her suspicions, Rosie was uncertain how to assist her, so she got each of them a cup of coffee, and they sat down in the front booth to discuss the matter.

"Hannah, even if the child...

"Josie...her name is Josie," Hannah interrupted.

"Yes...even if Josie is your child, it would take going to court to get custody of her, and I don't know if you could come up with enough proof that she's your child."

"What about her eyes?" Hannah said, as if that was the only proof she needed.

"I'm not saying that Josie isn't your child, I'm just saying that you'll need a lot more evidence...more proof than that to take her away from the couple who have raised her, and I'm sure have loved her very much. They've done nothing wrong. It would break their hearts to have their daughter taken away even if she wasn't their child."

Hannah looked down and sighed, "I know...I know."

"And remember, Hannah, nothing has changed about your ability to raise the child properly. You could still have a seizure and put her in jeopardy."

"You're right. I wouldn't want to be responsible for her getting hurt, but...but...I need to know for sure if she's my daughter."

"Okay, honey, I'll help you in any way I can to find out the truth."

***

Several hours later, Rosie and Hannah were sitting at the public library looking through an old newspaper dated February 13, 1946. When they found the Announcement section, Hannah ran her finger down the column until she reached the *Births-Reported* heading. This section was subdivided according to the name of the hospital reporting the birth. Rosie skipped over three sections to get to the part titled *Other Births*. This was for reporting births at home or at a midwife's facility.

"There it is, Rosie."

Mr. and Mrs. Chester Kessler – daughter.

They skipped over to the Obituaries in the same newspaper and found two words and a date: Infant Frazey - 2-12-1946.

Rosie's mind drifted back to the chaotic day Hannah gave birth. With three women having babies in the same room at nearly the same time, coupled with an incompetent assistant, it was possible that the babies were somehow switched in the added confusion of Hannah's seizure and stroke, but proving it now would be impossible. Rosie thought for a fleeting moment that she might go back to the midwife and the assistant to see what they remembered. If they had any doubts, they would have come forth when it happened, not now, not six years later.

"Hannah, if you just want Josie to be in your life, it might be best not to confront the Kesslers or the midwife. If they feel threatened, you might never get to see Josie."

"I know. I would never want Josie to feel scared or think that she has the wrong parents. I couldn't do that to her. I've made up my mind that I will see her from a distance when I have an opportunity without her ever knowing that I...that I...."

Hannah began to choke up and Rosie was afraid that the stress might bring on a seizure.

"Come on, let's go back to the diner, have some coffee, and make plans for seeing Josie from time to time."

With Rosie's help, it didn't take Hannah and Paddy long to agree on a plan that would allow them to see their daughter without anyone suspecting the relationship.

They soon found the Kessler's address on Caller Hill just a block or so from Kinney Elementary School. Hannah came up with a plan to see Josie nearly every day. She had her father inform the janitor at Kinney Elementary that she would be in the area in the afternoons sketching the school as part of a project to sketch all the schools in Fiddler's Point.

Each afternoon at two, when the diner closed, Hannah drove the motorcycle to Caller Hill where she half pretended to sketch the school. Each time she spotted Josie, she would sketch the little girl playing or walking home from school.

One autumn afternoon in 1954, Hannah had her motorcycle parked in front of Lane's Malt Shop just catty-corner to the school. As she positioned herself to begin sketching, she was startled for a moment when she saw Josie and two classmates walking directly toward her. They were all dressed in skirts and sweaters. Josie was carrying a Brownie Camera on a leather strap around her neck.

School's out...maybe she's coming over to the malt shop for some ice cream, Hannah thought.

As the three young girls approached, Hannah flipped her sketchbook back to the page with the drawing of the school.

"Are you the artist lady?" Josie asked as she and her friends stopped near Hannah.

"The artist lady? How would you know that?" Hannah asked, thrilled to hear Josie's voice.

"A long time ago, our teacher's told us that you were an artist and would be around our school drawing pictures. I've seen you lots of times."

"That's nice. What's your name?" Hannah asked, just wanting the conversation to continue.

It was the closest Hannah had ever been to her daughter. A rush went through her body at the thought of holding the little girl in her arms for just a moment.

"Josie's my name...what's yours?"

"My name's Hannah. It's good to meet you."

Hannah stuck her hand out hoping Josie would shake with her, and she did.

"Do you like to draw?" Hannah asked with a smile, patting the girl on the shoulder with her free hand.

"I've never tried it much, but I like to take pictures with the Brownie Camera my dad just bought me."

Josie's two friends were becoming impatient and beckoned Josie to come along into the soda shop. Hannah released her hand.

"Oh Jules, you and Ann shouldn't be in such a hurry," Josie said to her friends.

"I would love to see some of the pictures you've taken with your camera, Josie. Maybe sometime you can show me a few."

"Okay," Josie said, raising her camera and snapping a shot of Hannah. "I'll even let you see a picture of yourself if I see you here again sometime."

The three girls went into the soda shop and came back out a few minutes later with milkshakes.

"Goodbye, artist lady," two of the girls said.

"Goodbye, Hannah," Josie said, looking back and waving as she and her friends crossed the street and walked up Caller Hill.

Hannah quickly drew a likeness of Josie and her friends as they crossed the street. She knew she would remember this day for the rest of her life.

□

CHAPTER THIRTY-TWO

The friendship between Rosie, Hannah, and Paddy continued through the 50s as Rosie watched her son, Gib, grow into a teenager. In a small town like Fiddler's Point, it seemed inevitable that Gib would eventually cross paths with Josie Kessler. During the last week of summer vacation in 1960, this chance meeting occurred across the river in Kentucky at the Greeno County fair.

Gib, and his friend, Rick Shultz, were playfully guiding their newest girlfriends through the pitch-black spook house when they ran into another young couple that one of the girls knew. During introductions, and aided only by the light from Shultzy's Zippo, Josie Kessler officially met Gib Walters for the first time. More than ten years would pass before they would meet again.

Gib graduated from high school in 1962, and attended the local junior college for a year or so before enrolling at the University of Kentucky where he earned his bachelor's and master's degree. On the day that he was scheduled to leave for Georgia to pursue his doctorate degree in Human Relations, his 1950 Dodge quit running. He left it with Paddy to repair and took a Greyhound to Georgia.

***

Always from a distance, Hannah continued sketching Josie from time to time as she passed through her school years. On the evening of her high school graduation in 1964, Paddy drove Hannah and Rosie to the event in Gib's old Dodge that now ran like new. Hannah was able to complete several sketches as Josie moved through the various stages of the ceremony. Without realizing it, one of Hannah's sketches included Chester and Sadie Kessler. As much as Hannah and Paddy wanted to congratulate Josie with a hug, or at least a handshake, they kept their distance as they had always done.

***

After the ceremonies, the three went to Morgan's for coffee.

"This coffee is really good," Rosie said.

"That's because someone else made it," Hannah replied with a wry smile.

"Paddy, you'll never guess who stopped in at the diner this morning," Rosie said, casting her gaze at Paddy.

"I'm not very good at guessing. Who was it?" Paddy said with a typically sluggish response.

"Roe Cagney! I haven't seen that trouble maker around here for years."

Just the mention of his name jerked long suppressed memories from the deepest recesses of Paddy's mind. Paddy finished stirring his cup of coffee as his eyelids began to flutter rapidly. His gaze quickly shifted from Rosie's face to the small whirlpool of foam in his coffee cup.

"Roe...Roe Cagney?"

"Are you okay, honey?" Hannah asked, watching Paddy's eyes as they fixated on the mug of coffee in front of him. He didn't answer her.

His mind was racing back to the last time he and Roe Cagney worked the tugs together. They were moored near Marietta to make some emergency repairs to a broken gasket in the tug's engine. Since it was going to take the best part of a day to get the part, and another day to make the repair, most of the crew went ashore. Paddy did not.

Late that night, Roe Cagney returned to the barge. Paddy was still in the galley preparing his famous spaghetti and meatballs for the following day's lunch.

Roe suddenly barged into the galley complaining loudly about having a headache. He began ruffling through the cabinets looking for some Alka-Seltzer or aspirin.

"Where in the world did you get all that mud all over you?" Paddy asked.

"Roe's muddy shirt had several rips across the back and appeared to have blood stains around them.

"Your back's bleeding! You probably need someone to take a look at that," Paddy said, moving around Roe to get a better look.

"Mind your own damn business!" he shouted, turning his back away from Paddy.

"Suit yourself," Paddy replied, as Roe left the kitchen without an Alka-Seltzer.

The next morning, the crew again went ashore. This time, Paddy went along to see if he could find a card to send back to Hannah. He was on his way into a drug store when he spotted the morning newspaper headlines on a nearby rack. A young girl's nude body had been found along the riverbank a short distance south of town.

Paddy read the article, but it didn't give many details. One quote by an investigating officer brought chills to Paddy's spine:

"The victim must have fought back valiantly because they found *skin and blood under all of the victim's fingernails."*

My God, what if it was him, Paddy wondered.

He immediately returned to the tug. He was nervous and didn't know exactly what to do, but he needed to know. He walked past Roe's cabin several times before opening the door. He wondered what he would do if he was caught, but he had never known a crewmember to return to the tug until late at night.

He stepped inside the cabin and closed the door behind him. In the tugboat's small sleeper cabins, space was extremely limited, so most crewmembers kept their personal belongings under their bunk. That area was considered strictly off limits to other crewmembers unless the captain ordered an inspection. Paddy went directly to Roe's bunk and looked beneath it.

He felt a small suitcase, pulled it out, and opened it. He gasped as he saw a handful of girls' class rings in a cloth bag. Beneath the bag, he found a stack of newspaper articles covering murders of young girls along the Ohio River. He nervously put the news clippings and rings back where he got them, but did not notice that a small clipping had fallen out of his hand and landed in the shadows beneath the bunk. He put the case back under the bed without realizing that he was covering the dropped clipping from the Fiddler's Point Times. The article covered the murder and probable rape of the mayor's daughter the evening of her hlyh-school graduation.

All crewmembers were scheduled back on board by midnight and the first-shift crew would get the tug underway as soon as the fog lifted the next morning.

As the Lady Lexi got underway, everything seemed routine until Roe came into the Galley. He never spoke to anyone as he sat quietly at the end of the table sipping on a mug of coffee.

That night, Paddy went to bed early as the tug moved steadily past Steubenville, but he didn't sleep well—maybe because of the heat and humidity or maybe because of what he had seen under Roe's bunk. Just past midnight, he went into the galley and poured himself a mug of coffee. Dressed only in cutoff jeans

and a tee shirt, he went up on deck
to get some fresh air.

A voice came from somewhere in
the darkness.

"You've been in my stuff!"

Before Paddy could focus on
where the voice might be coming
from, something heavy hit him hard
behind the right ear and knocked
him overboard.

***

"Where do you suppose Josie is right now?" Paddy asked, coming out of his trance and lifting his gaze from the coffee cup first to Rosie's face and then to Hannah's.

"Most of the grads are going to Popcorn Beach from what I understand," Rosie said.

Paddy looked deeply into Hannah's eyes and knew she was thinking the same thing he was thinking.

"We need to leave, now!" Paddy said, instantly standing up and heading for the door. Hannah laid down some change for the coffee without trying to explain anything to Rosie.

"Rosie, tell me exactly where Roe's mother lives on the west side!" Paddy asked as he sped toward the diner.

"Uh...she lives in a small silver trailer just past Nell's soda shop on the right side of the highway, but I haven't seen or even heard anything about Mrs. Cagney in several years. She may not even live there anymore."

Moments later, Paddy parked the old Dodge beside the vacant barbershop and without a word, hopped on his Harley and headed west across the Soda Creek Bridge. He rode to Nell's and spotted the silver trailer across the road. Twilight was coming down hard as he parked his bike on Nell's lot and bought a hotdog and a Pepsi. He carried them to a picnic table sitting under a nearby shade tree. From there, he could see lights on in the trailer.

Paddy's mind was thinking clearer now than it had in years. His first thought had been to walk through the cornfield to the edge of the beach. From there, he could spot Josie and keep an eye on her from behind the cornrows. But what if I lost sight of her in the crowd? It would be easy to do that, he thought.

Finally, he decided that the best way to protect Josie from Roe Cagney was not to let him out of his sight. As Paddy sat watching the trailer, the last sliver of sunlight was bouncing off the field of dried cornhusks creating a sea of maize.

Up the road a short distance from the trailer, a dirt road led from the highway to Popcorn Beach. One car after another filled with young people turned onto the road and headed for the beach party.

It wasn't long until the trailer door opened and Roe walked out with a sack of trash and threw it into a nearby garbage can.

It's him! Paddy thought. He got up from the picnic table and walked into the cornrows. He moved nearer the trailer and hunkered down watching for Roe to open the door again. Moments later, he did.

Roe was wearing faded blue jeans, a white tee shirt, and a white Cincinnati Reds baseball cap. If the twilight held, it wouldn't be hard to follow him at a distance.

When they finally arrived at the edge of the cornfield where fertile soil met sand, Paddy watched as Roe Cagney crouched in the shadows about two cornrows deep. Paddy carefully surveyed the area to get a better feel for exactly where he was in relation to Roe and the beach area where the party was taking place. The cornrows were to his left and followed the snake-like contour of the creek. Roe's position was about fifteen paces in front of him where the creek cut back to his left forming the sandy cove that was Popcorn Beach.

No one swam in this stretch of Soda Creek because it was extremely dangerous. Not more than knee-deep in most places, the floor had several deep trenches that suddenly dropped down ten to fifteen feet. That's where the big catfish stayed, and where Paddy fished with his trotlines. Once he got his bearings, he realized, even in the darkness, that he was not far from one of those trenches now.

There must have been more than a hundred young boys and girls partying in the sand around several tall, blazing bonfires. There were packages of chips and pretzels, hot dogs to roast over the fire, and plenty of soft drinks and beer. The forecast was for a hot, dry evening.

Paddy finally spotted Josie and another girl talking with a couple of guys. They were all drinking beer and listening to music from dozens of transistor radios scattered around the beach.

In less than an hour, it became evident that the beer drinking was sending both girls and boys into the cornrows in search of the one thing Popcorn Beach did not have—bathrooms. It was also easy to figure out that the guys were stepping into the cornrows upstream a ways while the girls found a place downstream—a place very close to the hidden Roe Cagney.

If I can figure that out, Roe also has it figured out, Paddy thought. He slowly and quietly moved a step or two closer to Roe. He was glad he was wearing a brown and yellow plaid shirt and khaki pants. The only light now came from the crackling bonfires, and in the flickering light, Paddy's cloths blended in with the dried cornstalks. The problem was that Josie's burnt-orange Bermudas and matching blouse were also hard to see in the firelight.

Another hour or so went by and Paddy watched dozens of young girls walk into the cornrows, stay a few minutes, and then walk out—usually laughing about the primitive bathroom facilities. Josie and her friend also walked in and out without incident. Paddy wondered what Roe was waiting for if he was, indeed, a stalker. Then, it dawned on him—he was waiting for a girl to be in the cornrows alone.

Maybe parents remembered what happened to Mayor Lowe's daughter nearly twenty years earlier, Paddy thought. Maybe they warned their kids always to stay in pairs—maybe they didn't.

More time passed before Josie and her friend returned to the cornrows as their second or third beer began to run through their bodies.

"My gosh, I can't believe how quickly beer makes me have to pee," Josie's friend said as she pulled down her shorts.

"Me, either," Josie responded. "I've only had three beers, and I think I'm getting drunk already," she continued, giggling because she was having trouble getting her shorts unzipped.

"I'm done...are you ready to go?" her friend asked.

"Oh, God...I think I'm going to be sick. You go on, and I'll catch up with you in a minute. I don't want you listening to me throw up," Josie said, leaning over at the waist.

"That's fine with me. If I hear you getting sick, it'll make me throw up, too. I have a weak stomach."

Josie's friend stepped out of the cornrow and headed back to the bonfire as Josie began to throw up. This was the moment Roe was waiting for. Slowly and quietly, he closed the short gap between himself and the sick young girl. From behind, he slid his left hand over her mouth and grabbed her by the back of her hair with his right.

He tried to pull her backwards, but before he could, Paddy's two large hands shot under both of the smaller man's arms and jerked him into the air. Roe landed on his face near the bank that dropped sharply down to the water's edge.

Josie struggled to her feet and threw up again before staggering out of the cornrow onto the sandy beach. Seeing that she was safe, Paddy turned his attention back towards Roe Cagney.

Dazed and disoriented, Roe barely managed to get to his feet and open his pocketknife before the charging, angry Paddy blasted into him with two powerful forearms. Paddy felt something sharp penetrate his left side as he knocked Roe off the edge of the bank and into the creek. Paddy stood on the bank watching Roe step into one of the deep trenches.

The desperate man kicked and thrashed trying to stand up but suddenly began a series of short, shrieking sounds as treble hooks penetrated his clothing and skin. As he twisted violently, Paddy's trotline hooks dug deeper into his flesh, wrapping around his legs and arms until the thrashing stopped, the kicking stopped, and all efforts to scream were replaced by the gurgling sounds of a drowning man.

After the water was quiet for a while, Paddy stepped back into the cornrows. He walked slowly across the field to his Harley and rode it to town.

When he arrived at the diner, he was nervous, scared, and covered with mud. He told Hannah and Rosie exactly what happened. Rosie's first suggestion was to call the police and let them handle everything, but Hannah worried that Paddy would be questioned and maybe even charged with murder. As things stood now, there was no proof that Roe had ever attacked anyone.

"Have the police search his mother's trailer," Paddy said sluggishly.

"What do you mean, Paddy?" Rosie asked.

"At Morgan's this evening, I remembered everything about how I was injured years ago when I worked the tugs," Paddy said slowly but firmly. "I found a suitcase full of newspaper clippings and a sack of girls' class rings under Roe's bunk on the Lady Lexi. That was the same night I was knocked overboard. The clippings were about young girls being murdered from time to time along the Ohio River. I didn't take the time to look at all the dates, but I'd bet my life one of the girls was Mayor Lowe's daughter.

"Do you think Roe still has all those things?" Rosie asked.

"He might have them over at his mother's trailer. I don't think he would risk leaving them under his bunk on a tug while someone else uses his cabin for thirty days," Paddy said.

"You're right. He would want to keep his trophies close," Hannah said.

"His mother won't be any help. From what I understand, she lays around drunk most of the time. Roe wouldn't have any trouble keeping those things hidden from her. I doubt if she would understand what she was looking at even if she did find them," Rosie said.

"What should we do Rosie? I don't want Paddy to be in trouble," Hannah said.

"He won't be in trouble, Hannah, I'll call Mayor Lowe. He'll know what to do," Rosie said, hoping her assurance would help Hannah stay calm.

Rosie called the Mayor. After explaining that she had information that might concern his daughter's death, the mayor promised to come to the diner as quickly as possible. Rosie returned to the booth and assured Paddy and Hannah that things would be fine.

"What if the mayor doesn't believe Paddy?" Hannah said, still nervous about the possible consequences.

"Calm down, honey, before the stress gets you sick!" Paddy cautioned, weakly taking her hand.

"Paddy?" Is something wrong?" Hannah said, feeling something sticky on his hand.

Paddy didn't answer as his head slumped forward onto the booth.

"Oh my God!" Hannah shouted. "That's blood on his hand!"

"And that's blood on his side. He's bleeding badly," Rosie said, returning immediately to the telephone on the back wall to call the emergency squad.

It wasn't long before the ambulance arrived to find Paddy unconscious and Hannah sitting across from him with a glazed look across her eyes. She was pulling on her right ear. Shortly after they took Paddy away in the ambulance, Hannah regained consciousness from her seizure.

"Where's Paddy?" she asked, not remembering anything that had happened since she saw blood on Paddy.

"They just took him to the hospital to check him over and fix whatever is causing him to bleed," Rosie explained, glossing over the seriousness of his condition.

Moments later, the front door opened and Mayor Lowe walked in.

"What's going on, Mrs. Walters?"

Rosie explained the earlier events and the mayor immediate called the authorities and sent them on a search for Roe Cagney's body.

"Mayor Lowe, could you take us to the hospital to be with Paddy. Neither one of us can drive a car."

"Sure. Maybe I can talk with Paddy and find out more about what happened."

When they arrived at the hospital, they learned that Paddy had been rushed into surgery for a deep knife wound to his chest. They all sat in the waiting room until the doctor came out.

"We did all we could do. He's in God's hands now."

"Can I see him?" Hannah pleaded.

"It'll be several hours before he comes to. You'll have to wait until then."

A little while later, a nurse came out and told Hannah that Paddy was awake and asking for her, but she could only stay a few minutes.

Hannah walked up to the bed and took Paddy's hand.

"I love you, honey...don't you ever, ever forget that," he managed to say before his eyelids began to flutter.

"Paddy! Paddy! You promised to never leave me again!" Hannah said as the doctor came back into the room.

He checked Paddy's pulse before pulling the blanket up over his face.

"I'm sorry, ma'am, he's gone," he said, glancing at Hannah, but Hannah could not hear him as she collapsed to the floor with another seizure followed almost immediately with a stroke as she had done years earlier when giving birth to her daughter.

The doctors did what they could, but informed Rosie a short time later that the stroke was severe and that Hannah's chances of survival were not good. Rosie sat at Hannah's bedside the rest of the night. Shortly after dawn the next morning, Hannah regained consciousness.

"Rosie...Rosie...can you hear me?" Hannah said without opening her eyes.

"Yes, Hannah...I hear you."

"You've been such a dear friend, Rosie. I don't know how I would have ever made it without you in my life. I have one last favor to ask of you," Hannah said, her voice trailing off into a whisper.

Hannah began coughing and her breathing became more labored. With her right hand, she barely managed to motion for Rosie to come closer. Rosie leaned over to listen to Hannah's whispers. When the whispers stopped, so did Hannah's heart.

***

Just after dawn, the police and sheriff's deputies pulled the bloated body of Roe Cagney from the waters of Soda Creek. Mayor Lowe stood on the bank with a slight smile on his face, but tears in his eyes.

On the west side of the cornfields, other officers entered the silver trailer where they found Roe's mother passed out on the couch. She remained that way as the deputies searched the place. They soon found Roe's collection of girl's class rings and newspaper clippings.

The FBI was eventually called in to match the initials on the class rings with the names of the murdered girls in the clippings. There was no doubt in the minds of the authorities that Roe Cagney was guilty of dozens of murders across several decades.

Roe's death in Soda Creek was eventually ruled an accidental drowning while in the act of stalking another victim. That potential victim was never named.

□

CHAPTER THIRTY-THREE

Josie never remembered anything about the graduation party on Popcorn Beach. Having drunk the first two or three beers in her life, she could only remember becoming violently ill in the cornrows. Even that memory faded as the summer passed into autumn.

In the fall, Josie got a part-time job as a photojournalist trainee at the Fiddler's Point Times and enrolled in classes at the local branch college. Four years later, she completed her bachelor's degree and began a master's program in Visual Arts. She was often seen walking the streets of Fiddler's Point taking photos of interesting buildings that might be suitable to use for a master's degree project.

In early summer of 1969, Josie was walking in the far west end of Fiddler's Point when she spotted a gray-haired lady sitting alone on the front steps of Rosie's diner. She snapped several shots before approaching the lady.

"Hi...my name's Josie Kessler and I'm a photojournalist for the Times. I hope you don't mind my taking your picture."

"No, I don't mind at all," Rosie said as she studied Josie's face and marveled at how much the young woman looked like Hannah across the eyes.

"May I ask your name, ma'am?"

"Everyone just calls me Rosie—you can too."

Josie moved the camera around to her left shoulder and offered her right hand to shake.

Rosie smiled and shook hands with the pretty, young lady who unknowingly was still such a secret but integral part of Rosie's life. They talked for a while about the White Bear Inn and Josie asked for permission to take photos of the old building from all angles. When she finished, her first question was, "Why are all the rooms in the back half of the building all boarded up?"

"I don't really know why, but it's been that way since I got here in 1935. It was in my lease that the boards could never be removed."

"You mean you've never been in the back or upstairs?"

"I've been in the front half upstairs, but the back half has been walled off. Not much in the front except for boxes of receipts and tax records. I understand the upstairs was once used as an inn before the Civil War. Once the bigger hotels were built uptown, the White Bear apparently went out of business."

"How many rooms upstairs were used for the inn?"

Rosie chuckled a little before answering—not at the question, but at the answer she was about to give.

"Four! Only four rooms were used as the inn. That's probably why it was called an inn instead of a hotel."

"Rosie, I've got to get back to work now, but would you mind if I come back sometime and take some more shots of the building when the light is better?"

"You're welcome anytime. Do you drink coffee?"

"Oh yeah! Probably more than I should."

Rosie pulled her sweater up around her chin even though it was one of the hottest days of the year.

"I had better go inside; I'm feeling a little chilled. The next time you come by, we'll have a cup of hot coffee together and talk about all the secrets of this old place if you'd like," Rosie said.

Josie agreed and went on her way back to work. Her intentions were to take Rosie up on her offer, but work and school got in the way.

In August of that same summer, Rosie Walters took many of those secrets to her grave.

□

CHAPTER THIRTY-FOUR

Gib Walters returned to Fiddler's Point for his mother's funeral—as did many of his neighborhood friends who had left The Point shortly after high school. His cousin, Howser, was the new assistant principal at Cutter Elementary, Shultzy owned a farm near Cincinnati, Dewey was teaching up around Dayton, Bosley, Hiatt, and several of the others were working at the local plants or factories. Feller and Forgee joined the military. Eddie Creek became the head mechanic at the local Harley Motorcycle dealership.

A few days after the funeral, Creek pulled onto the parking lot in front of Rosie's while Gib was having breakfast in the front booth. Gib glanced out the window and saw that Creek was not riding his usual Harley motorcycle, so he walked outside. "Hey, Creek. Isn't that the old outfit Paddy and Hannah Phoot used to drive around town?"

"One and the same, ol' buddy."

"How did you come by it?"

"I'll tell you all about it for a cold beer."

They went into the diner and sat in the front booth. Sitting any place else would have been a sacrilege to guys from the halfpark.

"I promised your mother that I'd never tell anyone about how I got this cycle...except you. She even had a bill of sale made out for a dollar to make it official."

"You mean you asked her to sell it to you?"

"No...not at all! She gave it to me in return for a favor."

"A favor? What kind of favor?"

"It was kind of strange. She called me one day out of the blue and asked me to take her a ride on a friend's Harley. When I got down here, I saw that it was Paddy Phoot's cycle with the sidecar."

"I remember it well. They had it when I was just a kid. I'm surprised that it still runs."

"Oh, Paddy kept it in perfect shape. Still runs like a top," Creek said.

"So, my mom wanted you to take her a ride, huh?"

"Yes. And when I asked her why...she just said she was keeping a promise to an old friend."

"It must have been a promise to Hannah Phoot—she died several years ago."

Creek just smiled.

"It wasn't just a ride; she wanted me to take her up and down every street and alley from The

Point up to the Court Street Landing...even the gravel road behind the floodwall.

"Did she tell you why?"

"Didn't have to! I saw everything she did."

"What do you mean?"

"She got into the sidecar and put a large container on her lap. I guess you call it an urn. It was full of ashes. She didn't tell me who the ashes belonged to, but I finally figured it out."

"I'm guessing it was Paddy's ashes in the urn?" Gib said, associating the sidecar more with Paddy than with Hannah.

"Then, you'd only be partly correct—it was Hannah and Paddy's ashes mixed together."

"Wow! I knew they were very devoted to one another, but I would never have guessed that."

"Anyway, your mother had a scoop of some kind and she let the wind pull the ashes out of the scoop as we rode along. She had me slow down or stop in front of several places in town. A few times, she actually got out. At Cutter, she walked across the playground to the boiler room and then over to the little crooked house, scattering ashes as she went."

"Hannah Phoot's father worked at Cutter and lived in the little crooked house," Gib said, watching Creek grin a response to his comment.

"After she tossed ashes in front of nearly every tavern in the west end of town, she had me take her back to this diner where she got out and walked completely around your place tossing ashes."

"I'm beginning to see a pattern." Gib said, shaking his head in wonderment.

"Then we drove the entire perimeter of the sand and gravel lot doing the same thing. When she finished there, she got out of the sidecar again and told me to meet her at Morgan's in fifteen minutes. I watched her walk around the half-park and then up the levee. Gib, I think she tossed ashes on both sides of the levee all the way up to Morgan's where I was waiting."

"Was that her last stop?"

"No, she asked me to have a cup of coffee with her in Morgan's before we made our last stop. But, in case you want to know, she secretly scattered some ashes under our booth before we left."

Gib's mind was jumping back and forth to the different places Creek had mentioned, but he couldn't put much reasoning to his Mom's actions.

"We left Morgan's, and Rosie instructed me to take her up to Park Lawn Cemetery. When we got inside the gates, she guided me straight to where she wanted to go. I figured she'd been to this grave before. She emptied the remaining ashes on a grave before replacing the urn's lid and setting it on top of a flat marker."

"Did you see the marker?"

"Yes. I walked over with her. Infant Frazey – 2-12-1946 was the only thing printed on the marker.

With his story told, Creek and Gib soon drifted onto other subjects. They spent a while talking about old times, Creek's wife, Karen, their children, and the many changes that had slowly taken place in Fiddler's Point.

After Creek left, Gib thought about the journey his mother had taken on the sidecar. He had never given much thought to the relationship between his mother and the Phoots. They had just always been around.

Hannah had worked at the diner for as far back as Gib could remember, and his mom treated her more like a sister than an employee. He had no idea what connection his mother had with the infant at Park Lawn Cemetery, and it would be many years before he made that connection.

□

CHAPTER THIRTY-FIVE

On Monday morning, Gib had an appointment with his mother's lawyer. The attorney informed Gib that he had inherited her entire estate that included the old stone and frame building where he grew up, several acres around it, and even the half-park where he and his neighborhood friends played softball during their youth. He also inherited nearly a hundred thousand dollars in cash that represented Rosie's lifetime savings.

After his appointment with the attorney, Gib stopped by to see a former professor that he had during his freshman year at the branch college. The professor invited him to the new cafeteria for coffee and gave him a quick rundown about the former branch college's rapid growth into a full-fledged university. After learning that Gib had just earned a doctorate degree, one thing led to another, and Gib found himself a few weeks later teaching full-time at Southern Ohio University.

The semester passed quickly, and on Christmas Eve, Gib walked the few blocks from the diner to Main Street Hardware on Market Square to do some last minute shopping. He discovered that what used to be a meat market next door to the hardware was now a photographer's studio and gallery called Kessler's Kreations.

A fuzzy, fleeting image of a girl named Kessler teased his memory. Someone he met at a county fair while he was with an old girlfriend...maybe, but he didn't want to go there.

Gib pulled on the door handle of the new shop only to find it locked. He glanced at the towering town clock up the street to see that it was just past closing time for the Market Square shops. As he stood looking into the glass window, his gaze locked onto the eyes of a beautiful young lady inside the closed gallery. For the first time since high school, his heart thumped wildly at the first sight of a woman.

Walking back to the diner through the swirling snow, he could think of nothing but the woman who shared the magic moment he had been searching for throughout his college career.

On Christmas Day, that same woman was outside in the snow taking pictures of the diner. Gib invited her in for a hot mug of coffee. There was an instant mutual attraction and they soon became nearly inseparable. Less than two months later, on Valentine's Day, he proposed. A month after that, they were married.

***

The following spring, after the harsh winter snows had disappeared, Gib and Josie removed the heavy roughhewn lumber from the upstairs balcony of Angel's Manor. They immediately discovered a wall of French doors. One of them had been shattered, leaving small, jagged splinters of glass in the framing; however, there was no glass on the floor.

After stepping inside with their flashlights, they were shocked at the profound beauty of the room. Then, both light beams found three watercolors hanging above the fireplace. Each had a spray of faded brown stains that did not appear to be part of the original painting. Neither realized that the once bright red bloodspots were more than a century old. They moved slowly around to the next wall where they saw another watercolor that seemed frozen in time.

"Oh my God, Gib! That's...that's us isn't it"

Gib was speechless for a moment. He was looking at a watercolor of himself and Josie when they were children. Josie was inside her father's black panel truck and Gib was beside it. Josie appeared to be sharing her homemade valentine with him. They were both familiar with the valentine and why it was now framed and hanging in Josie's gallery.

"My God is right, Josie!" Gib finally blurted out.

Josie moved her light to her right and stopped at another watercolor hanging on the wall. It was Josie with Ann and Julie, two childhood classmates. They were in the crosswalk near her elementary school.

"I remember that day...it was after school and we went over to the soda shop for milkshakes. Honey, that's where I met the art lady. She was always somewhere around town sketching buildings...or at least I thought they were buildings."

Together, they walked slowly around the room shining their beams on one framed watercolor after another. There was one of Josie at a dance recital, one of her cheering at a junior-high football game, one sunbathing at the city pool, and another with her date as they walked into her junior prom.

"She's built a shrine to you, honey." Gib said, shaking his head in disbelief.

"Who's built a shrine to me, Gib?" Josie replied in a near frantic tone.

It suddenly dawned on Gib that prior to seeing her the past Christmas Eve, he and Josie had not crossed paths since that day at the fair. Maybe it was because she went to Catholic school, or maybe because there was a difference of over two years in their ages, but it was becoming obvious that Josie had never gotten to know the art lady whom he had known his entire life.

"The art lady's name is Hannah Phoot...she used to work for my mother at the diner. She lived in a back apartment."

"Why me? Why all these paintings of me?"

"Maybe because you were such a pretty little girl," Gib said, trying to lighten the moment.

Josie didn't respond. She immediately moved back to the mantel and removed one of the three paintings hanging there.

"Here's one of this building with a horse and buggy in front."

"All three are signed with the initials A.B. on the bottom right-hand corner. The other paintings are by a different artist."

Josie was thoroughly bewildered at the discovery of so many paintings with herself as the center of attention

"Did you ever finish going through all of those boxes of papers that your mom left behind?"

"No...not really."

"If your mom and Hannah Phoot worked together for years, maybe we can find something that will help us pull all this information together."

"Let's go down to the diner for some coffee and look through some of those boxes," Gib said. "Besides, I need to call someone to come fix that broken door glass."

***

Downstairs, Josie and Gib sorted through all of Rosie's personal effects, but found nothing to indicate why Hannah Phoot included Josie in so many of her watercolors.

It would be nearly forty years before they discovered answers to many of Josie's questions.

□

CHAPTER THIRTY-SIX

As the months turned into years, Josie and Gib renovated the back half of the old White Bear Inn into a splendid home. They began with the rear balcony and worked their way toward the front.

The only things that they refused to change were the barbershop and diner because they brought back so many good memories. Gib kept things just as they were in his youth. He even kept the coolers running and stocked with Pepsi. The records on the jukebox had not been changed since the late '50s or early '60s.

Old neighborhood friends stopped by to visit and they always sat in the front booth. Their conversations were often generated by various initials carved into the wooden tables and side panels. When Gib wasn't teaching, he spent much of his free time sitting at his laptop in that same front booth writing dozens of short stories about those carved initials and the people they represented. It was here during the late spring of 2007, that he discovered a treasure trove of information that has guided his writing ever since. Josie had just sat down across from him with two mugs of fresh, hot decaf.

"It's getting late, honey. Don't you think it's about time you wrapped up for the night," Josie said, removing one of her small earrings.

"I guess so...my eyes are getting a little tired."

"Oops!" Josie said as the earring slipped from her fingers and dropped to the floor under the booth.

"Be careful, Jo, you could step on it and break it. Lift both of your feet up and slide out of the booth. I'll do the same and get a flashlight."

Gib walked behind the coffee counter and got a flashlight. He looked under the booth but couldn't see the small earring.

"I can't see it from here. It's probably back toward the wall or in a corner. I'll have to get under the booth to find it."

He crawled under the table on his side and looked around. He spotted the earring in the back corner. After handing it to Josie, he saw something under the booth seat that he had never noticed before. It looked like a wooden flange of some sort below the center of the seat. He rolled over onto his back and looked at the opposite seat. It, too, had a flange.

"Josie...I don't believe what I think I'm seeing!"

"What, Gib?"

"I'm not sure...I've got to check it out closer. Hand me a screw driver...or a pocketknife...or something!"

Josie went behind the counter and looked, but the only thing she could find was a table knife. Gib took it and began tapping with the handle end. When he slid out from under the booth, he had a small wooden dowel pin in his hand.

"I've sat in this booth thousands of times and I've never noticed what I just found."

"What is it, Gib?" Josie asked, looking at the small piece of wood in his hand.

"This is what carpenters used years ago instead of nails. The pins are used to fasten two pieces of wood together. In this case, this pin was used to hold the booth seat in place on the box support underneath it."

He leaned over and grasped the wooden seat. He tugged on it gently causing it to slide off its base a few inches. Gib looked up at Josie who had a strange look of anticipation on her face, much like a child opening a Christmas gift.

"Here goes!" he said, sliding the seat completely off.

The flashlight wasn't needed now as the overhead lights flooded the inside of the wooden base. For a long moment, there was total silence as their eyes looked down upon dozens of stationary boxes with lids, a stack of hotel registers, and what appeared to be several cloth-bound journals. On top of them, Gib found a sealed envelope that did not appear as old as the other items.

"Are you going to open it now?"

"Okay...here goes nothing."

Inside the envelope, Gib found a short note from his mom dated August 2, 1969...just a couple of weeks before she died.

If you are reading this letter, son, it means I have gone to meet my maker, and that you have found this material just as I found it many years ago while repairing this booth. Of course, I read everything I found and added some material of my own. You may someday decide to do the same.

You will find the oldest diaries are on loose sheets of paper stored in the sealed boxes. They are all written by Waapa Jane Walters, a distant relative, who operated the White Bear Inn from the early 1800s until her death in 1901.

Your father and I moved into the building and began operating the diner and barbershop in 1935. As distant relatives of Landon and Waapa Jane Walters, I eventually became the owner of this old building.

There are stories of fortune and misfortune, love and loathing, joy and heartache, hope and despair, and cowardliness and heroism found in these pages that will reveal events kept secret to this day.

You have always been an aspiring writer, son, and I hope you will find the motivation in these pages and the conviction in your heart to write of these events. If not, add to it if you wish, but please put things where you found them.

Someday, maybe someone will reveal these secrets from the remarkable people who once dwelled within the walls of the White Bear Inn.

I love you,
Mom

Butterflies swarmed in Gib's stomach as he finished reading some of his mother's last thoughts. He glanced up at Josie and saw tears running down her cheeks.

"Apparently, a distant relative named Waapa Jane Walters kept her journals in these stationery boxes. Mom says they date back to the early 1800s. She apparently wants me to write about some of the events and people in the journals."

"That sounds fascinating. Do you think she's talking about you writing something academic like an historical account of this Waapa Jane person?"

"I don't know. I think we should read through all the material and then decide if we want to write about it or not."

"Gib, you once told me your mother and Hannah Phoot were best friends for many years. Her journals may reveal the truth about...well you know."

"About why Hannah included you in so many of her watercolors?"

"Yes."

"I think we should both read everything before we discuss anything. That way, we'll be able to look at the whole picture to see if there are stories to tell that others will want to read."

"I'd rather not," Josie said hesitantly. "I think you should read the material first. Then, I'll let you decide whether I should read it. Meanwhile, would you go up to the attic and bring down the crate with all of the watercolors we found?"

Gib nodded his understanding of her decision and began removing the material from the booth base. He seemed excited about getting started.

***

In the weeks that followed, Gib read every word more than once. He finally realized that there were numerous dramas played out in the journals that could be expanded into worthwhile short stories or even a novel.

Before he began writing, he sat down with Josie and explained his plans. He wanted and needed her approval concerning the information about Hannah and Paddy Phoot.

Rosie's journals confirmed that Paddy Phoot died shortly after his heroic actions that probably saved Josie's life—actions of which she still had no memory. Hannah died a few hours later from an epileptic seizure followed by a stroke. According to Rosie, Hannah was just as likely to have died from a broken heart.

"How do you want me to handle the details I found about the art lady and Mr. Phoot?" Gib asked, not knowing what Josie's answer might be.

"Honey, the day we first walked into Angel's Manor and saw the watercolors hanging on all the walls...I knew," she said, beginning to tear up. "Not the details, but the emotions.

"Josie, we can discuss this some other time, or never if you prefer."

"No! Now is the time...before you begin writing your novel. I know that the person who painted those scenes from my childhood...our childhoods...loved me. I felt the love in my heart and every fiber of my body. The actual circumstances that resulted in so many secrets no longer matter now," Josie said, her chin trembling.

"Then there's just one last thing that I need to tell you," Gib said, taking Josie's hand.

"And what's that?" she asked, squeezing Gib's hand in a valiant effort to hold back tears.

"Pddy Phoot loved you too...I have proof."

There was no holding back now at the realization that yet another stranger may have played an important role in her past. Gib pulled her into his arms and held her until the sobbing stopped. Finally, Josie was able to compose herself and speak again.

"Write your novel, honey, and have it turn out the way you want it to turn out. I have all the proof of love I'll ever need.

***

Several weeks later, Gib went into Josie's gallery to ask her to go to lunch, but she was busy with a customer. His eyes were immediately drawn to a new wall display that he had not yet seen. On that wall were Angelina Bonèt Walter's three watercolors. Surrounding them were dozens created by Hannah Phoot.

The White Bear Inn had given up a treasure of water-colored memories. Among the many paintings of Josie, were sketches of Rosie, Paddy, Hannah's Gaze, Market Square, and the colorful characters who frequented the area taverns. Scattered within the display were sketches of Gib, Howser, Dewey, Creek and Karen, and other neighborhood kids who spent much of their youth between the halfpark and Rosie's diner.

In the center of the display was Hannah's first sketch of Josie as she handed a valentine to Gib through the window of her father's panel truck.

In front of the display was a sign printed in all capital letters: WATERCOLORS-NOT FOR SALE.

The End

Made in the USA
Middletown, DE
15 August 2016